By Christina Dodd

CHRISTINA DODD

That Scandalous Evening

AVONBOOKS

An Imprint of HarperCollinsPublishers

AVON BOOKS
An Imprint of HarperCollins*Publishers*
195 Broadway
New York, New York 10007

Copyright © 1998 by Christina Dodd
ISBN 978-0-380-79091-3
www.avonromance.com

First Avon Books mass market printing: September 1998

Avon Trademark Reg. U.S. Pat. Off. and in Other Countries, Marca Registrada, Hecho en U.S.A.
HarperCollins® is a registered trademark of HarperCollins Publishers.

Printed in the U.S.A.

30 29 28 27 26 25 24 23 22

To Chet Gilmore,
a father and a friend to me

And to Lillian Gilmore
The whole world took a vote
and you're the best and kindest lady
we've ever had the privilege to know.

I love you both.

Chapter 1

"Let us hope no one remembers the scandal." Eleazer Morant stared down his quivering, rabbitlike nose at his sister-in-law. ''I will not have my daughter's good name tainted by the tincture of your disgrace.''

Already dressed in her outmoded brown traveling garments, Miss Jane Higgenbothem sat upright in the hard chair. She was, she knew, the picture of dignity and tranquillity. She worked hard to achieve that image, and for just such moments as these. Eleazer had not summoned her to this dimly lit parlor just to whine again about that ancient scandal, she was sure. So why was she here?

In well-modulated tones she answered, ''I cannot imagine the ton will be interested in anything that happened so long ago. They are ever on to some new tidbit.''

''Except that this scandal happened to Lord Blackburn.''

She lowered her gaze to her gloved hands. The carriage was waiting. Adorna was waiting. London was waiting.

And Eleazer droned on. "Lord Blackburn is one of the richest men in England. He sets the tone. Everything he does is copied." His knuckles turned white as he gripped the back of an old-fashioned high-backed chair. "Yet despite all that, I understand there are some who still call him 'Figgy.'"

Jane winced. "My behavior has been exemplary since my return from London," she answered stoutly.

"You *still* sketch," Eleazer said in a tone usually reserved for accusations of prostitution.

"All ladies sketch."

"Your skill betrays you."

"I'll try to do worse."

"Don't be saucy, miss. Those portraits you do are scathing, as you well know."

Her portraits were really nothing more than quick outlines, impressions Jane gathered from the people around her. But Eleazer had once seen one she'd done of him, and he had recognized the parsimony shining in his eyes. He had not forgotten—or forgiven.

Flipping open the fat book of accounts in his hand, he shook it at her. "I can scarcely yet believe I financed that ill-begotten season of yours. It was not my duty to stand the blunt, but I did it on my dear Melba's urging. As I told her then, nothing good can come of this." His fingernails scraped the leather binding. "I was correct, as usual. Nothing good did come of it."

She'd heard this refrain many times. Eleven years ago he had paid for her clothing and rented a house in a fashionable part of London. And how had she repaid him? With disaster. But he hadn't done anything for her. He'd done it for Melba. For Melba, her sister and his wife, whom he had revered with all the meager passion of his mean-spirited heart.

Jane had done it for Melba, too. For her beautiful older sister. Even at the age of eighteen Jane had known she was ill suited to society, but Melba had lightly dismissed her qualms. "Darling, you must marry. What else is there for a lady to do?"

Looking back, Jane suspected Melba had known she was dying, and maneuvered to move Jane from her home to her own household. Now, faced with Melba's widower, Jane knew her sister had been right. It would have been better to be *any* man's wife than to be Eleazer's mere dependent.

"I've been your housekeeper. I've raised your daughter." She took a quiet breath. "Now I'll be her companion."

He turned to the window and stared out at the street, then leaned forward as if he saw something that interested him. "I could have hired someone else to do those things, and more cheaply."

From outside she heard a shout. Rising, she saw across the street. A rag-clad woman had stolen an apple, and now she cowered from the blows of a street-cart vendor. Jane flinched at the sight. Only Eleazer's largesse stood between her and just such a scene.

"I have never been invited to invest in Blackburn's business concerns." He tossed her a malicious glance. "Because you embarrassed him."

She had embarrassed *him*? Jane bit her tongue. No

doubt that was true. But she wondered, sometimes, why no one cared that Lord Blackburn had *ruined* her. Why a female's reputation could be held so cheap.

Yet none of this mattered anymore. Eleven years had passed since she'd lost her respectability and her muse in one dreadful episode. "I question if Lord Blackburn's consequence has suffered unduly from the incident."

"Lord Blackburn's repute is ever growing." Eleazer craned his neck to watch the constable drag the woman away. "When he outfitted a regiment and led them to the Peninsula, a dozen young lords imitated him. When he was wounded and returned wearing an eye patch, every modish buck took to wearing an eye patch."

Jane sank back into her chair. "He was wounded?"

Eleazer turned from the window. "I said so, didn't I?"

She didn't want to display interest, yet she couldn't refrain. "Did he . . . lose the eye?"

"I don't know. How should I know? As I told you, we are not intimate."

She pressed her glove-clad palms together so tightly the muscles of her arms ached. Lord Blackburn's health was of no concern to her. She chanted in her head.

Yet in London she might see him, just from a distance, and despite her efforts, excitement wriggled along her nerves.

And her nerves leaped when a timid knock sounded and a lanky, ill-dressed Frenchman poked his head in. Monsieur Chasseur, Adorna's French tutor. He had arrived at last. Grateful for the interruption, Jane rose.

Seeing her, he stepped into the chamber, shoulders hunched, clutching a cream-colored, rumpled sheet of paper. "Mademoiselle, I have come to say—"

Eleazer gave a full-throated bellow. "What?"

The cowed son of a gentleman immigrant who had lost everything in the French Revolution, Monsieur Chasseur knew well of the bloody Reign of Terror. Yet he blanched at the sight of his irate employer. *"Je regrette, mademoiselle, je ne réalise—"*

"Oh, speak English, you stupid frog." Eleazer glared until the youth blushed, then turned to Jane. "I've already spent three hundred pounds on this debut, and part of it on this milksop tutor!"

"Eleazer, we have been through this before. Adorna must know how to dance, so we have a dancing tutor. She must know how to play an instrument, so we have an instructor for the pianoforte." Jane smiled at Monsieur Chasseur. "And she must speak French, for civilized people speak French."

"Oui." The young Frenchman laid his hand over his heart, straightened his shoulders, and struck a pose. "France and civilization are one."

Eleazer snorted rudely. "Frenchmen eat fungus dug up by pigs."

For a moment, Jane thought Monsieur Chasseur would erupt in a Gallic fury, for in spite of his poverty, he was very proud of his heritage. And should he speak insolently to Eleazer, she would lose the only tutor she could find who would willingly teach Adorna for a pittance—a matter of some importance to Eleazer—and one who had agreed to escort them to London and remain close to Adorna in a last ditch effort to bestow on her a sense of the French language.

The maligned tutor clenched his fist. The paper crinkled in his hand. Recalled from his fury by the sound, he looked down at it. His ruddy color faded and his shoulders drooped. He crept closer to Jane and, keeping one eye on Eleazer, he said in a low voice, "Mademoiselle, I must apologize, but I cannot travel to London with you and stay as I promised."

"What?" Eleazer cupped his ear. "What's that?"

Jane stared at Monsieur Chasseur in dismay. "But you wanted to return to London. You said you found many pupils there during the Season."

He ducked his head even lower and waved the paper. "I have received this *lettre*. Mademoiselle Cunningham, one of my *jeune* pupils . . . she is dead."

Eleazer heard *that*, for he bellowed, "What has a dead girl got to do with Adorna?"

The tutor confessed, "There is an investigation. They wish me to be there. She has been . . . murdered."

"Murdered?" Jane didn't know the Cunninghams, but she imagined how she would feel if it were Adorna. "How horrible. How? Why?"

He just stared at her, as if the sound of her voice could not quite penetrate his grief. Then his eyes focused, and he said, "Mademoiselle, I am only the tutor."

"If you're only the tutor, what do they want you there for?" Eleazer asked shrewdly. "You're a suspect, aren't you?"

Jane was horrified. "Oh, Eleazer! Really, can't you see . . . ?" See that the innocuous young man lived as most impoverished gentlemen lived, quietly, without hope, struggling for a trifling existence.

"No, mademoiselle, he is right." The tutor seemed to shrink even further. "But I do not know why. I taught her yesterday morning at her beautiful home. The sun was shining the last time I looked upon her *visage belle*, but the thick fog rolled in off the sea as I rode to my next lesson. It was so foreboding, I should have suspected I would never see her again." He snuffled, pulled out his handkerchief, and wiped his nose. "And now there is this *lettre* from the constable . . ."

Jane noticed his red-rimmed eyes. He was in pain, as would anyone be who knew a young woman's life had been snuffed out, and he was worried because he was under suspicion for having been in the vicinity, and because he was French. "I'm sorry for your loss."

"*Merci, mademoiselle.*" He snuffled again.

"Well, that takes care of that." Eleazer rubbed his hands in satisfaction. "We can't have a murderer teaching Adorna. Think what that will save me."

Not a thing, Jane thought. Unlike Eleazer, she would wait to convict the tutor. She walked Monsieur Chasseur to the door and in a low tone said, "If you make your way back to London, call on us. We are staying with Lady Tarlin in Cavendish Square. There we will arrange for lessons."

Monsieur Chasseur bowed. "Bless you. I do so wish to teach Mademoiselle Morant."

"I know you do." Adorna had once driven Monsieur Chasseur to frustrated tears over her inability to conjugate a simple verb. Still, despite his frustration, he had returned, again and again. Like all men, Monsieur Chasseur was in love with Adorna, and he now left reluctantly.

"A murderer, huh? And here I thought he was nothing but an impudent frog." Eleazer smirked, then scowled. "But for what I've paid him, Adorna should speak Chinese, too. Of course, she's too much of a ninnyhammer."

Jane couldn't argue with that, but Adorna's wit was of no consequence. "Adorna is as beautiful as her mother was, and with the proper training, she can make an advantageous marriage. You want that, don't you?"

"Of course I want it," he said irritably. "I need those benefits."

If Eleazer had ever displayed the least affection for his only child, Jane could have forgiven him much. But from the moment of her birth, he had entered Adorna in his debit column. Now he hoped to move her to the credit column, and his pettiness made Jane's voice sharp. "Then look upon the money you spend as an investment. Through Adorna you'll get the noble connections you want. The ones I failed to attain."

"Yes, you did fail miserably. I've placed the sum of ten thousand pounds in the Bank of England, but I expect an accounting of every cent."

"You shall have it. Adorna must have the best to outshine all the other debutantes."

"That's another thing." Eleazer poked his finger

toward her. "You needn't think I will buy *you* another wardrobe."

"Any clothing I have needed since my season, I have purchased myself," Jane said proudly. "I will continue to do so."

Her reminder irritated Eleazer all over again. He didn't know where she had come by her money. He would have preferred to have her beg him for every ha'penny. Any chance to wield power pleased Eleazer; thus Jane took every opportunity to thwart him.

No matter that her small store of funds was almost depleted.

"I still think you should stay here in Sittingbourne."

He didn't have to tell Jane that. She knew he had wanted to keep her here, imprisoned in this tall, thin, somber house until everything bright and hopeful in her had withered.

Sadly, she had wanted it, too. To go out and face the world again, after what she had done . . . She pressed her hand to her side where a stitch of fear stabbed at her.

She was twenty-eight years old, firmly on the shelf, and when she remembered The Disastrous Season in London, she knew she would rather beg on the streets than return to that scene of unspeakable humiliation.

But she *was* returning.

In these grim years of servitude, she had learned many lessons, not the least of which was a hard-won poise. So she would go to London. She would see the nobles who had peopled her nightmares. They would not even recognize her, but she would be there to witness Adorna's triumph. It was Adorna who mattered now.

"We told Lady Tarlin we would arrive this afternoon," she said. "I think it would be best if we left."

Eleazer leaned back in his chair and folded his hands across his chest. "Of course. Heaven forfend you leave your dear friend Lady Tarlin waiting."

"We are grateful to Lady Tarlin," Jane reminded him. "She is sponsoring Adorna on the strength of a very tenuous connection."

"Yes, she's *your* friend. *Your* noble friend," he said, pettishly. "You pretend to respect me, and all the time making sure I never forget you are a noblewoman and I am a lowly merchant."

"That is not true," Jane said in a clipped tone. She had not originally despised Eleazer; he earned her disdain.

"Well, it doesn't matter now." He smirked as if he knew something she didn't. "Go on. What are you waiting for?"

Startled by his sudden dismissal, Jane walked toward the entrance. He had threatened not to send her to London, but she still didn't understand why.

"Go on," he urged cordially.

Would she at last discover the reason for this interview?

As she opened the door, he asked, "Do you know Dame Olten?"

She paused, her fingers pressing into the trim. "The butcher's widow. Of course I know her." A mean, pinch-mouthed woman who delighted in tormenting her customers.

"She and I have come to an agreement. We will be married next month." He sounded pleasant as he uttered the damning words she'd feared to hear every day since Melba's death ten years ago. "You'll have to find somewhere else to live."

Chapter 2

"London is so vast." Since late afternoon, when they had entered the city proper, Adorna had kept her pretty face pressed to the glass of the carriage window. Now she turned away and covered her nose with her gloved hand. "And it stinks!"

"The Thames *is* quite pungent today." Jane held a perfumed handkerchief to her nose as she smiled. None of her sketches could do Adorna justice. Adorna's beauty was so bright it almost hurt the eyes. Her blond hair shone like platinum. Her piquant face was rounded. Her delft blue eyes slanted up at the corners, and her lids drooped over those eyes in a beckoning, come-hither way that drove men, both young and old, mad with desire.

When Jane looked at Adorna, she saw Melba. She saw her own dear sister, and she didn't comprehend how Eleazer could turn his back on the living incarnation of his wife. And to marry Dame Olten!

"Is something wrong, Aunt Jane?" Head tilted,

Adorna watched Jane. "You look as if you have dyspepsia."

"Would it be surprising after that meal at the inn?" Jane grimaced. "I own, the sausage meowed when we cut into it."

"How dreadful, Aunt Jane. Please don't say so."

Adorna looked faintly queasy, and Jane wanted no carriage sickness now. Not when they were so close to their goal. "I was jesting, dear. I'm sure the sausage was probably bovine."

Adorna fell back against the seat, her mouth agape with horror. "Not *bovine*!"

"That means a cow, dear," Jane said hastily.

"Oh. A cow. Why didn't you say so?" Adorna sat back up and tidied the ruffle on her bonnet. "But I still think you look odd. It was my father, wasn't it? He upset you."

Jane stared at Adorna, and wondered. How could the girl seem so simple, and yet at the same time be so shrewd?

I'm homeless. The bitter words fought to be said.

Yet she had ever protected Adorna from the worst of Eleazer's faults, and she wouldn't heap blame on the guileless girl for her father's actions, nor would she ask for assurances for the future. She was homeless, not witless; somehow she would make her way in the world. "Your father is concerned about economy."

"As always! That's never agitated you before." Adorna took Jane's gloved hand between her own. "Do tell me, Aunt Jane. Was it him, or is it me?"

"You?" The carriage jolted along the cobblestones, but Jane scarcely noticed. "Why would I be upset with you?"

Adorna's head drooped. "You didn't want to come, but I couldn't have a season without my dearest aunt. I would have been frightened without you."

She glanced up through her long, dark eyelashes, but Jane shook her head in disbelief. "My dear, I would never desert you. And I don't think anything frightens you."

Looking at her directly, Adorna said, "Then call it fondness, Aunt Jane. I love you too much to leave you behind."

Now, that, Jane *did* believe. Putting her arms around the affectionate girl, she said, "I couldn't bear to be left behind, either. I would worry."

Adorna placed her head on Jane's shoulder and hugged her back. "About what? This is the first step to a fabulous season!"

As a girl, Jane, too, had seen London as a stepping-stone. After she would see Rome, Paris, and the New World. She would live an unorthodox lifestyle, wherein charm and beauty mattered little, and talent and dedication measured a woman's worth.

Nothing had turned out as she had imagined, and now, ironically, it was Jane's responsibility to guide Adorna along a decorous path. "Do you not remember young Livermere and how he seized you when you refused his suit?"

"Oh, that." Adorna straightened and peered out the window once more. "He was a fool in love."

"The world is populated by just such fools," Jane

remembered the hours of worry when she thought Adorna had been kidnapped. "Men lose all sense when confronted with you."

"I can handle them. I can handle anything, and I can take care of you. She told me to take care of you."

"Who told you, dear?"

"Why, my mother, of course, when she was so ill." Adorna sounded matter-of-fact. "She talked to me about you a lot."

Jane's head buzzed with confusion. "Why would Melba tell a child of eight such a thing?"

"Because she loved you, of course."

Adorna seemed to think this explained everything, and while Jane longed to question her niece, she knew she would get no more coherent answer. "Why haven't you told me this before?"

"You never asked." Adorna quivered as the horses slowed. "Is this it, Aunt Jane? Is this Cavendish Square? The houses here are very grand."

Jane took a breath and delved into her memories. "Lady Tarlin is very grand, also. Very charming."

The carriage drew to a halt in front of the tallest home with the grandest door. Adorna said, "Just from her home, I can tell she's going to be charming."

Jane scarcely heard. With a flourish, Lady Tarlin's young, freckle-faced footman placed the step against the carriage and flung wide the portal. When she stepped outside this carriage, she would officially be in London. In London, where the ton fed on scandal and the insignificant Jane Higgenbothem had once been the main course. When she set foot on the step, she would be committed.

Then two things happened. Adorna took Jane's wrist and placed the limp hand in the young footman's white-gloved palm. And from the top of the stairs, Jane heard a call.

"Jane, dearest Jane, you're here at last!"

Framed in the doorway of the town house stood a fashionable woman, joy lighting her face.

A remembrance surfaced. Of a girl, tears streaming down her cheeks, crying out to Jane's retreating form, "Come back to London as soon as you can. We'll make Blackburn sorry, I promise you!"

Jane trod lightly down. She dipped into a curtsy. "Lady Tarlin, what a pleasure to see you."

"Enough! Jane, don't you start that 'Lady Tarlin' nonsense. I'm Violet." Violet bounded down the stairs, took Jane's arms, and looked into her face. "We are friends, are we not?"

Relief flooded Jane, and she smiled. "I do hope so. I have clung to that thought when it seemed all light had . . ." As quickly as the pleasure came, it faded. When the season was over, would she have a place to go?

Violet hugged her once, hard. "I'm glad to have you here after all these years of begging you to come." The advent of three children had changed Violet's petite figure from the perfect hourglass to one whose sand had run to the bottom. Her pale brown hair fell in ringlets around her full face, her brown eyes still sparkled with humor, and her thin lips were always tilted upward as if she found something secretly amusing in every situation.

Her lips tilted upward now as she asked, "Where is your ward about whom I've heard so much?"

Adorna had descended from the coach and waited. Now she stepped forward, curtsied, and said respectfully, "Lady Tarlin, my aunt and I are so grateful that you've consented to sponsor us for our season."

"She's not sponsoring me," Jane said. "My debut is long past."

Adorna spoke slowly and precisely. "I have planned a double wedding."

It took a minute for her meaning to sink in. Then, horrified and embarrassed, Jane exclaimed, "Adorna!"

"An excellent objective." Violet gave a chime of laughter at Jane's grimace.

"A ridiculous notion. I don't know what gave her that idea."

"Maybe she thought of it herself." With her hand under Adorna's chin, Violet considered the innocent countenance turned up to her trustingly. "She's lovely, and with a captivating manner, too. You were right, Jane. She'll be the toast of the season." Linking arms with both of them, she led them up the stairs. "We must get busy. We have less than a month to prepare." With a sideways glance, she said, "You'll both need new wardrobes."

"Not me," Jane said.

"New hairstyles," Adorna said.

"Dear, your father—" Jane began to remonstrate.

Adorna's chin jutted remarkably for such a rounded feature. "Papa's not here."

"You would hate to have Lord Blackburn think you had fallen on hard times," Violet interposed in what Jane thought was a quite unnecessary opinion.

Jane glanced at Adorna, but as they reached the door her niece had swiveled and faced the street, giving the appearance of having forgotten her companions. Jane whispered, "Is Lord Blackburn well?"

Violet tossed her head. "Better than he deserves, although I do my best to make him miserable. Do you really care?"

Pressing her lips together, Jane shook her head. She shouldn't care. She was a chaperone now. A spinster. A maiden aunt. Perhaps she'd wear a cap this season.

"Come, dear," she said to Adorna. "We mustn't loiter on the steps."

But in a burst of exuberance, Adorna threw out her arms as if to embrace the whole city and declared, "I'll take the ton by storm. I'll make you both proud of me. I swear I will!"

Her golden hair caught the rays of the setting sun, and Jane thought that with her arms outstretched and her cape tossed back, she looked like the embodiment of a triumphant goddess. Violet, too, gazed at her in appreciation, and murmured, "A pretty sentiment," while below them, the young, heretofore deferential footman stood with his mouth undeferentially agape.

Then their coachman shouted. On the street, a fashionable phaeton careened across the square. The gentleman driver sawed at the reins, his gaze still fastened to Adorna like a knight to the Holy Grail.

"Oh, no," Jane said. It had started already.

As their coachman and footmen tried desperately to back their horses, the gentleman swerved. Just in time. He missed their carriage, but his wheel struck the curbstone. His rotation was too sharp. With a crack that reverberated up the narrow street, the phaeton overturned.

Adorna squealed and averted her face.

The driver went flying, landing with a somersault on the cobblestones.

"Is he hurt?" Jane asked.

But he came to his feet at once. Tugging once at his cravat, he brushed his hair off his forehead, then gave a formal bow that, even from a distance, was obviously directed at Adorna.

As he hurried toward his struggling team, Adorna asked, "Are the *horsies* hurt?" She had her hands over her eyes.

Jane watched as the gentleman went to his team's heads and spoke to the creatures, calming them. "The horses are well. So is the man who drove them, although he deserves worse."

"I know." Adorna turned to her aunt and frowned ferociously. "Why do men insist on driving those dangerous vehicles when they can't control their horsies?"

"I would say that the problem is, they can't keep their eyes on the road," Jane answered.

"I don't understand what happened." Violet sounded truly bewildered. "Mr. Pennington is usually so careful with his team."

"Go on in, dear," Jane said to Adorna. "I know how these incidents upset you."

"Thank you, Aunt." Adorna glanced at Violet. "With your permission?"

Violet waved her inside.

Jane waited until the austere butler had bowed Adorna into the dim interior before saying meaningfully, "I did warn you."

Violet frowned. "You think Mr. Pennington saw Adorna and lost control of his team?"

"It happens all the time."

Violet's laughter chimed out. "This is all quite unbelievable. Between Adorna causing carriage wrecks and Blackburn's first sighting of you, I contemplate a very entertaining season."

Chapter 3

A month later, from the top of Lady Goodridge's broad stairway, Ransom Quincy, Marquess of Blackburn, removed his silver quizzing glass from the pocket of his dark blue waistcoat and lifted it to his face. Below him on the main floor of the garish, pink-painted ballroom, a glittering crowd seeped in and around the pillars. They leaned over the balcony, they trickled between the banquet hall and the gaming chambers. Only the dance floor was free as they waited for the orchestra to begin.

His sister Susan would be in ecstasy; not only had she succeeded in leading off with the season's first huge success, but she had convinced her insufferable brother to attend.

Or so she thought, and he had no intention of disillusioning her. He had his reasons for allowing himself to be so coerced, and they had nothing to do with making his sister happy.

"Blackburn!" Gerald Fitzgerald came from behind. "What are you doing here? Thought you gave these up."

"I thought so, too. I was wrong." Quizzing glass still up, Blackburn made a quick inspection of the former cavalry leader.

They had met at Eton, Fitz sent by a widowed mother who sacrificed everything to ensure her son's education, Ransom dispatched by a father determined to see his heir go through the phases of schooling required for a noble's son. Despite their disparate backgrounds, or perhaps because of them, they had become fast friends. Through the death of Ransom's father, through the early, frivolous years in society, through Mrs. Fitzgerald's decline into invalidism, they had remained companions.

Fitz wore his usual well tailored costume: a coat of claret velvet with high padded shoulders, a gleaming gold waistcoat, black trousers, and highly polished boots decorated with a gold metallic tassel. A bit garish, but Fitz wore it well. More important—"You seem healthy," Ransom said in delicate inquiry.

Fitz clapped his hand to his thigh. "Hardly giving me a twinge. Good surgeon you had with your unit. Thank you for loaning him to me." Taking advantage of a friend's privilege, he pushed Ransom's quizzing glass away from his face.

Ransom allowed it, turning his face toward Fitz so he could see as he wished. This was, after all, their first meeting since the battle of Talavera ten months ago.

Fitz was tall, almost Ransom's height, and apparently handsome if the reaction of the passing ladies was anything to go by. Yet when last Ransom had seen him, he'd been in a ragged hospital tent on the Spanish Peninsula, white with pain and afraid he would lose his leg to his "damnable heroics," as he called them. He hadn't, and Blackburn was glad to see him looking staunch and hearty.

Fitz apparently felt much the same. "Shrapnel scarcely left a scar," he observed.

"Surgeon saved the eye." Blackburn kept his expression impassive. "That's all I care about."

"Naturally." Fitz inspected the ballroom just as Ransom had a few moments earlier. "A crush! One can scarcely move down there."

"When the dancing starts, it'll break up." Blackburn lifted the quizzing glass again and stared at the teeming humanity below with the same affection he reserved for Spaniards and cockroaches. "I shall not dance, of course, and my sister will fret."

"Since when do you care what Lady Goodridge thinks?"

There spoke a man who had no siblings, Blackburn thought. "She's my sister, my eldest by ten years. She has her ways of making me uncomfortable."

Fitz smiled a small, secret smile. "She scares the good sense out of most people."

"But not you. You never had any."

Fitz laughed aloud this time, throwing back his head so that his fashionably curled hair bounced and the ton stared as they squirmed their way around.

"I'm glad I can amuse you," Blackburn said

coolly, but he watched his friend carefully. Fitz was up to something. That febrile glitter in his eye signaled mischief, or worse.

"So sorry! I'm the one who's supposed to amuse you, aren't I?" Fitz cuffed Blackburn on the arm. "What excuse will you give for not dancing?"

Blackburn leaned closer. "Lend me your wound in the thigh."

"Will not, b'God," Fitz said with equanimity. "Use it for sympathy from the ladies."

Ransom gave a bark of laughter. "You're a knave."

"It's better than being positively grim." Fitz stared meaningfully at his friend.

"Me?" Blackburn touched his fingers to his chest. "Grim? I prefer to think of myself as conservative."

Fitz ran his gaze over Blackburn's somber ensemble of black evening coat and trousers, black boots, snowy white shirt and cravat tied in the waterfall style. "Conservative. *I'll* say. I heard stories you were at the Foreign Office every day." He glowered. "*Working.*"

"Really?" Forgetting he was supposed to encourage the gossip, Ransom allowed his voice to chill. "Who's been reporting on me?"

"Everyone. You were the talk of London, wearing clothing from last season and exercising your horse at odd hours. In the early morning!"

Blackburn toyed with the silver chain that held his quizzing glass. "While on the continent, I discovered there *were* hours before noon."

"Speculation is, you're working the spy game."

The fine silver chain snapped in Blackburn's fingers, snapped as cleanly as a traitor's neck in a hangman's noose. "Spy?"

Fitz watched as Blackburn detached the chain. "So I told them. Blackburn, a spy? I said. Nonsense! He's too proper."

"Quite right."

"Too well-bred."

"I am a Quincy."

"Too . . . dull."

A faded blue eye. A quavering old voice. "England is depending on you, Lord Blackburn. That treacherous blighter's out there somewhere."

In as insufferable a tone as he knew—and Blackburn knew well how to be insufferable—he said, "If dull is knowing the worth of propriety, then yes, I am dull."

"Except for that business of working at the Foreign Office."

"A whim, long vanquished." Blackburn slipped the chain in his waistcoat pocket. "Or didn't the gossips report *that*?"

"I heard you were at Stockfish's house party in Sussex and hunting with the MacLeods in Scotland."

"Keep your blinkers open and your blinders off. We know about de Sainte-Amand, but the one who planned the whole operation—that one we really need. So watch. Find out how the information is passed. Find out how the information is getting out of the Foreign Office. Find out who the leader is."

The instructions echoed in Blackburn's brain, and he swept the chamber with his gaze. He tried to focus clearly. He could not. The shrapnel to the eye had destroyed more than his faultless features. He could see; oh, yes, he could see. But he'd lost the keenness of his vision. No longer could he squint down a barrel to aim a gun. Never again would he hunt deer on his estate in Scotland.

Never again would he stalk across the Iberian Peninsula and with faultless accuracy bring down one of Napoleon's soldiers.

So now, like a race horse forced to the bridle, he worked for Mr. Thomas Smith.

He spied for Mr. Thomas Smith.

What a bitter taste that left in his mouth, that a member of one of England's oldest and most patrician families would lower himself to such ignoble deception. Yet he could not say no. Not and keep the promise he had made to that lad who had died in his arms.

''Matchmaking mama off to the left,'' Fitz warned.

Blackburn glanced over. Lady Kinnard, formerly Miss Fairchild, was bearing down on them. Her he could see—Lady Kinnard's broad beam rolled behind her like a ship at sea. She towed another one of her beautiful, wide-eyed, man-eating daughters, and Blackburn said, ''Move on.''

Fitz lingered, a merry cast to his mouth. ''But why? Kinnard's daughter would do you well.''

They were getting uncomfortably close. ''Well for what?''

''For that bride you're seeking.''

Blackburn gave Fitz a push, and the incorrigible bastard fled down the stairs, laughing all the way. When they reached the bottom, Fitz dug an elbow into his ribs. "I meant to tell you, Blackburn, there's another tale making the rounds."

"What?" Blackburn asked in an ominous tone.

"That if it's not spies you're after, but a leg-shackle."

"Damn!" Blackburn hadn't expected this.

"Any appearance of furtiveness must be avoided. Instead, you must crash into society. Draw attention to yourself, like you did all those years ago. Create another scandal. That certainly gave the ton something to talk about. Or if you will not, tell them you're hanging out for a wife."

Fitz's features were a comical blend of indignation, dismay and wicked delight. "Never say it's true, man!"

Mr. Smith had chosen to start that rumor. Blackburn knew it would be impossible to halt.

Fitz interpreted his silence as he wished. "B'God, it *is* true. The great Blackburn is going to fall at last."

Better a rumor than another scandal, so Blackburn agreed, "So it would appear."

"At least you'll have no trouble plucking the heiress of your dreams." Fitz leavened his speech with a hint of brogue picked up from his Irish father. "But what am I thinking? You don't need another fortune. You should flush out the heiresses, then should leave them for those of us who do."

"So you're after a wife, too?" Blackburn mocked.

Fitz caught a passing footman, snatched a glass of brandy from his tray, and drank it down. "Suffering, I mean *matrimony*, is a man's lot in life."

Before, Fitz had sworn he did not care how much

the pockets pinched, he would not marry. "Creditors giving you a chase?" Blackburn asked.

"As always." Fitz grimaced with a little more derision than usual. "Parasites." He handed the glass back. "So we're hunting the softest, sweetest game of all," he mused.

"This is not a hunt." Blackburn clipped off the words. "It's nothing but a bunch of mares being paraded past stallions. When the stallion scents the right mare, he paws the ground and the stable master cobbles them together until they get the job done."

"Cynical, yet accurate." Fitz had heard it before. "But if you feel that way, why are you doing it?"

Others might question his sudden seeking of a wife, and Blackburn had to offer some reasonable explanation. "Got a bit too close to death over there. Occurred to me my sister was right. Life is short, and the Quincy name precious. I need an heir."

"The Quincy name. I should have known." Fitz laughed, then sobered. "Yes. The war has changed us all."

Startled, Ransom stared at his friend. He didn't look any different, except . . . perhaps Fitz displayed a niggle of discontent.

Then Fitz's countenance changed to merry dismay. "Oh, blast, everything you do becomes all the kick. That means every gentleman will marry this year. The pickings will be thin."

Ransom never meant anything so sincerely as when he said, "I have no interest in what others do."

"Which is why they copy you so assiduously. You do as you like and don't care what anyone thinks.

Like your sister.'' Fitz gestured toward the cardroom, where men sat on well-cushioned chairs of pink— Lady Goodridge's favorite color. Catching sight of a maiden, he said, "There's your type. The blushing one with the ivory headdress."

Ransom closed his eyes in pain. He hadn't had a woman for a long time. Yet these pink and white girls left him cold. They had no passion, no depth. They were untried, spoiled, rendered useless by a system that required nothing of them—much as he had been before the war.

Someone used an elbow to move him aside, and he opened his eyes. "No."

"You used to like the ones with the generous . . ." Fitz gestured.

"No." Blackburn walked away.

Fitz caught up with him. "Listen. I need your prestige to keep myself at the forefront of London society, and I can't do it if you walk away from me."

Blackburn slowed. How could he disparage so cheerfully insouciant a man? "Susan is right when she calls you a scoundrel."

Fitz preened. "But she said it affectionately, didn't she?"

"Very affectionately, although God knows why."

"Because she's a lonely widow. She appreciates a charming man, I'm a charmer. When a man is poor, he has to be, not like you glowering lords who have women fawn all over you." Fitz squinted through the haze created by a thousand candles. "There's a crowd over there."

Blackburn had never had patience with the simpering debutantes, the worshiping beaux, the downright dangerous mamas. But being with them, conversing with them, had become his duty. "A crowd."

Fitz picked up on Blackburn's hesitation, and read it as yielding. "Yes, a crowd, with a woman in their midst, a beautiful woman worthy even of the Marquess of Blackburn."

His damnable duty.

He scanned the throng as the crush became greater. Making his decision, he seized Fitz by the padding on his shoulders. "Come on then, man."

Fitz gave him a grin, then shoved his way into the crowd. He performed the service of breaker very efficiently, and Blackburn followed in his wake, ignoring the called greetings with the disdain for which he was well known. If he wanted to talk to someone, he would; there was no need to try and engage his attention.

"You're taller than I am. Can you see the newest belle?" Fitz asked.

Blackburn studied two younger sons, both better dressed than they had any right to be for their income.

"He's hiding in society where the only sin is unfashionable dress or a lack of blunt. And what better way to earn that blunt than to spy for the French?"

"Why do you keep ogling the men?" Fitz jostled him. "The women are over here! Women, Blackburn, women. Remember them? Smooth, scented, with all those interesting parts." Fitz gestured with both hands, illustrating a curve of hip and waist. "Wonderful, wily creatures who flee before the skillful hunter."

Listening to the delectation in Fitz's voice, Blackburn experienced a pang of envy. He had never felt that way about a woman. They'd always been easy for him, and once he had realized they were easy for every man blessed with a fortune, he had gained in contempt what he lost in gullibility.

Had any of them been different? Had he overlooked the one who was special?

But no, that could not be. For that to be true, he would have to admit he had been a blind fool. These women all looked the same, sounded the same, said the same things. "There's nothing worth having there."

"You'll find a diamond if you'd just search. A diamond, Blackburn!" Fitz paused in his onward charge. "Look at that bunch of slobbering hulks. They're huddled together, shoulder to shoulder, positively pawing the ground."

"Stallions," Blackburn reminded him.

Fitz called, "Let us through. There you go, lads. You can't keep her for yourselves." The constriction eased as the men turned, and Fitz slipped through the crowd, slighting each man as he spoke. "Southwick, does your wife know you're romancing a girl? Lord Mallery, you're not witty enough for this exalted group."

Blackburn followed close on Fitz's heels, protecting his friend's back and wondering why.

"Brockway, you old wigsby, you're too hoary for this game. No woman of taste would want"—the way parted, and Fitz stopped cold—"you."

He barely exhaled the last word, and Blackburn

trod on his heels. "Beg pardon, old man, but—"

"Your servant, ma'am!" Fitz snapped to attention, then bowed, leaving Blackburn a clear view of, not the diamond, but the profile of a tall, dignified lady. The fashionable lines of her green gown accentuated her excessive height. A lacy shawl covered only a modest bosom, and she held her gloved hands clasped at her waist like a singer waiting for a cue that never came. She wore a spinster's cap like a decoration of war, perched on the dark hair that had been cut to frame her face in wisps. Her composed mouth had never greeted a man invitingly. She was obviously an old maid. The chaperone.

Blackburn began to turn away.

Then she smiled at the woman beside her, a blond debutante with an exultant bosom. Filled with pride and pleasure, the smile lit the spinster's plain features and brought out the spark of jade in her fine eyes— and he'd seen those eyes before.

He jerked to a stop. He stared. It couldn't be her. She had to be a figment of his wary, suspicious mind.

He blinked and looked again.

Damn, it *was* her. Miss Jane Higgenbothem, the Scandal herself, risen from the depths of the past—to make his life hell once more.

Chapter 4

Eleven years before...

It was he, Jane thought with feverish pleasure.

Ransom Quincy, the Marquess of Blackburn, strode through the elite reception looking like a god who deigned to flatter unworthy mortals with his presence. He stood tall and proud, dwarfing the other gentlemen who minced between the ballroom and the cardroom. His blond hair was cut to perfection, each strand glowing like molten topaz flowing from Vulcan's furnace. His noble jaw jutted up at precisely the right angle; this god was arrogant and impatient with the perambulations of the marriage-minded mamas who shoved their daughters his way.

Jane hadn't expected to see him; he attended so few of these events. Though she always hoped she would. Ever since she'd first sighted him, she looked for him everywhere.

"Stop staring at him." Her sister, Melba, took Jane's drooping black ringlet and tried to coax curl back into the determinedly straight strand. "He's not for you."

"I know that," Jane answered. Of course she did. A god such as Blackburn deserved a goddess to match him. She ached to sketch him.

She surveyed the scene around her, despising the twittering debutantes. None of them was worthy to serve as his handmaiden, or even as a virgin sacrifice. Thus far in her first London season, she had seen no female worthy of him. Least of all herself, The Honorable Jane Higgenbothem, daughter of the impecunious and deceased Viscount Bavridge.

Blackburn lifted his silver quizzing glass. He scrutinized the white-gowned girls who stood along the wall, and they watched him anxiously, moths awaiting their call to the flame. One mother even gave her daughter a little push that sent her stumbling forward. He caught the chit, then carefully placed her back against the wall.

No one would make the selection for Blackburn. His glance fell on one of the Fairchilds, a Miss Redmond, and although she was beautiful, she clearly lacked character. He bowed to her, a sensuous exercise of muscle. Although Jane was too far away to hear him speak, she watched his beautiful lips move and knew they must be warm and soft, not at all like the cold clay with which she sculpted. He offered his arm; the chosen debutante giggled and covered her mouth with her gloved hand. He indicated his impatience with a sardonic lift of his brows, and Jane knew the girl would not be the recipient of another offer of a dance from Blackburn. Wiggling her smooth, white arms, she pranced off at his side.

She wasn't even cognizant of the honor done her.

Melba jiggled Jane's elbow. "Stop staring at Blackburn. Stand up straight. You're a lovely, tall girl and you deserve to stand above all the rest."

Jane straightened her shoulders and lifted her chin.

"And pay attention. Lord Athowe has arrived. He likes you, Jane. For pity's sake, make an effort to secure his suit."

Jane barely glanced at the handsome earl as he made his way through the crowd. "But I don't want to wed him. Besides"—she picked at the pearl button that closed her glove—"Miss Frederica Harpum has made it known that he is her beau."

"Miss Frederica Harpum has not yet received an offer, and that makes Lord Athowe fair game," Melba said, pragmatic in spite of her astounding beauty.

"But she's been friendly to me. Friendlier than anyone else in London."

"Friendly?" The word hovered, redolent with disapproval.

"Quite." Jane thought back on the girlish confidences exchanged over tea.

Melba snapped her ivory-handled fan shut. "Jane, you are remarkably naive. Frederica Harpum is about as friendly as a cobra in the zoo. Stay away from her. *Don't* discuss your unbecoming ambitions with her."

Jane opened her mouth to confess she already had.

"And *do* try to attach Lord Athowe." Melba must have seen the expression of mulish stubbornness for which Jane was famous, for she said softly, "Please, Jane, won't you at least try?"

Hearing the weary tone in her sister's voice, Jane said, "You're tired again. You've been tired a lot lately. Are you breeding at last?"

Melba placed her arm around Jane's shoulders. "No, I am not breeding. Eleazer would not have allowed me to come had I been so."

"Too bad," Jane muttered. She adored her seven-year-old niece, Adorna, and would have liked more.

"But you are not to make such blunt observations. Young women are not even supposed to know what that means."

She sounded severe, but Jane could see the dimple that blinked in and out of Melba's cheek. She had always amused Melba; Melba had always loved her. It was a good arrangement for two females with no supporting family.

"How silly." She tucked her arm around Melba's slim waist and hugged her close. "I am young, but I'm not stupid. Why, a woman who wishes to follow my calling must to the greatest of her ability seek to understand physical characteristics."

"Dearest." Melba picked her words carefully. "I know I've encouraged you with your little hobby, but I never meant that you should think it as anything but a pastime like needlework."

Offended to the core, Jane said hotly, "It's nothing like needlework! It's so much more. It's a God-given talent."

"It's unsuitable." Melba was ruthlessly practical.

"I must use it or the fates will destroy me."

"Don't be dramatic, dear." Turning Jane's face to her own, Melba said, "You're the daughter of a viscount, an impoverished one, so don't talk about your calling." She squeezed Jane hard and used the tone Jane would heed. "Especially not here!"

Athowe was approaching, Melba meant. Greeting the bowing earl, she said, "My lord, how good to see you! Have you once again come to whisk away my darling sister?"

"Yes, but what I found is even better." Stepping back, he lifted his thumb and studied them. "Two sister goddesses embracing! What a picture you make."

Immediately a portrait sprang to Jane's inner eye. Melba, truly a goddess and so brightly blond and fair, she shone with a nimbus. And Jane, a mortal, but taller, hardier, dark, with the big, strong hands that betrayed her vocation. It would be a magnificent painting, and Jane would do it for Melba as thanks for the years of insistent mothering.

"You have the most peculiar expression on your face, Miss Higgenbothem." Lord Athowe watched her with an indulgent, diverted expression. "I sometimes wonder if you even know where you are."

Jane blinked at him. "I do know. I simply don't always wish to be here."

"Jane!"

Chuckling, Lord Athowe raised his hand. "No, no, don't chide her. It's her delicious bluntness that has relieved the tedium of this endless season."

Jane didn't know about her delicious bluntness, but she certainly agreed about the tedium. How did the ton bear this? Year after year of fretting about the latest fashions, the newest dances, the design of one's jacket or a cut direct from a leader of society. Living in constant fear of being ostracized, yet avariciously waiting for someone to commit the least infraction of deportment, thus providing fodder for the gossip mill.

Jane hated it. She hated it all, and she had not been a success at first. Quite the opposite, for tall, capable women who looked a man in the eye were not modish. Then Lord Athowe had had his now famous quarrel with Miss Harpum, and had turned his attention to Jane. It had started out in a fit of pique to the stylish Miss Harpum, Jane was sure, but it was not that any longer. Lord Athowe liked Jane for her honesty, and his attention had engendered more attention until she found she was a small sensation among Athowe's contemporaries.

A distinct disadvantage for a woman who wished only to worship her hero—her inspiration—from afar. She glanced out on the dance floor and saw *him*, Lord Blackburn, preparing to perform a country dance with yet another undeserving twit.

Lord Athowe bowed before her, disrupting her view. "Miss Higgenbothem, would you please do me the honor of saving me a dance?"

Seeing the chance to be close to Blackburn, she said, "How about this one?"

Melba gasped beside her.

Lord Athowe jumped, too, but he gathered himself and offered his arm. "Refreshing and unique," he said.

Jane didn't care what he thought. She only cared about dancing near Lord Blackburn.

On the floor, lines formed, one for the men, one for the women, and Lord Athowe took his place opposite Jane. She was supposed to look only at him, but Blackburn stood almost within her range of sight, only two down, and she couldn't resist letting her hungry gaze wander his way.

The candles illuminated his high cheekbones and left his lower face in shadow, and Jane committed that characteristic to memory. There were so many facets to him, fascinating her in the variety of his emotions. She could willingly dedicate her life to catching his image, and still never get him right.

An elbow dug into her ribs. She turned and saw the lady next to her gesturing, and realized the music had begun. She was holding up the dance. Obediently she picked up her skirt and bustled to catch up.

Her skirt. It was a midnight blue velvet. Melba had not wanted her to have it, saying such a hue did not complement her coloring, but Jane had insisted. Although Blackburn did not know she was alive, each glance from him stroked her like velvet, and this gown was her own, private homage to the magnificence of Blackburn's fine midnight blue eyes.

As she looped through the dance, her nerves tightened. Each couple would change partners until they had danced with everyone in their set. That meant she would get to partner Blackburn. She would get to bow to him. She would get to touch his hand again, to look into his face again, as she had done on those rare and precious moments when she had shared the floor with the indifferent lord.

And that moment was fast approaching. Starting from opposite ends of the opposing lines, they advanced on each other. Jane distinctly noticed a tick of annoyance when Blackburn recognized her, but this time, she resolved, she would do nothing to embarrass him. She curtsied. He bowed. He offered his hand. She took it. And the excitement almost brought her into his arms.

But no. She recovered with nary a stumble. They stepped to the end of the line and separated. And the evening lost its savor.

She had seen him. She had touched him. She wanted to go back to the town house and work.

"Thank you for the dance, Miss Higgenbothem." Lord Athowe led her toward her sister. "It is always a privilege."

"You flatter me," Jane said with automatic civility. Melba would be proud.

"*Dear* Jane," Lord Athowe said. "I wish I could once have your full attention."

Jane blinked at him. "My full attention?"

"You're here, then you're gone, flitting off into another world where none of us dare follow. You look at me with those big, green eyes . . ."

Early in the season, when she had first met Blackburn, Jane had anxiously examined herself in the mirror. She was tall, thin, small-bosomed, rather muscular, with skin that tanned when exposed to the sun. She also had a pleasant smile, good teeth, and an abundance of long black hair which defied all efforts of the iron curler. She was not, and never would be, fashionable, but she had decided her eyes were jade, not green, and yes, even pretty surrounded by their dark, curled lashes. But they were not enough.

"*Jane.*" Pressing her hand between his, Lord Athowe called her back. "You've done it again. Won't you stay here with me?"

She looked around. He'd led her into an alcove where lovers visited when they could. But she was not his lover, nor did she wish to be. He was comely, wealthy, and seemed a kind man. He should have been a maiden's dream. But after eight years of observing Melba and her husband, Jane had no trouble recognizing a man both shallow and easily swayed. She would not have Athowe as a husband, nor any other man, for that matter. She had other, less conventional dreams. And her art. "Lord Athowe, I should go."

"You're correct to worry about the propriety." He leaned closer. "If you understood how I felt about you, you would tremble at the idea of being alone with me."

Jane thought he was trying to look dangerous and sensual, and failing badly. He ought to take lessons from Blackburn.

Then he unbuttoned her glove and pressed a wet kiss to her wrist, and she realized she had to escape.

She jerked her hand back, leaving her glove dangling between his fingers. Snatching it from him, she hurriedly replaced it. "Lord Athowe, please."

He edged closer. "Dear Jane, I know this is precipitate, but I ask, I beg—"

At that moment the orchestra gave a bleat much like a fanfare.

"What is that?" she quickly asked.

She snapped him out of his ardent performance, and his eyes narrowed with annoyance. "What?"

She stepped around him and looked into the ballroom.

"What . . ." Lord Athowe looked, also. "Oh, it's Frederica." He gave the name a particularly scornful intonation. "We don't need to be concerned about *her*. Not when we have each other."

Jane edged farther into the ballroom. "What is she doing on the orchestra stand?" She didn't really care, but curiosity about Frederica had just saved her from a very unpleasant scene.

Having concentrated attention on herself, Frederica smiled and gestured the crowd closer. "I have made the most extraordinary discovery." Her voice carried throughout the ballroom. "There is one among us who hides a pure, true talent."

Her gaze sought out Jane, then skipped to Athowe with a predatory hunger.

Four footmen struggled out of the door from the entry. They carried a square table on which was draped a large, upright, man-shaped form. Jane's heart gave an appalled thump. Could it be . . . ? And if it was, how she regretted doubting Melba's warnings about Frederica!

Bitterly Jane realized what a fool she was. A total unmitigated fool.

"It should not be hidden from society." Frederica smiled. "Not when it can bring us all such . . . entertainment.'' Malice lingered in the curve of her smooth, colored lips.

''So let me present you with''—she pulled the drape away—''Miss Jane Higgenbothem's own creation!''

Silence struck like a bolt of lightning. Like the thunder that follows, the ton gasped. Then, like the rustle of wind before a killing storm, Jane heard the whispers slip across the room. ''Blackburn.'' ''Lord Blackburn.'' ''It's Blackburn.'' ''He's *naked*!''

For one brief moment of gratification, Jane admired the statue she had created. Seen in the light of a thousand candles, it was superb. The features were firm, full of pride and disdain. The classic pose displayed every muscle, and they seemed to move sinuously beneath the smooth clay skin. It looked so real, she wanted to shout with pride.

This was *her* work. Her best work. The work into which she had poured her heart and soul and used her all her skill to create. Surely these people would recognize art and beauty when they saw it. Surely they would treat her statue with the reverence it deserved.

Dragging her gaze from her creation, Jane blinked hopefully around her.

But she saw no admiration. Only horror. Titillation. Contempt.

Then a path opened between her and Blackburn.

In the abstract, detached manner of one living a nightmare, she noted that Blackburn's forehead throbbed with a bright red vein. His beautifully generous mouth was compressed into a tight line. His hands, clad in snow white kid, flexed and unflexed as if Jane's neck rested between them. He was the incarnation of pure rage.

She swallowed convulsively and stepped back, reaching to steady herself against Lord Athowe's arm.

He was not there.

"Lord Blackburn, confess all." Frederica paused to snigger. "Did you . . . pose . . . for this statue?"

"No," Jane said. "Oh, no."

Blackburn whipped his head around and glared at Frederica.

She was insinuating that Blackburn had stood patiently, exposing himself to Jane's artistic scrutiny, when nothing could be further from the truth. The sculpting had been drawn from furtive observations and vivid imagination.

"I did not," Blackburn snapped.

But an amused, anonymous male voice called, "Blackburn won't admit to it. What man would?"

Like a dam breaking, the comment shattered the crowd's composure.

Laughter blasted forth from every throat. The lords and ladies of the ton pointed, their fingers trembling, at Jane's finest work. They laughed until dark threads of kohl dripped down the women's cheeks, until men's cravats withered under the force of their amusement, until Blackburn swore without caution, until Jane burned with mortification.

Until Jane's reputation was in shreds.

Chapter 5

Laughter. Jane could almost hear its echo in Lady Goodridge's ballroom. She would never forget. Could never forget. Not the laughter, nor the dreadful shattering of the Ming vase, nor the thump of Melba's body as she fainted.

Those sounds had signaled the end of Jane's reputation, her ambitions, and her life. Everything since had been grief and duty, and now every time she heard the laughter of merrymakers, she flinched, then turned to see if they were pointing at her.

They weren't. No one even looked at her. They all stared at Adorna.

And why not? Adorna's blond hair had been shaped by an artist's scissors and now curled cunningly around the nape of her long, slender neck. Violet's modiste had created a gown of simple white muslin, tied with a gold cord beneath Adorna's generous breasts. Her white kid slippers displayed her tiny feet, and silk stockings rustled against linen petticoats.

And as always, the curves of her body undulated

in a natural feminine rhythm as she walked, and that rhythm sounded the mating call to the male of the human species.

"Ma'am." A man of good height and close-cropped brown hair approached Jane and boldly took her hand. "If I were so forward as to introduce myself to you, and acquaint you with my credentials, would you introduce me to your ward?"

A chorus of boos from the other men distracted her from his pleasant, imploring face. Amused, she said, "Your friends scarcely approve."

"They're not friends, they're turncoats." He glanced around. "But I have the approval of a peer of the realm. Blackburn, tell this honorable chaperone who you are and explain that I'm respectable."

Jane didn't move, didn't look, but froze like a London street urchin who scented danger. From the corner of her eye, she noted a tall man step out of the pressing crowd while the other gentlemen fell back deferentially. She noted, too, that Blackburn stared at her as if she truly were a street urchin, streaked with soot and out of place.

She was. Oh, heavens, she was.

"I could hardly swear to your respectability, Fitz, without perjuring myself."

Blackburn sounded stiff and impatient, and Jane waited, quivering, for him to impugn her.

"But I have met this . . . lady before, and I can introduce you, if you like."

That was all.

Quietly he performed the courtesies, and his companion, Mr. Gerald Fitzgerald, seemed unaware of anything unusual in Blackburn's demeanor. Of course, that was because Adorna fixed his attention. Dear Adorna, who had blossomed beneath the concentrated fascination of so many men.

When he had done his duty, Blackburn did not step away. The well-remembered scent of lemon clung to him as he pulled her apart from the company. In a voice low and intense with contempt, he asked, "Stop quivering so! Did you expect me to denounce you?"

Slowly she looked up at him.

She could have sworn she hadn't forgotten anything about Ransom Quincy, the Marquess of Blackburn, but she must have, for his Viking beauty took her breath away. He seemed taller, although that was perhaps a function of her dismay. His blond hair seemed lighter, less golden, as white streaked it. He gazed through the silver quizzing glass she remembered so well, and his midnight blue eyes pierced her until she thought she must be bleeding.

"I would not explain to that crowd that you single-handedly exposed me to ridicule and humiliation." His upper-class accent grew more clipped as he spoke, and his voice deepened as he added, "For the most part, they have forgotten, and I have no wish to raise the specter of that scandal."

He probably hoped she would turn tail and run. He didn't comprehend that worse things had happened since that long-ago ball.

Her spine straightened, and flush with aplomb, she said, "You seem to forget, the scandal mortified more than one person."

"Who?" His gaze swept the babbling Fitz, the entire ballroom, before returning to rest on her.

Was he really so uncaring, or was he simply oblivious? "Such an inconvenience, my lord, to think of someone other than yourself," she said crisply. "So unusual for you, also."

His nostrils flared as he considered her. "You are impertinent."

"Following your example, my lord."

His rangy litheness had given way to a broader, more muscular build, and now he looked as cold and solid as marble. He didn't care what she thought or what she had suffered, but even for that, Jane was glad. Glad that she'd seen her nemesis. Glad that she'd found her tongue, uncovered her wit, and answered him smartly as he deserved. Any additional disgrace would be worth the self-respect she'd gained.

Then Adorna's beguiling voice shattered Jane's triumph. "Aunt Jane, would you introduce me to his lordship?"

Coming down to earth with a thump, Jane apprehended she couldn't afford the satisfaction of cutting Blackburn. He might be a rude beast, but he was wealthy, titled, and influential, and for Adorna's sake she had to preserve the fiction of mutual respect. She had perfected the unemotional mask; now she donned it, performed the introductions, and waited, torn between satisfaction and old heartache, for Blackburn to see Adorna. To really *see* Adorna and fall under the spell of her womanly charms.

The quizzing glass swept Adorna as she curtsied and murmured her pleasure at making his acquaintance. "How do you do, Miss Morant?" His smile, his courtesy, his bow, were everything a matchmaking mama could wish.

And that was what she was, Jane reminded herself. A matchmaker, seeking the best marriage possible for her niece. If that marriage happened to be with Blackburn, well—the fates had laughed at Jane before, and she had lived. She would survive this irony, too.

"Do you have a dance reserved?" he asked.

Jane scarcely winced.

Adorna lavished a smile on him, and with a wiggle of her shoulders, said, "Aren't you lucky. I have just one left."

"Then pray give it to my friend Fitz." Blackburn sighed as if the prospect of a country jig with a lovely maiden bored him beyond tears. "He's a war hero, but he can probably still hobble around to a slow tune."

Jane glared at the insufferable man. Did he think to avenge himself by his petty rudeness?

For the first time, he lowered the quizzing glass. A scar marred his face, drawing the inner corner of his eye down and streaking the brown skin of his brow with white. The disfiguration was slight, yet ten years ago he had been perfect, arrogant, and thoughtless to the point of cruelty. In her heart Jane had believed he was divine, untouchable by either emotion or injury. Now she had seen his marred face, and the earth shuddered beneath her feet.

"I say," Mr. Fitzgerald said, laughing in mock exasperation, "I can ask for myself."

"Of course, Lord Blackburn. I would be pleased to dance with Mr. Fitzgerald. He is surely the handsomest man in London.'' Adorna looked at Mr. Fitzgerald from beneath weighted eyelids, while the men around them protested in hearty, disbelieving voices.

Jane inventoried Blackburn's chiseled nose, his finely carved cheekbones, his granite chin. That face epitomized the best and finest of nobility and temperament. Yet she couldn't ignore the proof of his vulnerability.

Nor could she ignore the character his scar added to his features, or the artistic itch in her fingers.

She sought the words to express her outrage at Blackburn's pain, to demand to know why he had put himself into danger, to beg to worship as she had worshiped before.

But he was already turning away.

And thank God, she was coming to her senses.

''Lord Blackburn.'' Adorna's suddenly nononsense tone startled Jane. She sounded so much like Melba. ''You, in turn, must grant me a boon.''

Blackburn halted, and his quizzing glass rose again. He gazed on Adorna as if she were a puppy who had set her teeth in his coattails. ''I must?''

''The dancing will start soon, and my aunt will be left without an escort.''

Jane gasped. ''Adorna, no!''

The lord and the debutante ignored her.

''You'll care for her,'' Adorna said.

''I will?''

''Yes.''

Ten years ago, Jane had devoted her every waking moment to a study of Blackburn. She had hung on his every word; she had deciphered his every expression.

Now she saw him look around, noting the silence that had fallen. She knew he was weighing the consequences of a contemptuous refusal. She realized he was wondering if this scene would be gossiped about, and if the names of Miss Jane Higgenbothem and Blackburn would again be linked.

She saw the moment when he made his decision.

A tight smile thinned his generous lips. He bowed gracefully and extended his hand. "Escorting this . . . lady would be my dearest pleasure."

Chapter 6

Jane viewed Blackburn's white-gloved hand so dis-
dainfully he was tempted to check for a spot. "I can't
leave Adorna alone," she said.

"Of course you can." Her fingers were threaded
together, and he separated them with what he considered remarkable patience, then grasped one hand and
pulled. "All her dances are taken; your duty is done."

The foolish woman set her heels. "I truly can't.
Gentlemen are not gentlemen where she's concerned."

He glanced at Adorna, smiling and flirting. "I suspect that is true. However, scandal is seldom allowed
to rear its ugly head in my sister's home. In fact, it
has been almost ten years since the last scandal."

She tried to wrestle her hand free. "Eleven."

"Time flies." He gripped tightly. "Do you want
me to drag you across the ballroom? I believe that
would cause the kind of infamy you delight in."

She stumbled forward under the threat.

"Very wise," he murmured. Holding Jane Higgenbothem's hand once again sent an odd sensation of pleasure within him. Forcing her to do his bidding caused an even greater pleasure, and with notable deliberation, he placed her hand on his arm. "Now let us make a circle of the ballroom and squelch any rumors that may already be circulating."

"There are no rumors." Stiffly she walked beside him, obviously finding no gratification in his company.

"There will be if you don't smile." He grinned down at her, demonstrating *his* self-control and hoping he annoyed her as much as she disturbed him.

Yet she walked at his side through the crowd, her gaze resting on no one, serene as a black swan cruising through a pool of gabbling white geese.

The woman had no right to act so sedate. Not considering her *succès de scandale*. "Has anyone recognized you yet?"

"No."

"They will." Her fingers flexed just the slightest bit, and he felt an unworthy sense of triumph. Like a ragamuffin teasing a lost puppy, he picked at her, and he wondered at himself. He had scarcely thought about Miss Jane Higgenbothem in years. He could have sworn he hadn't. But when he saw her, all the old rancor came rushing back. He still wanted revenge, and on more than one level.

She was still as damnably tall. Her figure still put him in mind of the Valkyries, strong and curvaceous. She still spoke in that rich, clean voice with its lucid intonations, and her features were still too distinct for a feminine face.

Yet although Miss Higgenbothem appeared to be the same, she had matured. She no longer looked at him with worship-struck eyes. All those years ago, he had been immensely annoyed and embarrassed by her guileless adoration. Now he found himself speculating if she remembered that final scene in his home quite as well as he did.

"I have come face-to-face with three ladies who met me during my season. They looked right through me." Her chin was up. Her back was straight. As haughtily as ever his sister Susan had, she stared down the ill-mannered sots who dared observe them. "As a chaperone, I find I am invisible."

"What a fanciful flight." Imperiously he nodded to a classmate from Eton while guiding Miss Higgenbothem around him. He was not going to introduce her to that debaucher. "I might have expected as much from you."

"Indeed, I am not fanciful, my lord." Her voice contained frost. "Do you often notice a young lady's chaperone?"

He didn't, of course, but he was the Marquess of Blackburn. He didn't have to admit he was wrong.

She chuckled dryly.

"I'm doing this for your own good," he snapped.

"Ah. And I thought you were doing it because Adorna commanded you. It must be very uncomfortable, my lord, to be a leader of society and fear the memory of an old calumny."

"I would not find the recollection nearly as uncomfortable as you, Miss Higgenbothem."

She paused, then in a colorless tone, she said, "For Adorna's sake, you are correct."

For just a moment, she had been itching for a fight. His Jane had been acting like the creature of fire and passion with whom he had briefly skirmished. Now the dutiful chaperone had returned.

He was, of course, relieved. "I imagine the performance of your duties brings you great satisfaction."

"I can't imagine you care, my lord."

"I'm making conversation, Miss Higgenbothem." He paused beside one of the pink-painted pillars that ringed the ballroom, placed his palm against it, and leaned close.

"Ah. Conversation." Now she sounded bored. Bored! When before she would have been adoring.

She had not removed her hand from his sleeve, and he studied her.

As a girl, she had been bony, with angles of figure and face. Now he saw she had gained weight, enough to smooth out the angles and give her grace. Too, age had softened the raw vulnerability and untamed eagerness. Her determined chin, her enigmatic eyes, her placid brow, revealed nothing of her former fire. Only the mouth was the same: full, tender, and perhaps passionate—for the right man.

"Conversation," she repeated, "accompanied by a smile, is that not correct, my lord?" She smiled with those lips, but it did not pacify him; her attitude presently reminded him of his sister's. Jane was humoring him.

She asked, "How long must we keep up this charade?"

Humoring him, and none too politely, either. "Until I say we are done," he said from between clenched teeth.

"Very well. When we have spoken the proper amount of words, proper being defined by the Marquess of Blackburn, then you must sound the alert, and I will cease speaking at once."

"This is not a game, Miss Higgenbothem."

"I did not think so, my lord." They had circled the far end of the ballroom, and Jane was able to look across the dance floor to the crowd that surrounded Adorna. "Satisfaction, I believe you said. Yes, there is a great deal of satisfaction in chaperoneing Adorna. I have been her chaperone and companion since the death of my sister ten years ago, so I know the challenges. But tonight was a test of sorts, not for Adorna, who has always shown herself perfectly at ease in society, but for me. It has been so long, you remember, since I last visited London."

He started walking again. She fell in step. "Surely you have been back since—"

Jane whipped her head toward him and glared. "Don't be absurd. Who would have me?"

Indeed. Who would have her? She had been totally ruined by both her actions and his.

"Tonight appears to have been a success for you."

"A success for Adorna, at least." Jane glanced at him, then glanced away as if she could not stand to look at him for too long. "We are staying with Lady Tarlin. Do you remember Lady Tarlin, my lord?"

Remember her? They had been childhood friends,

the kind of friendship that never included romance and always included teasing. As he reached manhood and left to pursue the fair life as the leader of London's ton, they had drifted apart, and when next they'd met, it had been during Violet's first season.

Jane's season, too.

From his lofty position as ton leader, he had been vaguely glad to see Violet, yet not glad enough to really befriend her. After all, she was just a debutante. He had been carelessly kind, helping her find her feet as one of the season's successes, even introducing her to Tarlin, a rare chap with a good head on his shoulders.

For all the thanks he got. When scandal had struck, Violet had ripped a strip off of him that might have left a lesser man bleeding and uncertain. Responding now to Jane's question, he said, "Yes. I remember Lady Tarlin. I believe she was your friend during the . . ." He hesitated.

"The Disastrous Season, my lord, is how I have always referred to it. I find it apt, and it stops me from any romanticizing I might do."

He looked down at her again. She wore that spinster's cap with confidence. Her still hands, her calm eyes too, clearly indicated this woman would not romanticize anything.

"She is sponsoring Adorna, and when we first arrived tonight, she remained by our sides, introducing Adorna and easing me into my newfound duties." Humor warmed her voice. "I found it quite edifying to inspect the men with a judicious eye, and reach conclusions about their suitability for my niece."

It appeared she could laugh at herself now, as well as at him. Her young, earnest, humorless attitude had been modified, and he found his own attitude making an unwilling adjustment. He could honestly say he enjoyed her company—when she displayed a proper demeanor.

"I confess," she continued, "I took pleasure from deciding on the suitability of Adorna's companions. So I sent Lady Tarlin on her way to mingle with friends, and I remained."

Although Blackburn was looking down at Jane, he could have sworn he was steering a fair path. But someone bumped him from the side, and he turned to excuse himself. And found himself facing a disgruntled Lord Athowe.

"Sorry, Blackburn."

Blackburn didn't speak, but bowed slightly and moved on, well aware that Athowe was watching Jane with a slight frown wrinkling his pudgy face.

Apparently the little worm couldn't quite recall Jane's name.

But although Jane's expression remained unclouded, her quick, indrawn breath told Blackburn that she recognized Athowe. "Have we had enough conversation now?"

"Conversation is the accepted pastime for those who do not dance."

"You used to dance." She grimaced like someone who had betrayed interest where she should have none.

"I used to believe society's conviction that the best way to find a wife was to meet her at a ball and dance with her, much like a buyer who goes to market and rides the mare before he buys it.''

Damn! What had made him say *that*?

Through the noise of conversation and music, he distinctly felt her wince, and she removed her hand from his arm.

''I beg your pardon.'' He stopped and bowed stiffly. ''My friend Fitz says I am turning into a churl, and it would seem he is correct.''

''I've been saying that for years, Ransom, and you've never listened to me.'' The evening's hostess, Lady Goodridge, stepped around the pillar and offered her cheek. He kissed it while she scrutinized his companion. ''Miss Higgenbothem, you're back in London at last. I had begun to wonder if you would ever return.''

Chapter 7

```
～❧❦～
```

Lady Goodridge had identified her, and seemingly without difficulty. Jane could scarcely bear to look at Blackburn, and when she did he was smirking at her with what she considered quite a superior air.

"There's no need to be *obnoxious*, Ransom. Miss Higgenbothem might have remained unnoticed without *your* interference."

"Really, Susan?" Blackburn gazed at his sister demandingly.

She conceded, "Then again, perhaps not. And, Miss Higgenbothem, I see you've gotten over that *unfortunate* tendency to *worship* Ransom. So bad for his already-towering *conceit*." Lady Goodridge indicated two delicate, pink-cushioned chairs placed against the pillar. "Shall we?"

"Of course." A mixture of emotions tumbled through Jane. This imposing woman had never been anything less than kind; indeed, on the occasion of Jane's disgrace, she had been generous and supportive. But although she was stout, and wore pink in more shades than any one woman had the right, she bore a remarkable resemblance to her brother. The fair hair and firm features that looked so handsome on him gave Lady Goodridge a stern expression that had been known to send timid debutantes fleeing.

Jane subdued just such an instinct. She was, after all, a long way from a debutante. Still, she stood after Lady Goodridge took her seat.

"What are you waiting for?" Lady Goodridge waved an imperious hand at her brother. "Go. We are in need of sustenance."

He hovered, observing his sister through his silver quizzing glass. "I dread to leave Miss Higgenbothem alone with you."

"I have overcome my regrettable tendency toward *cannibalism*." Lady Goodridge smiled at him tightly. "At least as long as I am *fed*. I would like some pigeon, an apricot fritter, and the roast venison. Now, go *fetch* it!"

The force of the command surprised Jane, and she waited for an explosion of masculine temperament and injured pride. Instead he said, "Susan, you need a husband."

"A husband." Lady Goodridge reared back. "A husband! What would I do with a husband? I buried the first one within a year of our marriage. I don't look forward to repeating that experience."

"Get a young one this time," Blackburn advised. "Pick one you like. Papa can't arrange a betrothal for you this time, and a husband would curb your tendency to be overbearing."

"It runs in the family," she retorted.

He met Jane's eyes ruefully. "Sisters," he said in a tone that suggested she would comprehend his vexation, and with a bow, he marched toward the banquet room.

Lady Goodridge watched him with unmistakable pride. "One must be *firm* with him, or he'll stampede right over the top of one."

She seemed to expect an answer, so Jane murmured, "Yes, my lady."

"I understand *you're* that girl's chaperone," Lady Goodridge said as she adjusted her skirts.

Now Jane remembered Lady Goodridge's other attribute—she was remarkably blunt, as Jane had once been. "Adorna. Yes, she's my niece."

"Of course. Melba's girl. I sent my condolences. I was hoping you'd respond."

It was a reproach, but Jane would not allow herself to feel guilt. The time after Melba's death had been wrenching, and Jane had had to adjust to becoming Eleazer's unpaid housekeeper and Adorna's only parent, and a sense of loneliness that had never lessened.

With rare perspicacity, Lady Goodridge said, "But how rude of me to recall a time of such sorrow for you." Lifting her monocle, she looked across the ballroom. As if she had special powers, the crowd parted to show them Adorna, and Lady Goodridge looked her up and down. "Looks just like Melba."

"Yes. She is just as beautiful."

"But a widgeon where the mother was not." She turned a look on Jane. "Still, *you'll* do."

Jane didn't exactly know what that meant, but she said demurely, "Thank you, my lady."

"Now, stop hovering and sit."

Jane sat.

"I understand the father is a merchant," Lady Goodridge said.

Folding her hands in her lap, Jane answered, "Adorna's? Yes, he is."

"A misfortune," Lady Goodridge pronounced. "Still, her mother's *noble* background, combined with those *looks*, a *fortune*, and her *manner*, cannot fail to find its mark. How have you managed to raise the girl to be so unself-conscious?"

"She knows she's beautiful. She doesn't seem to realize that everyone is not similarly blessed."

"Harrumph." Lady Goodridge observed Adorna again.

This time the girl noticed the scrutiny. Her eyes widened when she saw the company Jane kept. Then she gifted them both with a smile.

Taken aback by the enhancement to an already extraordinary beauty, Lady Goodridge blinked. "I don't envy you guiding her through her first season. All *perdition* will break loose now that the bucks have *seen* her."

"It is frightening." Especially in view of that previous kidnapping attempt. "But she's a dear girl who loves and respects me, and she'll listen to my advice."

"About *nabbing* a *husband*?" Lady Goodridge asked meaningfully.

Pride rose on a gust of hostility, and she looked

Lady Goodridge right in the eyes. "About good manners."

A slight smile broke the severity of Lady Goodridge's features. "You've acquired the patina of maturity, Jane Higgenbothem."

Lady Goodridge had been testing her, Jane realized. For what reason?

Lady Goodridge watched her closely. "When my brother returned from the Peninsula, he almost *totally* abandoned society. Stupid thing, to go running off to defeat Napoleon when you haven't got an heir yet, and so I told him, I assure you. I told him, 'Figgy' "—Lady Goodridge patted Jane's hand—"I still call him 'Figgy.' "

With a composure that amazed her, Jane said, "I can't imagine he appreciates that."

"No, but when he's doing his arrogant marquess act, I find it quite effective in bringing him down to earth. At any rate, I said, 'Figgy, you're *thirty-four*, *titled*, still *unwed*, and, most important, *quite wealthy*. You need a wife.' "

Jane subdued a smile at the thought of Blackburn's reaction. "Did he agree?"

"He never agrees with me." Lady Goodridge smiled, her powder cracking. "I am the eldest by *quite* ten years. You would think by now he would understand I am *always* right. Miss Higgenbothem, the statue remained in my custody after the ball, and I examined it *closely*."

Jane blushed.

"I was much impressed, and I am now interested in the progress of your *art*."

A circumstance which did not surprise Jane at all. "I sketch."

"In a superior manner, I am sure. But how is your *sculpting*?"

Jane barely noticed the great emptiness the subject invoked. "I no longer work with clay."

"I feared as much. A great talent lost, and all because of my brother's *wounded* conceit. Of course, as serious as he is now, I would be glad of a return to his former *insufferability*."

"He seems to be insufferable enough."

"Hm." Her eyes narrowed on Jane in a most uncomfortable manner. "In his maturity, he does tend to do the things he thinks are right, regardless of how painful they may be. His reckless ardor during your ill-advised visit to his home laid the tombstone on your reputation. I daresay he will now seek to *redress* the *injury*."

Jane found herself stirring uncomfortably on her seat. "It wasn't ardor, my lady, but vengeance which drove him."

"Come, my dear, you can't cozen me! If you will recall, I was one of the women who found you." Lady Goodridge glanced around the ballroom, and her eyes narrowed. With a smile, she focused her attention on Jane. "I recognize *ardor* when I see it."

Heat swept Jane from toes to hairline, and she knew color burned in her cheeks.

After a short, poignant silence, Lady Goodridge laid a finger on Jane's chin and turned her face to hers. For a brief moment Jane met her eyes bravely. But only for a moment. She couldn't maintain her equanimity under that knowing scrutiny, and she dropped her gaze to stare blindly at Lady Goodridge's lap.

"Don't tell me." Lady Goodridge tapped her finger rather sharply. "You haven't kissed another man since."

Jane never thought she would wish for Blackburn's return, but she would court even that adversity to stop this dreadful conversation.

"You're the same green, untouched girl you were eleven years ago. You're still—"

Please don't say it, please don't say it!

"—a virgin!" Lady Goodridge concluded.

Jane glanced at her triumphant face, then looked hopefully toward the banquet room—and found Blackburn standing close by, holding two plates and impassively listening to the revelations.

She had wanted him to rescue her. She had *not* wanted him to overhear.

"Ransom." Lady Goodridge sounded demurely pleased. "You brought dinner."

"As you instructed." But he was looking at Jane.

"Good heavens, man, I don't have time to *eat*!" Lady Goodridge hefted herself out of the fragile chair. "I'm the *hostess*, and the dancing has started."

So it had. The orchestra had struck up a lilting air, and Jane had been unaware. Now she was aware of everything. The skipping dancers, the flirting debutantes, the predatory mamas. Most of all, she was aware of the insight Lord Blackburn had just been given, and she shuddered in embarrassment.

It was stupid, really, for of course she was a virgin.

She was not married, so virginity was assumed. But somehow the words changed Jane from a capable spinster into a woman of physical attributes. Where before she was sure Blackburn had no notion that beneath her gown she had a waist and hips and . . . other anatomical features, she now saw his gaze lingering on her bosom. Her hand crept up, and she tugged her shawl tighter.

Lady Goodridge pointed to the seat she had vacated. "Ransom, you sit *here* and eat that food *yourself.* You, Miss Higgenbothem, *enjoy* the *party*. I shall look forward to speaking with you *again*."

In sinking dismay, Jane stared after her departing tormentor. She would have given anything to think of an excuse to bolt, but her normal intelligence seemed to have fled under the weight of embarrassment.

"Your plate." Blackburn thrust it beneath her nose. "I hope you enjoy my selections. Susan was so busy giving instructions about her preferences, I forgot to ask yours."

"It looks lovely." Jane couldn't even discern its contents. She took the exquisitely decorated Chinese porcelain in her hand, careful not to touch him, desperate not to drop it, hoping for an obscure Oriental hex that would hurtle the holder into purgatory.

Yet when Blackburn released his grip, she was still in Lady Goodridge's ballroom. And really, what need of purgatory when she was here?

He seated himself beside her. "The almond biscuits are rather good, and I've found them quite useful in settling my stomach after any encounter with my sister."

Perhaps he was being amusing. She peeked at his frowning, downturned face.

Perhaps not. Picking up a round, flat, dry thing, she bit into it. "It's very good."

"That's the apricot fritter," he said gently.

"Well . . . it's good." Dabbing her mouth with the napkin he had provided, she braved a look across the ballroom. As she had feared, the attention of two of society's leaders had made her the cynosure of all eyes. The flapping fans waved a gust of speculation across her hot cheeks. What had started out as an ordeal with the end in sight—that is, of returning to Adorna's side after a circuit of the ballroom—now extended into eternity.

But she would not—could not—become the easily intimidated girl she had been before. She was no longer a foolish wallflower, but the sedate and dignified Jane Higgenbothem. Even when the ton discovered her identity, which she hated to admit, was now a distinct possibility, her composed demeanor, her spinster cap, most of all, her advanced age, kept her safe from vulgar speculation.

Again she risked a glance at Blackburn. Two deep lines dug their furrows between his brows, his lips were turned down, and she could see the faint white tracings of his scar. Surely its appearance, while distressing, conclusively proved he was not a god.

She would not allow him to manipulate her again.

Finding a biscuit, she bit into it and even tasted it. Yes, she would continue as Adorna's chaperone, dull and free of scandal, and any unwanted attention would quickly fade. "The almond biscuits *are* quite tasty."

"Miss Higgenbothem." Blackburn sounded as impatient as she felt. "I must apologize for my sister. She is remarkably outspoken, as though, because she is Lady Goodridge, she is above the most basic manners."

Jane found herself answering coolly, "It seems to be a trait in your family."

"Food has put heart into you." He stabbed a chunk of venison with his fork. "And a rather unwanted sauce, also. If you wish me to question you about your activities, or lack of them, in the past eleven years, I find myself as curious as my sister."

At that moment, Jane wondered what idiotic peculiarity of hers had once made this man seem irresistible.

But before she could reply, she heard a familiar voice call, "Jane." Violet hurried toward her, looking little like Countess of Tarlin and more like the madcap, informal friend she had been long ago. The light apple green cambric skirt fluttered around her as she walked, her hair had been swept up and crimped, and anxiety rode on her shoulder.

Bracing herself, Jane rose. She'd denied even the possibility that she might be recognized; Blackburn had forced her to face the truth. It was only a matter of time, and from the expression on Violet's pinched face, she suspected the time had come.

Violet did not even take the time to glare her dislike at him as he stood in polite response to her appearance. "Jane, she's gone."

Jane had braced herself for one debacle. Now she faced another, far worse disaster.

Violet's quiet voice shivered on the breathless edge of panic. "Adorna has disappeared."

Chapter 8

Is your entire family driven to misadventure?

The question hovered at the edge of Blackburn's mind, but he had too much mastery to say such a thing. Miss Higgenbothem looked much as she had all those years ago when her misguided infatuation had been revealed. White and shocked, and staring at him as if she expected him to swoop in and make everything better.

Now, as if that moment of connection had never been, she curtsied. "As always, my lord, I am humbled and honored by your attention."

Clearly she didn't need him; she had done without him for years.

He took the half-empty plate she held out. Turning from him, she linked arms with Violet, and they strolled away casually enough to fool any of the scandal-seeking matrons. Jane straightened her shoulders, and he remembered how she made just that gesture when her sister had collapsed. It was a sign of strength and independence, and he thoroughly approved.

Approved while he suffered a pang of guilt.

And for what? He had had nothing to do with this Adorna's disappearance.

Except that he had taken Jane away from her charge against her wishes, and dismissed her concerns as trivial. He found himself handing the two plates to a passing footman and walking after Jane as if he were a pull toy and she held the string.

The thought brought him up short. He was the Marquess of Blackburn. He was indifferent to any woman's needs and impervious to guilt. After all, it was the missing girl, Miss Morant, who had blackmailed him into escorting her aunt on this ill-fated tour of the ballroom.

Moreover, he had a duty to England which surpassed Jane and the fate of her charge.

He glanced around the ballroom. People who had no right to even gaze upon a nobleman of his stature were staring, and from somewhere behind, he heard the hiss of words. Words that sounded remarkably like "statue," and "scandal."

This was worse than he had expected. In his time at war, he had been wounded, not just by shrapnel, but with the sights and sounds of battle. He had thought that when he returned to England, he could return to his old self. He had thought he would once more become careless and uncaring, but on occasion he found himself being sensitive, almost . . . kind. It appalled him, and he hated exposing those newly painful parts of himself to this vulgar curiosity. The sooner he could find the traitor, the better.

And the revival of this old infamy could be utilized for that purpose.

His gaze darted to Miss Higgenbothem. She and Lady Tarlin stepped out of one of the many-paned glass doors that led to the garden. The month was March, the temperature cool, and as he stared at her slim figure, she shivered and clutched her shawl tighter.

If he were out with her, it would be good of him to offer her his coat. And an idea took hold of him.

If he appeared to be courting Jane, all of the ton would be so entertained to see the toplofty Lord Blackburn making a fool of himself, they would never think to examine his motives. Even the traitor himself would be unwary.

Yet to seek the whispers and the laughter! He clenched his gloved fist. He'd crushed the tattle once before with the sheer force of his personality. The recovery of his former position of glory had taken months, and his rage had only slowly dissipated. Court Jane, and the ridicule that accompanied it? He had better think long and hard before he took such a rash and painful action.

He glanced once through the windowed doors at Jane. Already she was in trouble, and at her first function! No, damn it! No, only if he had to would he use her as a distraction.

Then, just within earshot, he heard the whine of the matchmaking mosquito.

"I do so want your charming brother to meet my youngest," said Lady Kinnard in the high, nasal tone inherited by every one of her progeny.

"Of *course* you do," Susan replied with malice aplenty. "He stands alone. Shall we *intercept* him?"

From ten feet away, Blackburn met Susan's amused gaze. He had been dodging a succession of Kinnard's blond, avaricious daughters for years, and he would not succumb now.

The garden and his obligation to his country beckoned. With the swift resolution that made him a good officer, he determined to pursue Jane. Swiveling once more, he marched toward escape.

As he opened the door, he heard Jane ask fiercely, "Which of the men are missing?"

"Jane, there are hundreds of people here!" Violet said.

Blackburn shut the door without regard to Lady Kinnard's pursuit. "Who saw Adorna last?"

Violet looked at him, startled.

"I saw her last." Fitz stepped out of the shadows at the edge of the long, marble terrace.

Of course Fitz would be here, Blackburn thought. For all his former determination to remain single, he fell in love with obnoxious regularity. He would have to be fathoms deep in love with the inimitable Adorna.

"She danced off with Mr. Joyce," Fitz said, "and never returned."

"Mr. Joyce." Miss Higgenbothem tapped her foot, an intense rhythm. "Do I know him?"

"An unsavory character." Ransom held the door shut when Lady Kinnard tried to open it.

Fitz observed his friend's maneuver without undue interest. "Brockway has searched the gaming chambers, Herbert the banquet hall, and Lord Mallery has completed a circuit of the ballroom. No sign of her, but Southwick was dancing with another gel, and he heard Joyce say something about sundials.''

Lady Kinnard peered through one of the windows in the door, her nose smashed flat against the glass.

"Sundials." Ransom looked around at the darkened garden. "Miss Morant couldn't be so foolish as to follow him out at night."

"Adorna is not noted for her good sense," Jane said.

"Kinnard's moving to the left," Fitz advised him.

Blackburn grasped the handle to the next door.

Pounding on the panel with the flat of her hand, Lady Kinnard called, "Yoohoo. Lord Blackburn!"

Jane pulled her shawl tighter around her shoulders. "Does Lady Goodridge have a sundial?"

"Near the gazebo," Violet said.

Lady Kinnard threw her whole weight against the door, and it swayed outward.

"Shall we go?" Blackburn let go of the handle and offered his arm to Jane. She barely glanced at it and hurried down the stairs. Fitz followed close on her heels.

"Unusual for you to be ignored, isn't it, Blackburn?" Violet clasped the still-unclaimed arm. "Jane only cares about Adorna now."

If that was true, it would make his duty more difficult. He led Violet down the steps, and as they walked, he heard the impact of Lady Kinnard's body on the unlatched door. It opened with a slam that shattered the small windows. Blackburn glanced back in time to see her stagger across the terrace and career into a circle of chairs. The breakage, the shriek, and the clatter of furniture brought the music and the babble in the ballroom to a halt, and the guests moved toward the doors to see Lady Kinnard sprawled across a dainty table like a whole roasted hog.

Violet pinched his arm. "How obnoxious of you to find gratification in such a display."

"Quite. And how do you justify your own enjoyment of it?"

"I didn't say I enjoyed it!"

"Nor did you warn her."

"It would have been a futile attempt."

Jane turned on them and, in a tone he hadn't heard since he'd left the nursery, said, "We're here to find Adorna, not listen to your squabbling, so stop immediately!"

Blackburn didn't believe it. She dared reprimand him!

Jane paid him, and his outrage, no heed. "Mr. Fitzgerald, do you know the way to the sundials?"

"Indeed. Know Lady Goodridge's garden well."

Jane took his arm, and they rushed down the darkened path.

"Well!" Violet said. "I guess we've been put in our places."

Blackburn's fledgling plan seemed impossible. He had imagined that Jane still cherished a tendre for him, and that would make courtship easy. Instead, it appeared he would have to pursue Jane, and pursue her vigorously, too.

The thought was too much to bear. "I shouldn't have bothered."

Violet removed her hand from his arm. "You always did quit at the first sign of difficulty.''

She tried to hasten after Jane and Fitz, but Blackburn grabbed her elbow and swung her around. ''What do you mean by that?''

''Oh, please. As if you didn't know. Running away from Jane after you'd ruined her life.''

''Oh, that.'' He half thought she'd been talking about his ploy to use Jane as a screen. She wasn't, of course; it was only his own conscience speaking. ''I didn't run away from her.''

''You didn't offer for her, either, after thoroughly compromising her the first chance you got. A girl of good family—''

''Half-good!''

''So her father was a wastrel. What is *your* justification for *your* boorish behavior?'' She glared. ''Now, if you'll excuse me, I must help *my friends* search for Adorna.''

He ground his teeth as she hurried away from him. He didn't know how Tarlin put up with her. He didn't know why he occasionally regretted the loss of her friendship, either. Lately, since his return from the Peninsula, he seemed unable to distinguish the important from the trivial, his needs from his desires.

Smoky darkness shrouded the garden. Here and there a torch smoldered, put to shame by the sheen of a half-moon on the drooping tree branches. The night breeze smelt of pinks, which Susan's gardeners planted in profusion, and from outside the high wall he could hear the faint clatter of horses' hooves down a busy thoroughfare.

London was out there. The city was swallowing the

area around Susan's home, but in the exclusivity of her garden, one felt no concern—unless one was worried about a young woman lured to a secluded spot by a scoundrel, there to be abducted. And if Miss Morant was taken, she might have to marry before the season had truly started, and Jane would have to go back to . . . wherever it was she had come from.

He had decided she would suit his purposes, damn it. She would not foil his plans so easily. They had to find Miss Morant, and at once. Blackburn's long strides ate up the ground. He passed Violet and reached Jane and Fitz.

"The sundial is just ahead." He spoke in a low tone, his gaze probing the shadows. "But move quietly. This is the hub of the garden, and a multitude of paths converge. I have no wish to pursue our prey, and less wish to *quit* before our obligation is completed."

He thought Jane looked at him oddly, and he knew Violet snorted.

Touching Fitz on the shoulder, he indicated he should accompany him, then stepped forward, prepared to fight and listening with all the expertise of a seasoned warrior. A faint breeze wafted toward them, rustling the branches, but also carrying a burst of hushed French. Stiffening, he strained to hear; it was as if the gods of war had blessed him and his plot.

Turning to Fitz, he said, "Come on."

But it wasn't Fitz who stood by his side. Jane held herself like a long-legged doe ready to race after her fawn.

A low, breathless giggle sounded from the direction

of the gazebo. Jane brushed past, and Blackburn kept stride as they skirted the sundial. Behind them, he could hear Violet and Fitz. In front and off to the left, toward the gazebo, he could hear more of those seductive giggles.

Adorna did not sound as if she were struggling against a ravisher. Quite the opposite, in fact, and Blackburn wondered if he should be prepared to cover Jane's eyes.

Before he could make a decision, they rounded a corner and found Adorna standing in the middle of the path, her back to them, and giggling at—Blackburn strained his eyes—at a tall, dark, well-dressed gentleman. Sprawled between them on the ground lay Mr. Joyce, his eyes closed, a dark bruise marring his chin.

"J'ai un escalier," Adorna was saying.

"Do you?" The man sounded bemused to hear she had a stair.

"And . . . *je veux parler avec d'épaule.*"

Jane sighed with what sounded like both relief and exasperation. "She would talk to his shoulder," she murmured. "She would talk to anything." Stopping Blackburn with her hand on his chest, she said, "Adorna!"

Without showing an ounce of remorse or guilt, the girl cried, "Aunt Jane!" She tripped forward, her hands outstretched. "You found me. I told Lord de Sainte-Amand that you would!"

De Sainte-Amand. Blackburn slipped to cold alertness. Of course. He had met him before, this immigrant from France, but Blackburn had not recognized him. The man had a way of blending into his surroundings. And what had Mr. Smith said?

We know about the Vicomte de Sainte-Amand, but how's the information passed to him? How's the information being taken from the Foreign Office?

"He speaks French like Monsieur Chasseur, even though he doesn't know him," Adorna said enthusiastically. "And he's been letting me practice!"

"De Sainte-Amand is only one in a long chain, and while a long chain is easy to break, it is also easy to repair. We've broken it before. Someone is cleverly reforging it. We depend on you to find out who."

Jane placed her hands into Adorna's and brought her close. "I found you, but I wonder why you have disobeyed my instructions to remain inside."

Adorna hung her head, then looked up through the veil of her lashes. "I know you told me not to believe a gentleman when he said he had something to show me, but Mr. Joyce seemed so nice, and he knew a way to tell time by the moonlight on the sundial, and I thought that would be something you'd be interested in."

Fitz leaped to her defense. "You must not scold her, Miss Higgenbothem. She meant only the best."

As if seeking support, Jane glanced at Blackburn, and he smiled mechanically. Truth to tell, he scarcely listened, pierced by a sharp fragment of battle memory. A hail of cross-fire had cut down his regiment. Bullets had whizzed past his ears, men had screamed around him as they fell, and cannonballs had thundered the undeniable message—the French had expected their offensive.

Looking up at the moon, he noted that the pure white edge wavered slightly. He could see, and he wasn't stupid enough to lament the loss of total acuity. He spied for the lads he'd brought from his estate, and lost in a futile battle on the Peninsula.

Jane's exasperation sounded in her voice. "I *would* be interested in telling time by the moonlight, if it were possible." She gestured toward the scene Adorna had just left. "When did you discover Mr. Joyce had ulterior motives?"

"He didn't have ulterior motives; he wanted to kiss me, and . . . and . . . do lewd things to me. I told him no, but he wouldn't listen, and then, and then"—she held out her hand to de Sainte-Amand, and he stepped over Joyce's supine body to take it—"this gentleman came to my rescue."

"It was an honor," de Sainte-Amand murmured, his French accent lilting in his speech, his French cologne despoiling English air.

"He knocked Mr. Joyce right on his head."

Fitz stepped over to Joyce and prodded him. "He's alive."

"But I took care not to kill him." De Sainte-Amand oozed continental smiles and suave hand-kissing. "The English authorities frown when a French immigrant dispatches a British citizen, regardless of how richly he may deserve it."

Showing an immense amount of good sense, Jane looked at de Sainte-Amand without favor. "I don't believe I know you."

"Allow me." Blackburn moved to Jane's right

shoulder. "Miss Jane Higgenbothem, may I present the Vicomte de Sainte-Amand."

Jane murmured, "Charmed," in her most matronly tone.

But de Sainte-Amand clasped his chest and staggered back as if he were having a seizure. "Miss Jane Higgenbothem? *You* are Mademoiselle Jane Higgenbothem?"

"Yes." Jane edged closer to Ransom, away from de Sainte-Amand's inexplicable enthusiasm.

Blackburn touched her. Just a brush of the fingers against her shoulder blades, but enough to encourage her, to let her know he was there.

Then he wondered why. It was an unusual social situation, true, but she was in no danger. Yet she, apparently, felt the need for protection, and he had instinctively responded, even though he could not start a rumor of a courtship while in the garden with only his discreet friends observing.

"Mademoiselle, this is such an honor!" The slimy frog took Jane's hand and cupped it between his own. "I have seen your work."

Absolute quiet descended on the garden, smothering all sound with its stifling blanket.

The statue. Pure horror thrummed through Blackburn's veins. De Sainte-Amand had seen the statue.

Sounding as alarmed as Blackburn felt, Jane sputtered, "My . . . work?"

But how could de Sainte-Amand have seen the statue? That wretched piece of work remained hidden from all but a chosen few.

De Sainte-Amand seemed puzzled by both the silence and Jane's consternation. "Yes. I saw your splendid painting."

Relief choked Blackburn, and he stepped back. Than another possibility, more horrifying than the first, occurred to him. Had she been painting him as she had once sculpted? In staccato demand, he said, "A painting. Of what?"

De Sainte-Amand sighed in extravagant homage. "Of sister goddesses, the blond beauty is so frail and the other, you, Miss Higgenbothem, so strong, and the final parting so near."

Whatever this painting was, wherever it hung, it could not embarrass Blackburn. "The painting is of Miss Higgenbothem and her sister, then."

"*Oui*. I have seen grown men wipe tears away from the sight of such pain and such dignity." De Sainte-Amand flicked an invisible tear away with the tip of his finger. "Your brush is genius, mademoiselle, genius."

"Isn't it?" Adorna wrapped her arm through her aunt's and tilted her head onto the taller woman's shoulder. "I remember the picture. She painted it for Mama, but Papa didn't like it, so after Mama died, it disappeared."

Everything about de Sainte-Amand made Blackburn's skin crawl with loathing, and although his original fear had been settled, distrust rose to take its place. "Where did you view this work of . . . genius, my lord?" he asked.

As if to confirm his suspicions, de Sainte-Amand's

smug, villainous, insolent smile flashed in the dark. "Why, where it belongs—in the only place where true civilization exists. In France, my lord. In France."

Chapter 9

Blackburn had seen the effects of hatred on other men.
They swore, and stomped their feet, and picked vulgar
brawls.

But hatred didn't stir him to histrionics. Hatred, for
him, came on a frozen wind, chilling his emotions,
sharpening his mind, whetting his appetite for revenge.

France. De Sainte-Amand merely said the word
"France," and hatred clutched at Blackburn. Yet no
one knew, for he had a care that they would not. Self-
possessed as usual, he asked, "When were you in
France, de Sainte-Amand?"

"A mere six months ago, I went to my dear home-
land."

"To view the art."

"I did not go to see the art." De Sainte-Amand
laid a hand on his chest in a parody of sorrow. "My
beloved father sent me to the emperor to plead for the
return of our hereditary lands. While there, I saw the

painting.'' With a sly grin, he added, ''At Fontainebleau.''

''At Fontainebleau,'' Jane breathed. ''How splendid.''

Splendid indeed. Her painting hung in one of Napoleon's homes where his intimates went to hunt and
play. Why had de Sainte-Amand been there? Blackburn longed to interrogate him, but the slippery bastard might be suspicious, and in fact might himself be
using Jane's artistic achievements to distract Ransom.

Two could play that game. Blackburn would appear
to take the bait.

Grasping Jane by the elbow, he turned her to face
him. ''How did your painting get to France, and to
Fontainebleau?''

The pale moonlight played over her features.
''Your question is an intrusion, my lord.''

''It is so simple, Blackburn,'' de Sainte-Amand
said.

Blackburn looked only at the culprit he held in his
clutches. ''I didn't ask you, sir.''

De Sainte-Amand paid him no heed. ''Bonaparte
might not have the breeding to offer my lands back
without payment, but he has excellent taste in art.''

''So true.'' Fitz made his contempt obvious. ''He
'acquires' it from the countries he conquers.''

''Miss Higgenbothem's country has not been con-
quered,'' Blackburn pointed out with chilly precision.
''But perhaps Miss Higgenbothem nourishes a surrep-
titious admiration for this emperor.''

Violet took an audible breath. ''Ransom, apologize!''

Jane jerked her arm out of his grasp. "My lord, you are offensive."

Untouched by the tense atmosphere, Adorna gurgled with laughter. "Oh, Lord Blackburn, you're so silly! Aunt Jane didn't give the painting away. If you knew my father—"

"Adorna," Jane said sternly. "This is private."

"He didn't want to support Aunt Jane, so she had to—"

Putting her hand over Adorna's mouth, Jane said, "That's enough."

Apparently Jane had reached the end of her endurance. Locking her gaze with his, she said, "I won't have you harrying her for an answer, Lord Blackburn, nor will Adorna volunteer any more information about my painting or my circumstances. It is, quite simply, none of your affair."

Silence fell over the garden as he stared at her. She was trying to dictate to him, yet his curiosity had been awakened.

"I am sorry, mademoiselle." De Sainte-Amand bowed over her hand, then let it go with such obvious regret, Blackburn wanted to ruin his smiling, froggy face. "I would not have mentioned your marvelous painting if I had known it would cause you annoyance."

Annoyance? Blackburn thought. Was that what he was?

"Not at all," she replied.

She sounded a little emotional. Upset, perhaps, because he had learned of the parsimony of her brother-in-law? But why should she feel anguish? Most women he knew would use it as a whip over his head. Yet perhaps she was cleverer than he realized, for if anything, her reticence worked to produce a sense of responsibility where her nagging would not.

Sounding revoltingly sincere, de Sainte-Amand said, ''My only thought was to tell you of the pleasure I found in your brilliance.''

''Thank you. I'm gladdened that someone''— Jane's voice wavered—''that you were able to discern the emotion I painted into the canvas.''

Adorna dug in her drawstring bag and presented Jane with a handkerchief.

Confounded, Blackburn stared. Jane was close to tears. But why? She had never wept eleven years ago. Not in Susan's ballroom. Not in his study. In the most shameful of circumstances she'd shown remarkable pluck. Why would a simple compliment make her cry?

Yet she was moved, for Adorna hugged her tighter. Violet laid a hand on her shoulder. Fitz uncomfortably cleared his throat.

Someone had to take charge before this scene disintegrated into a morass of sticky emotion. ''We shall go back to the ballroom now.'' Blackburn noted that he sounded a little pompous.

De Sainte-Amand's smile flashed again, this time in scorn.

''We shall act as if our little group chose to take a walk in the garden to escape the heat,'' Blackburn continued. ''With so many respected chaperones, Adorna will be safe from gossip.''

''What about Mr. Joyce?'' Violet asked.

"I'll send some of the servants out to scoop him up and put him in his carriage." Blackburn didn't bother to glance Joyce's way. "Fitz, will you take care of explaining to Mr. Joyce the inadvisability of further disturbing Miss Morant?"

Fitz grinned with all the good humor of a born rakehell. "I would be delighted. Tomorrow, I think, would be a good day to call on him."

As the small group strolled toward the ballroom, Blackburn found himself thinking that Fitz could be similarly employed after every party, should he choose to be.

De Sainte-Amand moved close to Jane. "Who is it that teaches Mademoiselle Morant her French?"

"His name is Monsieur Chasseur." To Ransom's relief, Jane's voice sounded normal and steady. "He is a better teacher than Adorna's performance would indicate."

"Ah, Pierre Chasseur. I know of him." De Sainte-Amand sounded politely indifferent. "A pleasant young man. An immigrant, like me, but he is not, of course, an aristocrat."

His arrogance grated on Blackburn. Who was de Sainte-Amand, after all, but a Frenchman flaunting an inexplicable haughtiness and the faint stench of garlic?

As Blackburn trod the steps to the terrace, Violet brushed close. In a voice so hushed it barely reached his ears, she said, "Jane sold it."

He stopped, and Violet stopped with him. "For her living expenses, you mean."

"Yes." She watched Jane trod up the stairs. "Mr. Morant grudged her every penny."

"That's not surprising. Morant is known as being a cheat and a braggart, and I've taken care to stay away from him." This was his chance to discover the truth of Jane's circumstances, and he chose his words carefully. "But it's a shame Miss Higgenbothem burdened you with her miseries."

"Burdened me?" Fists on her hips, Violet glared at him. "Tarlin saw her one day, gazing longingly at a set of new drawing pencils. She put a brave face on it, but it was obvious that Mr. Morant shamefully abused her."

"Abused her? So she was bruised?"

"No, just ill clad and thin, and her palms had calluses."

When Violet drew in a shaky breath, Blackburn realized another woman was close to tears. It must be in the air tonight. "Still, it seems improbable an English gentlewoman would sell a painting to that upstart Bonaparte," he said.

"I don't suppose she sold it to the emperor herself." Violet's voice grew stronger as she spoke. "You worked in the Foreign Office too long, Ransom, if you're seeing treachery in Jane. Oh, when she was a girl she wanted to go to the continent. She wanted to live in Rome in a garret and support herself with her art."

He chuckled. "Madness."

"Maybe. Maybe it would have been better than the way she lived."

There it was. That guilt again.

"Jane probably sold her painting to one of Napoleon's agents, or to a collector who knows good work when he sees it. And her work is very good, Ransom. You have to admit that."

"*I* have to admit that?"

Violet opened her mouth, then shut it. "I suppose you still hold a petty grudge about that statue, but Jane paid for her mistake."

"You want me to pity her?"

"Compassion? From the great Lord Blackburn?" Violet laughed briefly, bitterly. "How foolish of me. Of course not."

She swept on, but Blackburn barely noticed. Instead, he watched Jane's silhouette as she stopped in the light streaming from the doors.

So the woman had experienced poverty. Yet look at her now! Her glacé silk gown was *au courant*. That skirt which hugged her slender bottom with such loving care had been designed by a master. Her shawl covered her modestly, true, but it was Belgian lace. Either she had made quite a lot on her paintings, and his pride would not allow him to believe that, or someone else had paid. Who? And why?

De Sainte-Amand moved to her side and spoke in a barely audible voice. She shook her head in rejection, but de Sainte-Amand insisted, pressing something into her hand. She looked down at it—a piece of paper, Blackburn thought—then tried to give it back. De Sainte-Amand insisted, closing his fingers around hers to make a fist, and with a show of reluctance, Jane slipped it into her handbag.

Then, as if nothing had happened, she said, "We

shall go in as if we've had a nice walk outside.'' She had a hint of Wellington in her posture. ''Adorna, let me look at you. No, you're none the worse for your experience. Now, smile, everyone.''

De Sainte-Amand opened the door, and music and laughter blasted out.

Jane led the way inside with such a semblance of gaiety, surely everyone inside would be fooled. Adorna followed, and Violet.

Blackburn leaped up the stairs before de Sainte-Amand could relinquish his hold on the door. Smiling at de Sainte-Amand, he said, ''So good of you.''

Inside, the heat and the odor of a hundred sweaty bodies assaulted him. Eyes darted back and forth, seeking amusement, looking for scandal.

With Jane's help, he would provide it.

''A lovely evening,'' he said, making sure his voice carried into the crowd at the edge of the dance floor. ''A pleasant walk in pleasant company.''

''And, Adorna, here comes quite a large contingent of gentlemen,'' Jane said.

''They are no doubt looking for you, Miss Morant.'' Fitz curled his lip in disgust. ''Blast them.''

The breath Miss Morant took brought her bosom to quivering attention, and the gentlemen, and Fitz, and de Sainte-Amand—all seemed stricken by a great, enveloping stupidity at the sight.

Blackburn didn't understand it. Yes, the bosom and everything else about Miss Morant exuded sexuality, but it was obvious, garish. He preferred women who utilized clothing to camouflage the length of their legs. Who manipulated their expressions to hide their vulnerability. Who acted as if ardor did not burn in their souls.

Jane, for instance.

He couldn't believe he was thinking that!

The skillful hunter recognized such a masquerade, and captured the unwary quarry, and reveled in her hidden treasures. Her legs extended far beyond the length any one woman's had the right to be. Only a fool would complain about legs that could wrap a man close and hold him while he thrust deep inside her.

Blackburn was not a fool. His mouth curled in self-derision. Or maybe he was, for recalling the range of her legs, for reliving the taste of her mouth, and for wanting more of her than mere duty allowed.

Yet if he must create a scandal and imitate a court-ship to disguise his hunt for the traitor, he should also take what pleasure he could from them.

The crowd of men surrounded them, jostling for position near Miss Morant. Jane's ramrod-straight spine stiffened, and purposefully, Blackburn moved to her side. Whenever she was near, her scent teased his nostrils. He would have denied that he remembered, but a faint aroma of spice on warm flesh transported him back in time, to his drawing room.

He laid his hand on her waist, near the small of her back.

She looked up at him, her green eyes wide and startled.

Her eyes had looked the same that morning so long ago. Wide. Startled. Unsure and frightened and, finally, passionate.

"Blackburn!"

Jolted out of his unwelcome reverie, he found himself facing a grinning, perspiring Athowe.

"Who would have thought such a prunes and prisms as you would deign to reintroduce Miss Higgenbothem into society!" Athowe extended his hand past Blackburn and toward Jane. "Miss Higgenbothem, I would recognize you anywhere."

Heads turned. Athowe's voice carried, and the name Higgenbothem attracted attention. Her hope for anonymity toppled, and while Blackburn applauded the success of his plan, he at the same time braced himself for the unwelcome attention.

Jane allowed the obnoxious man to kiss her hand, then withdrew it without warmth. "How good to see you again, Lord Athowe. It has been a long time."

Simple words. Courteous words. Kinder words than she'd yet deigned to speak to him. Blackburn ran his gaze up and down Athowe's well-cut outfit and refrained from asking the name of his corset-maker, and whether he still wore shoes that allowed him to run at the first sign of trouble.

"A long time indeed," Athowe said heartily. "Tonight we should dance as we did so many years ago."

"Thank you, Lord Athowe, but I no longer dance. I am a chaperone now."

"A chaperone." He burst into robust laughter. "You jest. The daughter of the late Viscount Bavridge can't lower herself to be a chaperone!"

Susan's guests were drifting closer, attracted by the first signs of a scene, and Blackburn heard one of the dowagers murmur in prurient tones, "The daughter of Viscount Bavridge? Oh, my dear. Not *that* daughter!"

Jane pleated the fringe on her shawl.

"Athowe, what have you done?" Frederica, Lady Athowe, squeezed through the throng. As always, she was beautifully coifed and gowned, yet to Blackburn she resembled an Egyptian scorpion, sleek-shelled, slender, and with a sting that brought death. "You've embarrassed Miss Higgenbothem. Miss *Jane* Higgenbothem." Frederica's poisonous gaze flicked at Blackburn, and she projected her voice with full-bodied delight. "So good to see *you* with *her*, Lord Blackburn. And what a surprise after all these years."

Blackburn could have sworn he felt the heat of Jane's blush as it swept from her toes past his hand to her forehead.

Athowe sputtered uselessly, as incompetent to control his wife as he had been incompetent about everything in his life.

But no one used Blackburn to further a vendetta; most especially not the former Frederica Harpum. He waited until the titters had died down. With incisive authority he said, "If I have chosen to escort Miss Higgenbothem for the gratification of her company, no one will question my decision."

Jaws dropped in unison, so that all he saw was a series of gaping mouths.

Fitz looked as poleaxed as anyone. "B'God, Blackburn, do you realize what you've said?"

"Yes. I do." Blackburn watched Frederica until she flushed, then he allowed his voice to carry over the increased muttering. "However, I'm not sure you know what you have done. All you have accomplished by revealing your knowledge of such an ancient tale, Lady Athowe, is divulge your age in quite an unattractive manner.''

Frederica still smiled, but tightly, her lips pressed together so hard one could only see a single red slash between nose and chin. "*Our* ages, Lord Blackburn. Or should I call you—*Figgy*?"

With one extravagant insult, Frederica drove Blackburn into genuine, burning fury. He didn't show it, of course. He simply waited until the tittering generated by Frederica's remark had faded before he said, "My friends call me Ransom, or Blackburn. *You* may call me 'my lord.' ''.

"What *is* happening here?" Susan's voice boomed out. The pink feathers in her hair bobbed as she strode forward. "Are you making *trouble*, Freddie?"

Although Frederica's eyes flashed at the sobriquet, she didn't dare protest.

Susan summed up the situation in one glance. "Freddie, I told you last time what would happen if you authored another *scandal* involving one of my *family*. You'd better take her home, Athowe."

Athowe grabbed Frederica's arm and tugged. She stumbled backward, glaring. Under Susan's gimlet eye, the crowd dispersed. The men around Adorna reassembled to wait on her return from Jane's side, and Susan said to Violet, "Lord Tarlin is looking for you."

Violet hesitated, clearly unhappy about leaving Jane with Blackburn, but Susan gave her a little push. "You'll have to leave Ransom *alone* with Miss Higgenbothem *sometime*, and really, what can he do *here*?"

Susan knew. His sister recognized the signs of his ire, but for some reason she chose to leave Jane to his tender mercies.

And he had none.

With slow deliberation, he slipped his fingers under Jane's shawl and up her bare upper arm. He saw her swallow as his flesh met hers, and when his palm slid back down to her elbow, she seemed to forget to breathe.

Yes, she was aware of him, bound by memories, as he was—and if she was not, he would soon create new remembrances to tangle in her mind.

He knew that every eye in the ballroom clung to him and his nemesis in avid fascination. He affixed a tender, lightly amused smile to his lips, leaned close to and quoted her in an undertone. "None will recognize you. No one will recall The Disastrous Season. And you certainly will not be called to account for the trouble you have caused me."

Steadily she watched him, her emotions well guarded. If he had not been holding her, he might have thought her impassive before his wrath. But her taut biceps strained away from the heat and threat of him.

"Guard yourself well, my darling Jane."

She flinched as, for the first time, he used her given name.

"For I right now see no reason why I should not take the rumors to truth, and take you to my bed."

"I haven't invited you." Her answer was made up of equal parts of determination and dismay.

He relished both the challenge and the consternation. "I can persuade you, Jane."

"No. I wouldn't be so foolish twice."

"If that were a wager, Jane, I would not advise you to take it." Letting her go, he bowed with every visible indication of respect. "Watch behind you, Jane. I'll be there."

Chapter 10

At three in the morning, Fitz leaned against the door–
post of the shabby rented town house to take off his
shoes, uncaring of the soot that coated the steps and,
no doubt, his white stockings. Taking his key, he tried
to set it in the lock, but this wretched street was dark
as Hades and he'd had enough wine to make insertion
difficult. The iron clanked until he found the keyhole,
then the key went right in. Stealthily he turned it, but
despite his care, the tumblers clanked as they fell into
place. Holding his breath, he opened the door. Surely
she was asleep.

But she called him. "Gerald? Son, how was the
ball?"

She was still awake. That meant she was in pain,
and he stared through the darkened rooms, his soul
heavy with despair. If only he had the money to . . .

"Son?"

"Wonderful, Mother." Lighting one of the precious candles, he impaled it on a stick and limped
through the study to her makeshift bedchamber.

"Lady Goodridge had her usual gala festivities, and everyone was there."

As the glow touched his mother's face, he saw the premature lines suffering had set there. Her breath labored; he saw the blankets rising like a mounded grave over the frail body. He saw the feeble hands clutching the book she had read until the candle beside her had guttered out. He also saw his mother's love for him shining through the aged ivory complexion, and the shimmering excitement as she waited to hear the latest gossip about old friends. He obliged her, of course, making himself comfortable in a chair by her bedside as he recounted tales of debutantes and old roués. He finished with, "Blackburn met his match tonight, too. Do you remember that scandal, oh, ten years ago, with that gel who loved Blackburn so much she made a statue of him?"

His mother giggled, a sound Fitz had not heard for too many weeks. "How could I ever forget?"

"Yes, well, she's back as a chaperone to a deb, and Blackburn escorted her around the ballroom, out into the garden—in company, of course—and back. *I'd* say he's smitten."

"What does *he* say?" Mrs. Fitzgerald asked shrewdly.

Fitz leaned close and tapped his nose with his index finger. "He defended Miss Higgenbothem when she was attacked by Lady Athowe."

"Interesting." Thoughtfully his mother slid her gnarled fingers along the counterpane. "One wonders whether he did so to protect Miss Higgenbothem, or to spite Lady Athowe."

Fitz smiled at his mother. The daughter of an English baron, she had married his Irish father for love and never regretted it, or so she said. Still, although she did not mingle with the crème de la crème, her wisdom about human behavior had more than once saved him from disaster. "I say, to protect Miss Higgenbothem. She's at her last prayers, but he's never paid Frederica the slightest mind before."

"No doubt you are right." She studied him in the feeble illumination of the candle. "How did *your* evening go?"

"Very well. I was hunting the greatest game of all—an heiress."

She bit her lip. Extending her hand to him, she said, "You don't have to do that. We're doing well by ourselves, aren't we?"

He stared at her, at the beautiful eyes which were too big in her thin face, and wondered how she could ask that as she lay in this hovel, tended only by one servant who left at nightfall to go home to her family. Concealing his bitterness, he smiled jauntily. "Indeed we are, but I'd like to do it in better circumstances."

"Did the beautiful Miss Morant capture your wayward heart? She must be young and innocent."

"And I'm an old roué," he teased her.

She started to chuckle, but a spasm of coughing caught her. The book went flying, and she grabbed for her handkerchief, covering her mouth.

He could do nothing, of course, but he leaped to his feet anyway and wrapped his arm around her bony shoulders and held her until it subsided.

God, how he hated this! He had been nothing but

a shallow, careless boy his whole life, seeking fun and adventure. Now fate had seized his precious mother, shaking her in its bony grasp, and he had to find a way to take her away where the wind blew clean and the sun shone.

There was a way. A way other than the heiress. And he was without morals or honor, damn it. Surely that other way shouldn't bother him.

"I'm fine now." Her voice was hoarse and shaking.

He glanced at the handkerchief she held. No blood, thank God. Not yet.

Carefully he set her back against the pillows and broached the invitation issued not an hour since. "Lady Goodridge wondered if you would be so good as to pay her a visit at Goodridge Manor. It's beautiful there, overlooking the sea. The fresh air would be good for you."

"Of course. Then I would return the favor by asking her here?" Her head lolled toward him, and she smiled to ease the sting. "I won't take charity, Gerald, you know that."

"Lady Goodridge is a genuinely kind woman, Mother."

"And formidable, and rich, with impeccable ancestry. That's well to remember, son."

"She's lonely," he said baldly.

"You'd know that, would you?"

"Sometimes a woman's heart is not so difficult to read."

"You're just like your father." Her hand moved toward his, and he grasped it. "A charmer."

He hadn't a chance of winning against her implacable will, but he had to try once more. "So you'll go."

"So I won't." With a swift change of subject, she said, "You were limping when you came in."

"Dancing with Miss Morant."

"Your wound is too recent. You shouldn't dance on that leg of yours."

"When have I ever done what I should?" Taking the book, he examined the leather spine with false interest. "*Robinson Crusoe,* heh?"

"Is she your heiress?"

"Shall I read to you?"

"You worry me with your plans." A fretful note colored her voice.

He noted it. She was tiring at last. Soothingly he said, "Don't worry, dear. All will come right, you'll see. Now where did you leave off?"

He read until her chin dropped, then allowed his voice to trail away. Brooding, he stared at her.

When his father died, income from the estate had been nothing more than a dribble, and Mrs. Fitzgerald had mortgaged it to put Fitz into Oxford and to provide herself with a stipend to last her, she said, for the rest of her days.

A good son would have applied himself to his books and earned himself a post somewhere as a curate for some rich lord.

Fitz was not a good son. He knew it despite Mrs. Fitzgerald's assurances to the opposite. He had no aptitude for study, and he had jauntily wormed his way into the top ranks of English society. Until Mrs. Fitzgerald had been forced to tell him they were gone to pigs and whistles. They'd spent the last of the money to buy Fitz his commission in the Cavalry.

He was a damned good officer, gaining ground for the English on the Peninsula when none thought it possible. Soon the generals noticed, and Fitz had found himself facing a trembly old man who had offered a proposition. Fitz would seek information for English Intelligence. Spying would be dangerous, and as an English officer, Fitz would be killed if caught.

''Why should I risk my neck?'' Fitz asked baldly.

''For the glory of your country.''

''Glory won't feed my mother if I'm dead.''

So he had wangled an ''incentive,'' payable for each mission successfully executed, and because he knew the unreliability of the Foreign Office's promises, he had insisted on being reimbursed immediately on completion. The money had gone back to his mother, and she had written glowing letters about his munificence, and those letters had encouraged him to take more and greater risks.

Oh, Blackburn wouldn't have approved, but Blackburn was a stick. Fitz had needed the money, and until the leg . . .

Dejected, he rubbed the wound. Ah, he and his mother were a fine pair, one given over to consumption, one crippled to the point he could never again do the one thing he did well.

There was no avoiding the issue. Regardless of his mother's censure, he was going to have to toss the handkerchief toward his heiress, and soon. That was all he was good for now: courting a woman, charming her into marriage, and servicing her until she was satisfied. He'd already chosen his quarry; he had her in his sights, and soon she would be his. By fair means or foul, he would have her.

But he had to admit, here in the wee hours of the morning, that French offer looked tempting. Very, very tempting.

Chapter 11

❧❦

Eleven years before . . .

Late morning sun peeked through the fog as Jane walked up the stairs. She lifted the lion's-head knocker and dropped it. The thump sounded as loud as the beat of her heart, but she allowed herself no nervous start as she gazed steadily at the dark green door and waited.

The butler answered, and she stared down at the bald crown on his head. "I would like to speak to Lord Blackburn," she said.

"Lord Blackburn?" He quickly assessed her gown and accoutrements. She wore her best morning gown, her most fashionable feathered bonnet, and her finest gloves. Her pocketbook hung from her arm and she held a lace handkerchief in one hand. She had no doubt about her appearance. But she knew a lady never called on a gentleman. And certainly never alone!

Then the butler glanced to the street for evidence of her conveyance.

There was none. She had hired a sedan chair and dismissed it on arrival.

"Yes, Lord Blackburn. This is his residence, is it not?"

"He isn't receiving guests. If you would leave your calling card—"

Jane pushed past him and strode into the foyer.

"Miss!" The butler scuttled after her. "You may not enter."

"I already have," Jane pointed out with impeccable logic. "And I intend to see Lord Blackburn."

While the butler gobbled in nervous dismay, she coolly took note of her surroundings. Blackburn's residence easily outshone the rather forlorn town house she and Melba had taken for the season. The staircase to the upper story glistened, a straight and haughty testimony to beeswax. A Chinese vase of some long-vanished dynasty stood on the floor filled with peacock feathers of blue, purple, and glistening gold. Jane's foot sank into the plush thickness of carpet, and everything about this home spoke of wealth, elegance, and lineage.

She had only lineage. Impeccable lineage, in fact, but that couldn't save her from dishonor.

She and Melba were to leave London, of course. Melba wasn't well, Jane had disgraced them, and there was no reason to remain. But in the miserable week since Lady Goodridge's party, Jane had relived the moment she saw Frederica Harpum gesturing and announcing, "Miss Jane Higgenbothem's own creation!"

In her mind, she experienced the heat of Blackburn's fury.

And she heard the laughter.

Not until Melba had fainted had the ton stopped roaring, and then only to crowd around and whisper with cruel curiosity as Jane arranged to have her sister taken back to the town house. Without Lady Goodridge, Jane did not know how she would have managed. Lord Athowe had disappeared, and Blackburn had certainly been nowhere in attendance.

But during the hours of tending Melba through her bout of the sweats, Jane had brooded. The force of Blackburn's anger had etched itself into her soul, and in the dark of the night, she had resolved to go to him, to elucidate why she had offered her small talents on the altar of his perfection.

To try and minimize the disaster, if only for her sister's sake.

The butler took up a protective stance in front of one glossily painted white door. "You cannot go in."

A dramatic little man, and none too bright, Jane judged. With a cool look of contempt, she pushed him aside, wrenched open the door, and stepped within.

And knew she'd found the right chamber when a voice drawled, "What are *you* doing here?"

The sun shone through multipaned doors that led to a small garden. Books lined the room, as well as paintings and cleverly placed sculptures.

Jane could see only Blackburn.

The most impeccable of God's creations, he

lounged in a high-backed chair placed before the fire. His exquisite lips were turned down in a frown. His blue eyes pierced her like the hottest flame, only now the flame held contempt. His crisp shirt was open, his collar and cravat crumpled and tossed aside. A steaming cup rested on the table by his elbow. He held a book in his broad hand. One blunt finger held his place in the volume, as if he planned to dismiss her and go back to his reading.

And so he could, after she had had her say.

But to be here with him, alone, to feast her eyes on him without interference—this was greater than she had dared to dream.

He leaned forward. "McMenemy, why did you let her in here?"

"She insisted, my lord, and I could not hinder her."

Lord Blackburn said softly, "Then I will have to hire a butler who can stop unwanted visitors. You may go."

"Yes, my lord." McMenemy sounded subdued, and the heels of his glossy shoes clattered on the wooden floor as he left, shutting the door behind him.

"An idiot." In a long, sinewy movement, Blackburn came to his feet and stalked toward the improperly closed portal. "I am surrounded by idiots."

Jane grabbed his arm as he walked past. "It doesn't matter."

He looked down at her hand with such scorn, she hastily removed it and rushed into speech. "I won't be here long."

"You're right about that."

"I just came to say . . . to try and tell you . . ."

"Hasn't there been enough said about you and me in the last week?" he asked cuttingly. "Where is your sister?"

"At the town house."

"Is she still too ill to attend you?"

"She's better, thank you for inquiring."

" 'Thank you for inquiring,' " he mimicked savagely. "You're here alone. Without a chaperone."

She had held her handkerchief in one palm. Now like a sculptress gripping a stone mallet in search of balance, she used both hands.

"You're trying to trap me into a compromising position."

She lurched in horror, and her pocketbook slapped against her arm. "Oh, no!"

"Why not? I'll wager Athowe has not called to offer you the protection of his name."

"We have not seen Lord Athowe since the night of Lady Goodridge's party," she said. Not that it mattered. She had not wished to marry him. But she recognized disloyalty when she saw it; Athowe dared not stain his precious name by even writing a letter inquiring of Melba's health.

"Such a surprise! The ever-inconstant Athowe has abandoned you." His mockery was not directed at her, but at Athowe. Until he focused on her once more. "So I am your only hope. A marriage to me would retrieve your reputation."

Straightening her shoulders, she glared at him for so misinterpreting her actions. "Such a thought never crossed my mind. I am not so guileful, my lord, and you may be sure I've brought no one to burst in upon us.''

Pinching her chin between his fingers, he brought her face up and scrutinized each feature. What he saw there apparently satisfied him, for he said, ''Excellent, for it would do you no good. I will not wed for any reasons but my own, and if that ruins us both, so be it. Your sister doesn't know you're here.''

A niggle of conscience made her turn her head away.

''Or else she taught you nothing of propriety.''

This injustice made Jane cry out. ''Yes, she did! A proper lady never visits a single man in his home. She told me so often.''

''But you don't heed her.''

''My reputation is already destroyed. What worse can possibly happen to me?''

He laughed, a short, bitter chortle. ''She didn't teach you enough, you foolish girl, if that's what you think.''

Jane digested his comment. He wasn't referring only to decorum, she realized, but to the real reason women avoided being alone with men. Except for that brief, uncomfortable moment with Athowe, she had never been burdened by such concerns—her height protected her—so she answered Blackburn honestly. ''She of course told me of men's baser natures, that I should avoid being alone with them, but you're angry and you've never cared for me, and you are so *perfect*—''

''Oh, for God's sake!'' His hands reached for her,

but he pulled them back at the last moment and paced away.

"—I know you command your passions in a way lesser men cannot."

He circled his chair and looked at his fingers. With unnatural tension, they gripped the curlicues carved into the wood. "I would not depend on that."

She didn't believe him, for if what he said was true, then he was not a god, but only a man.

Yet she was an artist. She studied people for their expressions, their stances, their nuances, and Blackburn seemed to be laboring under a great strain.

Chin down, he looked at her with the menace of a bull about to charge, and rend, and destroy. "You don't understand. I would do anything to cause you as much humiliation as you've caused me." His guttural voice rang with conviction. "Run away, little girl, before I forget I am a gentleman."

A chill prickled along her spine, but she reminded herself of her mission, and that she had not yet explained herself. "I resolved to come here. I must make clear why I dared to try to depict you in clay."

He shuddered as if he were in pain, and Jane took an alarmed step toward him.

Then she noticed how his mouth curled, like the smile of a cat who sees its prey within reach, and she took that step back.

"It was obvious to all *why* you dared." Circling the chair, he stalked toward her. "It was the *how* that was inexcusable."

She watched him cautiously as she admitted, "I did

a poor job." How it wrenched at her to admit it! "I know that now."

"If it was a poor job, no one would have recognized me." Her patent lack of comprehension drove him to clarify. "It was the . . . lack of clothing which caused the flurry."

Her heart sank. She had suspected that was the truth, yet he was so grand, so imposing, she could comprehend no other manner to sculpt him. "It is a classic format used by the Greeks and Romans, and in my own defense, I would like to say I had no reason to believe anyone would ever see that statue except me."

"You were inaccurate!"

She couldn't help it. Her gaze skimmed his form, seeking the error that so infuriated him. She knew she was not untalented. The proportions looked right, yet still he paced toward her. "I have studied the human form as much as possible in my limited circumstances, but I was hampered by not having a model."

Standing so that his toes met the points of her shoes, he snapped, "You're here to ask that I model for you?"

She tried to step back, away from his deliberate intrusion. "No. I would not dare such disrespect! I'm only trying to justify any . . . miscalculations I may have made which caused you anguish."

"Miscalculations." He enunciated each syllable separately. "Miscalculations." His hands shot out, and he grasped her shoulders and pulled her close. "Your miscalculations are now legion, Miss Higgenbothem, and the worst of them was coming here today.''

They had touched before—in the dance, today when she grasped his arm, and when he pinched her chin. She treasured each contact, each moment.

But this . . . this was different. He didn't plan to kill her. He could have done that, ordered his servants to dispose of the body, and been back to his reading by now. Instead, his fingers kneaded her collarbones almost painfully. His throat worked, and the scent of him was close and sharp: last night's brandy, today's lemon soap, and masculine flesh both warm and eager.

But eager for what? She wanted to look into his face, to demand his plans, but she found herself staring at the place where his shirt gaped. The edge of pure white cotton drew her gaze, then the amber sheen of his skin brought a sigh of satisfaction to her lips.

She had never seen the place where his collarbone dipped and formed a hollow, but she knew it. She had never seen the faint curls of blond hair at the loftiest part of his chest, or the glide of his Adam's apple as he swallowed, or even his throat, muscled and strong. But she had guessed the shapes, the colors, the textures, with uncanny accuracy. She had drawn them, then formed them from cold clay with as much devotion and pleasure as Blackburn's Creator had at his conception.

Yet she was wary.

Wary. Of Blackburn. And why? She had never been a cautious girl. That had been part of the problem, an exasperated Melba had said. She looked every man in the eye as if she were his equal, and men retreated before such a novel concept.

But before, the armor of Blackburn's concentrated indifference had stood between them. Now it was absent, and his attention swept her, as marked as cool breeze on naked skin.

What should she do with her hands? They still clutched the handkerchief close against her waist, and they seemed extraneous, in the way, not hers at all.

She was in his arms—a locale so exotic she had scarcely dared dream of it—and she was worried about her hands! But she didn't understand what revenge he was seeking. "My lord, why are you holding me?" With an almost physical effort, she tore her gaze away from the gaping edge of his shirt and forced herself to look up.

Into eyes so dark they had swallowed the midnight sky. He fought demons with those eyes, demons she didn't recognize, but could only acknowledge.

"My lord?"

"Damn you for coming. Damn you for placing yourself into my dominion."

He squeezed with bruising intensity, and she cried out, jerking her hands up. Her fists struck his forearms, breaking his hold, and he sucked in a quick, startled breath.

Then he laughed. "You're strong." He grabbed her wrists and turned her hands over. Taking the fingertip of each glove, he jerked, freeing her hands from their concealment. He dropped the gloves to the floor, and she found her fingers uncurling to show him her naked palm.

Vulnerability.

She *was* strong. She lifted heavy clay, molded it for hours, found the satisfaction of creating with her hands. Yet she wanted him to see the other side of her, to know how the strength had grown from her unguarded heart.

And he did see it. Her god was so sensitive, he knew her mind.

"You love me, don't you?" His voice was vibrant, vehement.

Her gaze worshiped the flare of his nostrils, the heavy-lidded satisfaction of his gaze.

"Good. That makes it so much better." Still grasping her wrists, he lowered his face to hers.

And kissed her.

A kiss. Rough, faintly bruising, heatedly angry. She trembled at being the recipient of such an honor.

They were almost touching along the length of their bodies, so she tucked herself into him, into a submissive position, trying to tell him in every way possible that she was his. His to do with as he liked.

Lifting his head, he stared at her, his eyebrows forming a vee of derision. "Stupid." He looked less like Apollo now, and more like Hades. "Stupid little virgin. You don't know what you're asking for."

He gave it to her anyway. His next kiss was harder, pushing her head back. Her hat tilted crazily, and he scowled at the unoffending headgear. "Take it off."

He released one hand so she could obey him, and she did. Her fingers shook as she untied the bow, but when she would have taken it and placed it gently on a rack, he lost patience. Casually he knocked her best bonnet to the floor.

"Don't dare protest," he told her.

She had to answer him, but her lips felt odd: swollen, tender, even wanting. She didn't know if she could perform such a routine task as speech. Not when she'd just been kissed. Slowly, with great care, she enunciated, "I'm not protesting."

His mouth cocked up in a half smile. Delicately he stroked the planes of her lips with the ball of his thumb. "You're almost sweet." Then, as if he didn't wish to think about that, once again he kissed her.

This time he required something from her.

She tried to ask what, but he snapped, "Give over, gel!" Depositing her wrists over his shoulders, he wrapped one arm around her waist and slid his fingers into her hair at the back of her head.

The demand was clear. Bewildered, she opened her lips, and he tasted her. *Tasted* her.

Inevitably she tasted him, too. He'd had coffee in that cup he'd been drinking. Not tea, coffee. How extraordinary. She knew a detail of his life because he kissed her. *Was* kissing her.

What had he found out about her? She began to quiver, brief little tremors of astonishment. Melba had warned her clearly enough about what happens between a man and a woman. Yet she had said nothing of this excruciating intimacy, where scent and taste mixed to form a brew of sensation. Jane shut her eyes to quiet the commotion in her veins, but the lack of sight only accentuated her tumult.

Alarmed, she opened her eyes and tried to move

back, but he still held her, and his grip tightened. He growled, like a dog whose tasty meal was threatened, and he nipped at her.

The nibble of his teeth against her lip shocked her, and she wanted to fight him or demur. But how? He seemed so sure, and she had resolved to let him take what punishment he would. Certainly she could not complain when he chastised her with that which she longed for. Yet when his hand slipped from her head to her throat, and he caressed the skin beneath her ear, she squirmed against him.

"Be still," he murmured. His mouth moved from hers to the place where his fingers touched, and she could hear his breath, light and uneven. "I'm not hurting you."

"No." She breathed. He wasn't hurting her.

But he took her word as refusal and lifted his head. "Yes."

Was he still angry? She couldn't tell. She only knew he looked different; less like a devil, and more like a lover. He turned her, walking her backward until the length of a table pressed at the rear of her thighs.

He gave her no choice; she was strong, but not as strong as he was. He treated her as if *she* were clay and he were the artist, and perhaps it was true. In this arena, he had mastered the art. He crowded her, his hips firm against hers, his chest flattened against hers, his legs restless and moving beside, along, between. His constraint should have blocked her breathing, but he held her just lightly enough that she did not feel imprisoned. Rather, he embraced her, and of all the stimulation he forced on her, that feeling was the best.

In her wildest imaginings, she had not imagined this. But she resolved to follow wherever he led.

So he did as he wished, touching first her hips, cupping them, stroking them to memorize their shape. He spanned her waist, smiling as if the contrast of womanly hips and slender waist pleased him. He grazed each rib, his blunt fingers counting upward over the top of her clothing.

She let him. She had decided she would. If such familiarity gave him pleasure, then she was privileged to accommodate him.

Yet still he watched her intently, waiting for, almost anticipating, escape.

And to her surprise, as his hands caressed the underside of her breast, she experienced a jump of panic, a need to bolt.

"You're frightened." He wasn't asking. He knew.

She swallowed, and her voice was hoarse. "I don't like that."

"Why not?" His whole hand cupped her.

She grabbed his thick wrist, her fingers rippling across the knob of bone at one corner. "You are touching a place where only a husband should touch."

Still he held his hand there, and in a warm tone, said, "Or a lover."

She gripped the joint so hard she felt the pulse in his veins. Her voice, usually strong and coherent, wavered abominably. "Surely it is understandable that I should be shocked and wary and"—she took a breath—"uncomfortable."

His other hand cupped her other breast. "How uncomfortable?"

She closed her eyes to escape from his scrutiny. From his amusement. Because he knew she was lying. It wasn't discomfort that made her want to move her hips, to seek after this adventure with all the zest that was in her. It was something different, stronger, something greater than she was herself. It was an impulse almost primeval in its strength; a directive.

Like sculpting.

His thumb moved over her nipple, and it contracted. So did every feminine part of her. Totally involved, impervious to sight and sound, she found herself digging her nails into his shoulders.

He laughed, soft and uneven, each stroke becoming more brazen until she whimpered. As if that were a signal, his hands grasped her hands. He moved them to his groin, and he held them to the tight cloth of his trousers.

Her eyes sprang open, and she stared at him. His eyes glistened with some great emotion, and he asked, "Note the difference."

"Yes." She agreed because he seemed to expect it of her, but she didn't understand why he laughed softly.

Like a greedy boy, he clutched a handful of her skirt, then another, and raised it. He stared at her garters tied just above the knee, and she let go of him to clasp the edge of the table. His breathing was fast and shallow, like hers, and he kept tugging at her skirt until she thought he would have it over her head.

But no. Still clutching the material, he clasped her

bottom and boosted her onto the table. She sprawled on the cold, hard surface, tousled with incredulity, confusion, and with his demands.

Voices sounded outside the door—the servants, perhaps, or worse, visitors. Sanity blasted through her. She grabbed for her hem.

"Give it to me, darling." The midnight blue of his eyes sparkled with stars as he tried to tug her hand away.

She hung on. "This isn't right. There are others—"

"No one else matters."

"Please listen, my lord!"

"Call me Ransom." He was coaxing now, wanting her skirt and the freedom of her body and God only knew what else.

McMenemy was speaking loudly, and being answered just as loudly. Jane couldn't believe Blackburn didn't hear. "Listen," she urged.

Changing tactics, he abandoned her skirt and slid his fingers along her outer thigh. "Darling," he crooned.

The door slammed against the wall.

He whirled to face it as Lady Goodridge stepped into the chamber.

In her ringing tone, she said, "Ransom, this butler is totally unacceptable. You'll have to . . ." Her voice trailed off as she observed her brother, Jane, and their dishevelment. Her eyes widened, and her substantial frame shivered.

Blackburn moved to stand in front of Jane, but it was too late. Lady Goodridge had brought companions. A gentleman and two ladies crowded forward, and one of the ladies screamed.

A draft of air from the open door ruffled Jane's hair and sent a hairpin spinning. It tinked as it struck the tabletop, as ominously as Jane's own death knell.

Chapter 12

The morning after an encounter with Blackburn, Jane thought blearily, hadn't improved in eleven years. Memories of last night brought forth other memories, memories she thought she had successfully suppressed.

And that particular memory, of her unsanctioned visit to Blackburn's home—that was the most hurtful remembrance. As she descended the stairs, following the scent of grilling sausage, she shuddered and hunched her shoulders. The retained humiliation made her want to curl up in a ball and hide.

But she could no longer be a coward. She had spent years hiding, and if she'd learned one thing, it was that the memories would always hurt her. She had also learned there were worse things than memories— the loss of a sister, the deliberate unkindness of a brother-in-law, being cast from her home and left to make her way in the world as best she could.

Memories? What were mere memories in comparison? She wouldn't be beaten by them.

Straightening her spine, she took a breath and stepped into the breakfast room.

A soft patter of applause greeted her entrance.

Startled, she looked around for the reason, and found Violet, Lord Tarlin, and Adorna gazing at her and smiling.

"What was that in honor of?" Seating herself at her usual place, she nodded at Lord Tarlin. Tall, thin, and balding, he was a man of good sense and honor, but Jane found herself uncomfortable in his presence. Not because of anything he did, but because she lived in his house, ate his food, and rode in his carriage. He thought nothing of her sojourn here, she knew. Violet described him as the most generous man alive, but the years of living under Eleazer's thumb had left their mark. Unconsciously Jane waited for the demand for payment.

"You did it. Jane, you did it!" Violet crowed. "I have never seen Blackburn as maddened and discomfited as he appeared last night."

"I have," Jane said dryly. "I had hoped never to see such a thing again."

"Those of us who know him rather enjoyed his annoyance," Lord Tarlin said.

"I liked him," Adorna said.

"Oh, so do I." Lord Tarlin sat still as Violet wiped a crumb from his lip. Smiling at his wife, he added, "But on occasion, he is too aware of his consequence."

"Aunt Jane will take care of that." Adorna wore a crisp morning gown of lawn green, and looked as fresh as if she had not imbibed wine, eaten supper at twelve, and danced until three.

It was, Jane decided, one of the many unfair advantages of youth.

"He is very handsome," Adorna continued. "No wonder you fell in love with him, Aunt Jane."

Jane shouldn't have been surprised at Adorna's sudden acquisition of knowledge, but she was, and with a thrust of dread, she wondered how much her niece really knew. For how could a chaperone moralize when she'd once created a scandal great enough to live through the ages? "Who told you such nonsense, dear?"

"By the time we came in from the garden, everyone had heard, and lots of people told me." Adorna sighed pleasurably.

Tensely Jane said, "You were told about the statue?"

"Yes. They said you made a good likeness of Lord Blackburn." Adorna blinked, the picture of an innocent babe.

"That's all?"

"A very, very good likeness is what I heard." Adorna frowned. "Was there more?"

Jane met Violet's gaze and recognized the relief there. "No, nothing else."

"I thought the tale romantic, and I wish you would sculpt again."

"Well, I can't. I have no place to do it and probably don't remember enough of the art anyway." A footman placed a loaded plate in front of Jane, and she murmured her thanks.

"That's awful." Adorna's eyes were two big, round, mournful pools. "They say you were so good."

As Jane took a scone, she answered Adorna crisply. "*They* said a lot of things, the least of which was that I was good. And 'romantic' is the last word I would use to describe that whole, hideous episode."

"*My* friends thought it so." Adorna dimpled. "I saw to that."

Currants dotted the split scone, and as Jane placed a dab of quince jelly on the textured surface, she marveled at her own extravagance. To put jelly on an already rich bread seemed almost sinful. "I don't think your young suitors are the ones who decide society's policies."

"No, but Lord Blackburn is." Violet crushed her napkin in her fist. "It's time he paid restitution for his actions. He has brought you nothing but pain."

Nothing but pain? Once again the memory of that day in Blackburn's study rose before Jane's eyes, but this time it wasn't the humiliation she remembered. She remembered the passion, unbidden and unwanted. She might deny the yearning, but her body's evidence would not be refuted. The warmth within her, the dampness between her legs, the ache in her breasts— seeing him had rekindled it all. All the desire. All the yearning.

And all the need to give vent to her artistic talent.

She couldn't. She shouldn't. But the address the Vicomte de Sainte-Amand had slipped her burned in her pocketbook like a coal of live craving.

"For him to pay restitution, he would have to feel

guilt,'' Jane said. ''Can you truly see Lord Blackburn feeling guilt about anything, especially about trivial events which took place so long ago? And besides, I committed the first offense.''

''He's not a bad chap,'' Lord Tarlin objected. ''I think if he hadn't been so angry with you, those events would have had a proper ending. But no man would have taken so pointed an insult so lightly.''

Jane put down her scone and asked the same question she had asked so many times before. ''What insult?''

''Yes, what insult?'' Adorna asked.

''I meant no insult,'' Jane said.

Jane received the same answer she had received so many times before. Lord Tarlin opened his mouth, then looked at his wife. She shook her head, and he shut his mouth again. Looking both uncomfortable and amused, he said, ''Yes, well, it's after eleven and I have duties to perform. Must get going.'' Standing, he bent and pecked a kiss on Violet's upturned face. ''I'll see you later, my love, shall I?''

''You're taking us to the ball at Lady Ethan's tonight, aren't you?''

Lord Tarlin sagged. ''Another? So soon?''

''The season is just started,'' Violet reminded him.

''I shall have to find some urgent need to go to Tarlin House.''

Smiling serenely at him, Violet said, ''Whatever you think is best, dear.''

After he left, Jane said, ''I hope he doesn't resent escorting us.''

Violet chuckled. ''Not at all. He always threatens

to run away from the season, I always offer my gracious willingness that he should leave, and he always stays to escort me.''

''He is truly caged,'' Adorna said thoughtfully. ''Not by you, but by his desire to be with you.''

Violet examined her voluptuous guest. ''What amazing insight.''

Adorna shrugged. ''You flatter me, my lady, but that must be obvious to all.''

It hadn't been to Jane, but over the years, she had grown used to Adorna's inherent shrewdness in all things concerning men. If only Jane had been as shrewd . . . She closed her mind to Lord Blackburn and his incredible threat. She would not think of him, nor would she look behind as he commanded. He had been angry at the reawakening of the scandal, but he did not really wish to take her to his bed.

The butler arrived, carrying a salver piled high with cream-colored sheets of sealed and elegant paper.

Adorna gurgled with laughter.

''Look at this!'' Violet lifted several in her fingers, then cracked the seal on a few. ''I have never seen so many invitations. Our little Adorna is a success!''

Jane nodded and smiled. She had never doubted that.

Violet's mouth twisted, and she picked up one folded paper with just her fingertips. ''And another letter from Mr. Morant.''

''I'll take it.'' Jane accepted it from Violet. Eleazer hadn't been jesting when he said he wanted a detailed reckoning of their expenditures; he wrote once a week demanding an accounting of his investment. Jane always acknowledged him promptly, although some of the purchases Adorna had insisted on making on Jane's behalf required carefully worded replies.

"Also," the butler intoned, "Monsieur Chasseur has arrived."

Only a few days after they arrived, the young tutor had arrived in London. Miss Cunningham's death, he assured Jane, had been ruled an accident, one that, the constable acknowledged, he had had no part in. He could now give Miss Morant his full attention, and looked forward to working with such a winning and intelligent lady.

Yet between fittings and teas and the theater, Adorna had little time left, so Monsieur Chasseur came weekly to teach her as he did so many of the other young people in London for the Season.

"Ooh, my lesson." Adorna wilted back into her chair. "French is too hard. I will never learn it."

"Of course you will, dear. You just must keep trying," Jane said mechanically.

She was an adult, with a responsibility toward Adorna. Last night's incident in the garden proved the girl attracted disaster like a flower attracts bees. So until the girl was settled with a good husband, Jane would continue to act as befitting a spinster, and then she would see about employment—as a governess, perhaps.

Yet inevitably her mind turned away from that thought and to Blackburn, and her fingertips tingled in that manner which had brought her so much grief. She wanted to paint. She wanted to sculpt. She wanted to be who she was and not who society commanded.

But—

She would not go to de Sainte-Amand's. She would not.

"Got a new report, m'lord."

Blackburn looked up from the paper before him and placed his pen carefully on the blotter. "You always sneak up on me, Wiggens."

"It's me job, m'lord. What ye pay me for." Wiggens smiled a gap-toothed grin. "But ye never jump, do ye?"

"Not much makes me jump anymore." Holding out his hand, Blackburn waited while Wiggens dug through the ragged layers of his clothing. In any of the Blackburn homes, garments so old and tattered would have been burned in the trash barrel, but on the streets of London, no one gave Wiggens a second glance. An invaluable tool, was Wiggens.

The report, when Wiggens handed it across, was stained, and Blackburn blew a thin, fine layer of soot off the top sheet before setting it before him. "Did the clerk give you any trouble this time?" he asked as he perused the contents.

"No, m'lord. Ye scared 'im fully last time, ye did." Wiggens nodded wisely. "Thank ye."

Blackburn paid for Wiggens's phenomenal memory, not for any literary skills, and when the secretary who inscribed those memories had cuffed Wiggens, Blackburn had been quite succinct and to the point. Employment was precious; perhaps the clerk wished to seek it elsewhere. The clerk did not.

Wiggens was now as cocky as ever, the best of the

battalion of miniature sleuths Blackburn employed.

As Blackburn read the exacting descriptions Wiggens had given, he recognized most of the people who entered and exited the de Sainte-Amand home. One, however, he did not know. Tapping his finger on the bottom of the page, he asked, "Who is this lady?"

"The one what went in this mornin'?" Wiggens grinned at Blackburn's nod. "I *thought* ye'd be interested. That's why I brung the report right away. Funny lady, she was, scared to death, by the way she acted. Walked past me corner first, comin' from Oxford Street, and walked along lookin' at the 'ouses as if she didn't know where she was goin'. Got right to the stairs leadin' to the Frenchie's door, and I thought, Aha! A new one! Then she took off like a shot. Walked down to the corner and around. Then 'ere she comes back again, walkin' slow-like, talkin' to 'erself!"

"What was she saying?"

"I wasn't that close, m'lord. Only watched 'er wipe 'er 'ands on 'er skirt, like she wasn't wearin' gloves, which she was, and put 'er foot on the bottom step. Then off she goes again! Back to me corner." Wiggens vigorously paced across the small chamber, imitating her.

Leaning back in his leather chair, Blackburn observed the performance. "But she finally decided to go in."

Wiggens frowned, unhappy at having the tale cut short. "Aye. After the third pass, she goes to the far corner, turns all military-like on 'er heel, and marches back up to the 'ouse, up the steps, and raps on the door.''

''They let her in.''

''I'd say they did! The Frenchie's butler made all goo-goo over 'er, smilin' and bowin' like she was somebody important. So I scoot a little closer, and peek in, and what do I see? The man 'imself comes into the entry and bows and kisses 'er fingers like she was a doochess or somethin'.''

Suspicion snaked up Blackburn's spine. ''Fascinating.''

''Then they shut the door.'' Wiggens collapsed in a chair and slouched down, presentation over.

Blackburn read the description of the lady again, then again, his brain clicking.

But it couldn't be Jane. The memory of last evening weighed heavy on his mind, that was all. He could still, when he wished, bring forth her image, breathe in her scent, feel the warmth of her skin, and want more. ''Tall woman, you said.''

''Tall enough to stand out in a crowd.'' Wiggens scratched in a manner that made Blackburn resolve to wash thoroughly when he was once again alone. ''Well dressed, no longer in the bloom of youth, if ye get me meanin', but pretty enough and quality. I could tell that.''

''Dark, short hair,'' Blackburn guessed.

''Curled around 'er face under the bonnet.''

Blackburn noted that his fingers were cold, and the faint buzz in his head disturbed him.

It was unlikely to be Jane. Only the false courtship he had resolved to perpetrate made him even consider her. That, the fact he respected her intelligence—and the fact he wanted her enough to threaten to make the rumors of their affair into truth. "Did you happen to notice the color of her eyes?"

"Naw. Too far away." Then Wiggens sat up straight. "But that's not right. I did note 'em, because they were as green as the moss in the gutters."

Staring at the paper, Blackburn saw Jane, silhouetted against the light at his sister's house. De Sainte-Amand had handed her a slip of paper. She had first tried to refuse it, as if her better instincts were fighting to maintain their hold. Then she had taken it.

Wetting his lips, Blackburn asked, "Did you hear her name?"

"No, m'lord."

She had no income, and a brother-in-law who apparently begrudged her every farthing. Yet her gown last night had cost more than Wiggens earned in a year.

"Was she dressed to seduce?"

Wiggens looked startled. "No, m'lord. A plain brown pelisse over a plain brown gown."

Had Jane sold her soul?

"Ye're lookin' a little peaked, m'lord." Wiggens peered at him through big blue eyes. "Ye might need to eat."

"Yes." Blackburn opened his desk drawer and drew out five shillings. Then, remembering the value of Jane's gown, he added another five. "I have a new mission for you."

Wiggens bowed, bony elbows akimbo. "At yer service, m'lord."

''I want you to go to Cavendish Square and set up shop there. See if the lady who acted so oddly at de Sainte-Amand's lives in the Tarlin home.''

''But I'm yer best!'' Wiggens said indignantly. ''Why would ye send me to Cavendish Square where all the toffs is?''

''We may have a problem developing there, possibly connected with the Frenchies.'' Blackburn placed the money in Wiggens's skinny, outstretched hand. ''I depend on you. You know that.''

As he glanced at the amount Blackburn had handed over, Wiggens's reluctance turned to enthusiasm. ''Aye, m'lord. I won't fail ye.''

Wiggens swaggered out, leaving Blackburn to his bitter thoughts.

The Vicomte de Sainte-Amand was one of the many Frenchmen who had immigrated fourteen years ago, escaping the Reign of Terror that had taken almost his entire family to the guillotine. Proud, vain, and poverty-stricken for the first time in his life, the son had found it difficult to adjust to English life. He needed money—a lot of money—and that was what de Sainte-Amand did not have.

Until recently.

De Sainte-Amand did not understand the term *discretion*. He had flaunted his newfound wealth; the Foreign Office had noted it. With a little investigation, the source of his new fortune became clear. He spied for Bonaparte.

Blackburn despised de Sainte-Amand for his ingratitude at the country that had offered refuge, yet in a strange way, he understood de Sainte-Amand's defection. De Sainte-Amand longed for a return to the old times, when he had a fortune and could command respect by his very position in society.

Yet many had lost much in their lives, and still they lived upstanding lives.

And then there was Jane.

She, too, had the right to be bitter. Her reputation had been destroyed by her own youthful stupidity, her art denied her, and respectability consumed in the bonfire of Blackburn's own desire. And she was destitute. Could de Sainte-Amand have recruited her? Every gentlemanly instinct rebelled, but in the cold logic of his mind, he knew the answer to be *yes*.

Standing, Blackburn picked up his beaver hat and carefully placed it on his head. It would appear it was time to renew his ignoble courtship of Jane.

A prospect that caused him too much pleasure.

Chapter 13

Jane put her finger to her lips, signifying silence.

Springall, the Tarlins' butler, shut the outer door as quietly as he could, but shook his head. "Not likely, miss. My lady has been asking for you every five minutes."

"I'll change out of my street clothes and be down as soon as I can." Humming a tune she'd heard on the avenue, Jane handed her redingote to the footman.

But before she could take a step toward the stairs, Violet said, "Jane, where have you been?" Her cotton skirt rustled as she hurried out of the drawing room. "Men are everywhere, like fleas on a dog. Adorna has a dozen gentleman callers already!"

Buoyed by an odd sense of exhilaration, Jane smiled at Violet. "And isn't that what we want?"

"Yes, but you must be here, too." With a proprietary air, Violet untied the ribbon under Jane's chin. "We daren't encourage the rumor you are hiding yourself away."

"Why not?" Jane couldn't keep the smile off her

face as Violet tugged at her bonnet. "It's Adorna they've come to see."

"And Adorna they've come to court." Handing Jane's bonnet to the hovering butler, Violet said, "They'll not be serious if they think her family is not up to snuff."

The comment made Jane flush with sudden fire. "I wouldn't do anything to harm Adorna."

"I know that."

Jane looked at Violet closely, and realized she had fallen for a trick. Violet feared Jane would be afraid to face the whispers and the gibing. And perhaps, before Jane's experience today, she would have hesitated. But right now, joy buffered her, and quick as a cat, she tugged on one of Violet's curls. "You would do anything to put me into society."

Startled, Violet stood back and looked her over. "So I would. Jane, you're looking very smug and very pretty. Where *have* you been?"

Without a qualm, Jane met her friend's eyes. "For a walk."

"And you come back looking like that? Whom did you meet? A long-lost lover?"

Jane chuckled. "In a manner of speaking."

Grabbing Jane's shoulders, Violet shook her. "Who? Was it Blackburn?"

"No. I'm sure he has dismissed me completely." Only more than once this morning, she had heard booted feet behind her, and imagined she felt the slice of Lord Blackburn's gaze. Such a stupid thing, to think he would do as he threatened, and hunt her down and use her.

Violet stepped away and viewed Jane with more suspicion. ''Is it some other lover I know nothing about?''

Jane wasn't going to answer. Oh, no, not and risk her dear friend's disapproval. For disapprove, Violet would, and in this instance Jane would risk all for a little satisfaction. Just a little. Just for a while.

''I must go change,'' Jane said. ''Then I promise I will come down and be a chaperone once more.''

Violet started to follow as Jane ascended the stairs, but a knock sounded on the outer door, another gentleman arrived for his visit to the magnificent Miss Morant, and Violet was drawn away to her responsibilities as hostess.

For all her exhilaration, Jane well knew her duty and was determined not to neglect it. She summoned the maid. She washed her hands until no trace of anything that could betray her remained on the skin or under the fingernails. She changed into an unadorned gown of steel blue cambric, then sat before the mirror and allowed the maid to arrange her windblown hair into a more mature style. Still, nothing could dim the rosy color in her cheeks and the shimmering stars in her eyes. Jane had not felt this animated for years, and she welcomed joy's return.

Yet she knew when she went into the drawing room, that woman must disappear, for she'd once again be Miss Higgenbothem, with old scandal clattering behind her like rusted laughter.

The trip down the stairs seemed longer and more arduous than the trip up, and as she descended, she allowed her mask to settle into place. She was the most proper chaperone ever to grace London drawing rooms. That, she could never forget.

She crossed the polished floor, her tread firm, and paused in the drawing room doorway. Inside, a veritable forest of suitors greeted her. Southwick and Mallery had donned their capes and were prepared to leave. They had overstayed the recommended twenty-minute visit, yet still they hovered, unwilling to abandon Adorna to the charms of Brockway and Brown. Those gentlemen had just arrived, and smirked at their departing rivals. Some whose names Jane could not recall had brought their sisters to make Miss Adorna Morant's acquaintance. Others had their mothers in tow—or their mothers had them.

Jane knew very well mothers were notorious for wanting to meet their sons' newest inamoratas.

In the midst sat Adorna, the image of feminine pulchritude and modesty. For a moment Jane was struck by the rightness of the picture, and she experienced a twitch of her fingers. With a pencil and sketch pad, she could capture this scene. The sharp contrast of black and white in the gentlemen's clothing. The rainbow of gowns on chattering ladies, heads leaned close as they gossiped. The pale-clad debutantes, nervous and hiding it well, or nervous and not. Adorna, outshining them all, secure in the knowledge she had been created for this society.

Then all eyes turned toward Jane, and a silence fell. Lady Kinnard sniffed, a telling comment in the stifling quiet. Everyone had heard about the scandal, and today Jane was alone, with no Blackburn to threaten her—or protect her.

"Good afternoon," she said, her voice low and cultured as Melba had taught her. "It is a pleasant day, is it not?"

For one dreadful moment no one replied. Then Mr. Fitzgerald stepped forward and bowed, and flashed an impudent smile, which Jane found vastly reassuring. "Indeed it is. Quite suitable for an outing, as I've just been telling Miss Morant."

"Oh, yes, dear Aunt, so he has." Adorna came to her feet, her gown of soft gold molding her body, her breasts shivering with the motion.

The men in the room shivered in unison.

"These ladies and gentlemen have been so kind as to make me welcome." Adorna held out her hand, and Jane put hers in it. Then Adorna faced the chamber and smiled, breathed, and charmed. "I know they'll make you welcome, too."

"Yes, Miss Morant," the men chanted.

Violet made her way to Jane's side, and murmured, "They're mesmerized."

"Not the women," practical Jane answered. If anything, the hostility among the ladies had heightened. Some of these women had daughters out this season. They envied Adorna's success, and if they could undermine her by rejecting her chaperone, they would count the afternoon well spent.

It was frightening, to see that phalanx of rouged and powdered faces tighten with unified disapproval, and Jane grasped the enormity of this challenge. No one, not amiable Mr. Fitzgerald nor prestigious Violet, could stem the tide of condemnation.

Only Blackburn could, but Blackburn was not here.

Lady Kinnard stood.

"No," Violet breathed.

Lady Kinnard's three married daughters stood with her. Through the years, each of them had sought Blackburn's attentions; each had been rejected in her turn. For them, the snub to Jane was more than social. For these women, it was personal.

After a brief hissing match, Miss Redmond, the latest Kinnard debutante, reluctantly rose also. With a great rustling of silks and many venomous sideways glances, the women prepared to leave.

Others followed suit, some smiling, some embarrassed. It was to be an exodus. Jane would have to abandon London, and go . . . where?

Then, from behind her, her savior spoke.

"Miss Higgenbothem." Blackburn's voice was smooth and deep, rich with meaning and rife with innuendo. "I have come to call on you."

Jane heard a gasp, and wondered if it had been her own.

I have come to call on you. With this visit, and with those words, he had reaffirmed his intentions of the night before. He had made Jane the pointed object of his pursuit.

She stood frozen, unable to move, afraid to look out at the gawking guests, more afraid to turn and look at Blackburn.

I have come to call on you. He was courting her. He was chasing her. It was her every fantasy, her every nightmare, come true.

Violet and Adorna, working together, hurriedly shoved her around to face him. Blackburn. The man who had stalked Jane in her dreams. The man who had threatened to take her to his bed. Would his purpose show in his countenance?

But no. He looked perfectly amiable. Exquisitely civilized. Utterly sartorial.

Until she looked into his eyes. They were blue and hot, intent on her to the exclusion of all else. He wasn't a *gentle*man. He was a *man* with one thing on his mind.

Violet didn't seem to see what was so obvious to Jane. With a smooth curtsy, she said, "Lord Blackburn. How good to see you."

As he turned to Violet, his face lost all expression, and he bowed with the respect due his hostess. "I hope the day finds you well." He lifted his quizzing glass. His gaze traveled to the suddenly gracious Lady Kinnard, then moved to each of her daughters. With a flounce, the youngest sat back on the sofa. The older three walked to the pianoforte and pretended an interest in the music set there. The other women tried to turn their motions into a natural restlessness, then settled back to watch the show. "You have, as usual, the finest gathering in all of London society."

If he sounded insincere, it did not matter. Violet knew how to play the diplomatic game, and she played it with a gratified vengeance. "Thank you, my lord, but I fear it is my houseguests who have garnered the crème de la crème. Miss Morant and Miss Higgenbothem are assuredly the draw."

"Lady Tarlin, you allow yourself too little credit." Yet Blackburn bowed, first to Jane, then to Adorna. And then to Jane again.

His marked gallantry was a sign of particular attention, perhaps even more pointed than his use of the phrase *I have come to call on you.*

Jane found herself mute before his waiting gaze. He mocked her, she thought, well aware he had saved her from social annihilation and smugly daring her to reject his assistance.

She wouldn't. She couldn't. Yet hard experience had taught her he would demand repayment, and to sign the contract without knowing the terms was the act of a desperate woman.

She should say something, she supposed, make some conversation, challenge him with words. But the scent of starch and lemon that clung to him clogged all channels in her brain, and she could feel only the surging resentment in her blood.

"Curtsy," Violet whispered in her ear.

Jane did so.

"Let me in, Jane."

The phrase was so faint, she thought she must have hallucinated. But no, Blackburn was leaning forward, close to her ear, and smiling.

He never smiled. Only now, and not with mirth or kindness. It was more of a baring of fangs, a signal she should run.

Violet pinched Jane's arm. "You're blocking the door, Jane. Let him in!"

Stupidly Jane stood still for one more moment. Then Blackburn stepped forward, so close their clothing brushed and she heard the beat of his heart.

Or was it hers, pounding in her ears?

She moved back so quickly Blackburn smiled

again, and she pressed herself against the wall as he strolled into the drawing room. As she faced the ladies and gentlemen, she saw they eyed her with belated approval. They saw no further than the surface; they thought Blackburn smiled because he valued her.

Simpletons, every one.

With the ease that marked all her moments in society, Adorna took the situation in hand. "Lord Blackburn, Mr. Fitzgerald has been enthusiastically suggesting an outing, one that would allow Miss Higgenbothem and me to leave the city for a short afternoon. Perhaps you could suggest a destination."

"Of course." Lord Blackburn saluted Mr. Fitzgerald.

Mr. Fitzgerald saluted him back, but warily, as if he could not quite comprehend Blackburn's attachment.

Mr. Fitzgerald had much in common with Jane.

"The weather is warm and dry, and one never knows how long we will be so blessed." Blackburn surveyed the company, using his quizzing glass like a weapon. As he trained the lenses on each lady, on each gentleman, they one by one sat straighter, stood taller, became more courteous because Blackburn would accept nothing else. He was a leader of society, and no one was allowed to thwart his desires. Right now he desired that Miss Higgenbothem be accepted without question, so accept, her they would.

"A picnic would be ideal," he said.

A murmur of polite agreement swept the company.

"Yes, a picnic." Adorna clapped her hands. *"Mangez le souris."*

Startled, Jane asked, "Adorna? Dear, what did you say?"

"Monsieur Chasseur taught me this morning. I said, 'We'll eat as we desire.' "

"Not . . . quite. I believe you said, 'Eat a mouse.' "

"Oh." Adorna faced the room and giggled. "I'm so silly."

Half the gentlemen giggled, too. The other half cooed.

Adorna turned to Blackburn. "My aunt speaks French very well. She is so accomplished." She sighed.

Her skill with languages, Jane did not deny. All those years ago, she had imagined she might someday leave the confines of the English shore and conquer the continent with her art. So she had studied the romance languages, Spanish, Italian, and French. Yet all she had gained was the ability to speak to Adorna's French tutor, and Adorna's hope that such skill would impress Lord Blackburn.

"My tutor loves to talk to her, because he says she's so polished she makes him think he's in France."

"Does she."

It wasn't a question. More of a statement, and it was accompanied by a cool, thoughtful stare that ran like a chill over Jane's skin. Blackburn's gaze lingered on her breasts, and they tightened, too, until she felt stupid, casting innocent lures where none was needed.

"I myself do not speak French well," Blackburn said.

Violet sputtered. "Modesty, Blackburn?"

He glared, and her mouth snapped shut.

"Not well at all," he repeated. "So I find Miss Morant's mistake as charming as herself. Might I proffer my sister's estate, Goodridge Manor, for a picnic tomorrow?"

"Capital!" Mr. Fitzgerald said.

"Goodridge Manor?" Adorna clasped her hands. "How kind of you, my lord. Will there be room to picnic?"

The gentlemen coughed to hide their amusement. The women tittered.

"Oh." Adorna gazed around with wide, surprised eyes. "Did I say something funny?"

"There's no reason you should know." Blackburn leaned his elbow against the mantel, a fine display of breeding, muscle, and tailoring. "Goodridge Manor is quite a large estate on the Thames near the coast. The house is on a hill. A park surrounds it, and extends to the shore."

"I love the shore," Adorna said.

"Then it's settled." Blackburn turned to Jane. "Or it is if your chaperone is amenable. Do these arrangements meet with your approval, Miss Higgenbothem?"

As if it mattered. Blackburn had, after all, just saved her from disaster once again. Yet no one remembered he was the author of the disaster. She must fall in with Blackburn's wishes, and she was expected to be grateful; the inequity of it grated on her. "It is quite a distance, is it not?" she asked coolly.

She had the diversion of seeing Blackburn look surprised. ''A three-hour drive.''

Jane turned to her charge. ''We'll have to be on our way early, Adorna, and there is a ball tonight.''

''I'll leave the dancing early. Oh, please, Aunt Jane, mayn't we go?''

It was a pretty appeal, and Jane suffered a pang when she saw it. ''We will be delighted.'' Jane directed her gaze over Blackburn's right shoulder. ''Thank you, my lord.''

''Tomorrow, Blackburn?'' Violet's satisfaction seemed greater than the good deed deserved. ''Your impetuosity is fitting, but will Lady Goodridge be receptive at such short notice?''

''Lady Goodridge is, of course, a woman of refinement and gentility. But I assure you, should her servants be unprepared at any time, she would flay their skins from their hides.''

Everyone—Lady Kinnard, her daughters, the suitors, Adorna, Violet—nodded solemnly.

Jane chuckled.

She couldn't help it; she thought Blackburn was joking, for Lady Goodridge was always so civil. But the bevy of disapproving stares silenced her, and like a child reproved in church, she hastily sobered.

That rare smile again played around Blackburn's mouth. ''Miss Higgenbothem is a dear friend of my sister's,'' he said to the company. ''She is not at all in awe of Lady Goodridge.''

Jane wished she could fade into the green striped wallpaper. She would never be so bold as to call herself a good friend of Lady Goodridge's.

Mr. Fitzgerald comforted Jane with a wink. "Lady G. has always been an admirer of Miss Higgenbothem's, I believe."

"No one would ever dispute that Lady Goodridge is the soul of benevolence." Violet did not want it said she allowed any malediction of Lady Goodridge. She was not so brave.

"Sometimes," her unrepentant brother said. "When she's not making my life hell. For instance, she has been quite outspoken about my need for a wife."

Jane groped for a sofa and seated herself. Since Blackburn's entry, so many women had gasped, she found the air quite thin.

Adorna sounded deceptively innocent. "Lady Goodridge is ever wise."

"Yes. After all these years, she has prevailed on me to agree."

Closing her eyes, Jane took deep breaths and tried to think of something, anything, that would change the subject. Certainly no one else was speaking; they all hung on each word with the avaricious interest of a beggar.

Mr. Fitzgerald rescued her. "Going to the country tomorrow, then. I'll call on Lady Goodridge and beg she accompany us. Fresh air will do her well."

"I doubt she will go," Blackburn said repressively.

"*I'm* sure she will," Fitz answered.

Raising his eyebrows, Blackburn stared at his friend. "Perhaps you know her better than I do."

Fitz bowed. "Indeed, Blackburn, a brother is hardly the best judge of a woman's character, and certainly not a woman as charming and lovely as Lady Goodridge.''

What Blackburn would have replied, Jane did not know, for Lady Kinnard interrupted by asking coyly, ''Are my daughters invited, too, my lord?''

Blackburn slowly turned his head and looked on Lady Kinnard and her progeny. ''Invited?''

''To Lady Goodridge's estate!'' Lady Kinnard's Fairchild background was never so clear as now, when she thrust herself where she was not wanted in pursuit of moneyed connections. Eyes gleaming with rapacious greed, she said, ''It would be so convivial to visit dear Lady Goodridge's home with a party of just these close friends.''

Everyone in the room held their breath, waiting. Would Blackburn issue one of his famous set-downs? Instead, he nodded slowly and in measured tones said, ''An excellent idea, Lady Kinnard. The greater the party, the greater the chance for . . . entertainment. Allow me to extend an invitation to any who would wish a day in the country, be they here''—his gaze swept the assemblage—''or not.''

With Blackburn's words, that breathless excitement that afflicted Jane disappeared. Whether she wished it or not, she knew Blackburn, she had studied Blackburn, and she did not believe anything, certainly not love, could change him into an amiable man who offered hospitality to all, especially not the brummish Lady Kinnard.

Something was definitely odd.

Chapter 14

"*Would everyone please stop smiling at me?*" Jane glared at her companions in the Tarlin carriage with an annoyance that increased with every mile.

"But why?" Violet jostled close to Jane as the carriage spun off the turnpike and onto the rutted road leading to Goodridge Manor. "Unrequited love for you has so overset Blackburn's emotions, he has developed windmills in the head."

"Or somewhere else," Lord Tarlin muttered.

"George!" Violet said, scandalized.

Her husband just grinned at her, and after a moment she grinned back. But she still reproved, "There are young ladies present," with a nod to Adorna.

Turning to the girl at his side, Lord Tarlin asked, "You didn't understand that, did you, puss?"

"Understand what, my lord?" Adorna asked.

"Don't smirk at me, George," Violet commanded. "And, Jane, look at the carriages ahead of us. Look at the carriages behind us." She tapped her hand against the window. "Other than love, what explanation can you give for Blackburn's generous open invitation?''

Jane wished she saw life as simply as Violet. Violet would be offended if Jane accused her of being an innocent, yet Violet's privileged life had insulated her from the realities of life.

If Lord Blackburn had changed his ways, it was not for love; of that Jane felt certain. Some other reason lurked behind his sudden amiability.

''I think it's romantic.'' Adorna's normally unfocused gaze sharpened on Jane. ''And he's so handsome. So debonair. Don't you think so, Aunt Jane?''

''Yes,'' Jane said shortly.

''He's old, of course.''

''I say!'' Lord Tarlin sputtered.

''But handsome. His hair is a very unusual color. Not quite gold, and not quite yellow . . . What color would you use if you painted him, Aunt Jane?''

''I don't know,'' Jane said with ill grace. ''Goldish yellow.''

Adorna placed her finger on the cleft of her chin. ''Maybe it's bronze.''

''Yellow ocher,'' Jane corrected. ''The base pigment would be yellow ocher.''

Adorna stared at her.

''Blond,'' Jane elucidated.

''That's right! Blond. And his eyes are such a blue color. So blue, just blue, almost purple-blue. Aunt Jane, if you were going to—''

''Midnight.'' Jane didn't want to think about him, but Adorna's questions forced her to. ''His eyes are midnight.''

"Like the sky. Yes, that sounds right." Adorna fanned herself with her hand. "If I were an artist, I'd want to paint him. He's well formed. It's not all padding and corsets, like some of the lords. I'd wager he boxes. How else would he get such a sinful body?" Gazing off into the rolling hills, Adorna seemed unaware of Jane's growing irritation. "What I really like about Lord Blackburn is his face. He looks so stern, almost angry all the time, except when he looks at you, Aunt Jane."

"How does he look then?" Violet asked.

"I think the word is . . . lustful."

"That's enough, Adorna," Jane said sternly.

She couldn't remember when she'd been this vexed with her niece, and she remained trapped in this carriage until journey's end. Worse, she couldn't even look forward to journey's end, because then she'd be at Goodridge Manor with half of London staring at her and wondering what madness afflicted Blackburn that he should show his devotion so blatantly.

Jane had, she realized, totally lost her sense of humor.

"Oh." Adorna looked downcast. "Did I say something wrong?"

The carriage jerked to a halt, saving Jane from an answer and Lord Tarlin from his impending explosion of mirth. One by one they exited the carriage onto Lady Goodridge's estate near the mouth of the Thames. The ocean wasn't far, and sent its fresh breeze up the river to fill Jane's lungs. The open spaces around them made her soul expand. The sunshine, the clear sky, the azure water that frothed beyond the scrub hills and sandy dunes—all fed a wild part of her starved by the city's claustrophobic envelopment.

When Jane turned her back to the river, she saw Goodridge Manor rising as a monument to civilization. A fine example of Georgian dignity, the house was constructed of a flaxen stone that glowed in the sun. Around it, the well-cut lawn slid away in a silken stretch of green, interrupted only by an occasional gazebo, or covered walk, or walled garden for privacy and shelter.

Yet the hand of modern man reached only so far. Eventually the lawn grew tall and coarser grass took over. Then the river and the wind took control, and sculpted the hills from the lower, rolling promontories along this stretch of the shore.

This blissful place formed the perfect blend of impetuosity and caution, and for one selfish moment, Jane coveted it.

Violet might have read Jane's mind. "Lord Blackburn's country estate is Tourbillon, on the sea down the coast. The house looks quite different, for it's older and harsher, and perched right on the cliffs. Still, the atmosphere is much the same. The whole place rather makes one want to visit and sip tea and watch the ocean forever."

Jane knew where Tourbillon was. At one time, she'd made it her business to discover that Tourbillon was close to Sittingbourne where she resided in Eleazer's house. But she didn't care now, and it irked her that Violet thought she did. "Your fancy has gotten away from you, Violet," she said disdainfully.

Tying the ribbons of her bonnet with determined gestures, she snatched her filled satchel from the footman and threaded her way along the ridge that ran parallel to the beach, seeking somewhere she could sit in private.

The others followed her, speaking in low voices, and she began to be sorry she had snapped. But she didn't need Adorna pointing out how handsome Blackburn was, and she didn't need Violet to imagine how much she would like to live in such a house. This whole situation had gotten out of hand, and Jane needed to set it right.

To do so, she would have to ascertain if Blackburn suffered from lunacy or was simply toying with her affections as an immature means of revenge.

A figure coming from the house caught her attention, and indeed she could scarcely ignore it. Only Lady Goodridge's upright figure could have prevailed over the vibrancy of her pink gown. Her matching parasol lent a rosy tinge to her skin. She walked briskly, not allowing the ankle-deep grass to slow her progress, and Mr. Fitzgerald walked with her, a little apart and dragging his feet like a recalcitrant lad.

As she made her way on an interceptive course from the house, her voice boomed out. "Miss Higgenbothem, I understand I have *you* to thank for this *invasion*."

Jane's resolution wavered, then strengthened again as she turned to meet her hostess. Someone needed to teach this domineering family a lesson, and Jane seemed the likely candidate. Dipping into a curtsy, she said, "It is not me you should blame, my lady, but your brother."

"Bah! He *scarcely* knows *good sense* when he's with you. Good to see you, Tarlin, Violet. Miss Morant, you're looking beautiful as ever."

"Thank you, my lady," Adorna said in her sweet, vibrant voice. "But my aunt Jane reminds me that beauty is only skin-deep."

Lady Goodridge snorted. "What do you want? An adorable liver?"

Adorna's eyes rounded. "I thought I had one."

Barely subduing a smile, Lady Goodridge said, "I'm sure you do, dear."

She waved them on. Mr. Fitzgerald remained. Turning her attention back to Jane, Lady Goodridge said, "You—*you* have intelligence."

Jane had heard it before, and no longer considered it a compliment. "Surely it's better for a girl to have beauty than brains."

"Yes, men do see better than they think." Lady Goodridge glared at Mr. Fitzgerald, then indicated the lorgnette that hung from a pink ribbon around her neck. "Luckily for you, Miss Higgenbothem, Ransom's eyesight has faltered with his injury."

"I am not so cold as to call that luck, my lady," Jane said. "Nor to seek pleasure in another's misfortune."

"Of course not. If you didn't display every gentle quality, along with your spirit, I would not be interested in you at all." Lady Goodridge gestured widely. "He's around here somewhere, and he's condescended to speak *even* with the *cits* who dared appear.

Miss Higgenbothem, you've driven him *insane* with *passion*.''

''He has always been mad,'' Jane replied frostily.

Tossing back his head, Mr. Fitzgerald burst into laughter. ''That's telling her.''

''Stop that!'' Lady Goodridge took her closed fan and slapped him across the arm with it. ''It's *your* fault I was dragged along *today*!''

Still grinning, Mr. Fitzgerald evaded her. ''I freely admit that, but I'm dancing attendance on you as penance.''

Lady Goodridge abandoned her attack, and something—in another woman, Jane would have called it hurt—flashed in her eyes. ''Insolent boy, you call caring for your hostess penance?''

''It is when I could be flying my kite on the beach.''

''I *told* you to go.''

''And I told you to go with me.''

Lady Goodridge stared at him, outrage puffing her ample bosom to impressive heights. ''A woman of my age does *not* fly a kite.''

''A woman of your age could watch.''

''A woman of my age does *not* walk on the sand and dirt. It gets in one's shoes and makes one's knees wobble unattractively.''

''You could take off your shoes.''

''Mr. Fitzgerald, you are *brazen,* and very . . . you are very young. Much too young.'' Lady Goodridge stared at her companion as if she wished it otherwise.

''Not so young as all that, my lady.'' Fitz moved closer to her. ''But young enough to keep you busy.''

Lady Goodridge stepped back and in a formal tone, said, "I'm busy enough." Then she rounded on Jane. "You, miss, will catch *flies* with that mouth hanging *open*."

Jane shut it with a snap.

"As I was trying to say, Miss Higgenbothem, I would *strongly* suggest you *marry* Ransom during this brief flash of *sanity*. With a man"—she glared at her companion—"one never knows how long it will *last*."

"You just said Lord Blackburn was insane." But Jane spoke to Lady Goodridge's back.

Mr. Fitzgerald grinned over his shoulder at her as he trailed after Lady Goodridge. "You'll not win an argument with her, Miss Higgenbothem, nor with her brother. They're both stubborn as mules and twice as fractious."

Lady Goodridge stopped dead in her path. "*Mr.* Fitzgerald!"

Slanting a wicked look at his companion, he called to Jane, "There's only one way to deal with these noble folk."

She didn't want to ask, but no one important could hear, and she couldn't help herself. "What is it?"

"A quick wit. A fast dodge." He laughed aloud as he glanced from the indignant Lady Goodridge to a shocked Jane. "And a good loving."

Chapter 15

One by one, multicolored kites caught the breeze and lifted jerkily into the air, soaring above the dunes under the guidance of dandies who wanted to impress the resplendent parade of young ladies. Blankets of the primary colors, of red and blue and yellow, had been stretched across the grass and weighted with rocks and picnic baskets for any matron who wished to sit. The murmur of the river formed a constant background for the laughter of a hundred people, all out of the City for a celebration.

Under Lord Tarlin's direction, the footman had spread their plaid blanket a little away from the crowd. Perhaps Lord Tarlin feared Jane, in her present mood, would alienate someone important.

Hardly likely. When she got too impatient with the triviality of London society, she had only to remember Adorna, and she tucked up her opinions.

"Will you sit, Jane?" Violet called as she came close. "I want to walk with George."

"Of course." Jane placed her satchel at the foot of the blanket and waved them on.

Catching Lord Tarlin's arm, Violet wrapped her own through it and smiled up at him, and he looked down on her with such affection, Jane turned her face away. She was glad Violet was happy, but sometimes she couldn't watch. Violet's bliss only made Jane's lonely heart ache.

Adorna laid her bright head on Jane's shoulder. "I'll settle down right here with you."

The girl's empathy pleased Jane. She loved the child, trouble that she was. Of course, Adorna would attract attention—was already attracting attention—and soon this peaceful stretch of the ridge would be swarming with young lords.

"It's warm here. Will you hold my pelisse?" Adorna asked.

As Adorna shed her jacket, it seemed the laughter, the talk, even the wind, died. Just as Jane suspected—even the elements would cease for a glimpse of Adorna.

"Better." Adorna took a breath of air, and one young kite-flying gentleman fell right on his face. "Are you warm too, Aunt Jane?"

Jane was, and her gown was constructed for outdoor wear. The long sleeves and high neck protected her from the sun, and no one, certainly not Blackburn or any of the inveterate gossips, could call the dull sage color alluring. Jane unfastened the buttons, and Adorna helped free her.

Sinking onto the blanket, they sat side by side, facing the beach. They tucked the hems firmly around their ankles as the breeze snatched at their skirts, and they watched the ripples curling on the shore, and the rush of wind teasing the sand.

At least, Jane did. Adorna's gaze followed the clumps of laughing gentlemen showing off for the ladies. She glanced occasionally at the road, and kept up a running commentary on the new arrivals. "Look! Mr. Southwick is wearing full evening dress, doesn't he look silly? The Andersons have arrived, they got married just last year and they say he has already found a ladybird. There's Mr. Brown courting Miss Clapton. She's got a face like a horse, but he must marry soon, or his estate will be put to the hammer."

"You have a remarkable memory for names. Why aren't you as adept at French as at tattling?"

"Because remembering their names is easy. You just look at their faces and"—Adorna wiggled her shoulders—"remember. French doesn't *mean* anything."

"Oh, but it does." Jane's fervor showed her love of the language. "It's romantic, and when it's spoken it sounds just like music."

"Very nasal music, then." Adorna gave a quivering sigh. "Monsieur Chasseur has started teaching me one phrase every day which I must remember. He said as long as I remember that one phrase, he'll be satisfied with my progress."

Jane didn't know if she approved, but all aristocrats spoke at least a smattering of French, and something had to be done to help Adorna learn it. If he thought that would work, she wouldn't gainsay him.

"Sometimes I'll make an exception and forget a face." Disdain tightened Adorna's rosebud mouth. "Like now. Lord and Lady Athowe have arrived."

Jane started to glance toward the carriages, but Adorna grabbed her. "Don't look. Maybe they won't see us."

"You don't like them?" Jane stared fixedly at the sea.

"After what they said to you at Lady Goodridge's ball?" Adorna tossed her head. "Beasts."

"*She* was rude, but I don't remember him saying anything objectionable."

"I suppose he didn't. I wager he's never said anything objectionable in his life. But he's the worst kind of worm."

Remembering his disappearance so many years before, Jane agreed.

"Who is *that* old man?" Adorna cocked her head toward the man walking along the ridge, and for once her extreme youth had not misread the situation.

He was indeed ancient. Bent and gnarled, he walked with a cane, followed by a footman who lunged whenever the old man tottered.

"That's Viscount Ruskin, formerly plain Mister Daniel McCausland." Jane nudged Adorna. "Stop staring. He's a solicitor, very rich. Rumor is he invented a machine that helped the war, so Prinny gave him a title."

"He was born a commoner, then."

"Very common. He wouldn't have gotten the title at all, except he's old and without male heirs, so the title will die with him." Jane smiled at Adorna and whispered, "It's the way the peerage keep their class exclusive and free of plebs, you know."

"Like me." Adorna tossed her head. "He really ought to marry a young woman and father an heir to spite them all."

Jane laughed. "A delicious thought."

"I wish my mother had found him when she had to marry."

Jane thought she detected wistfulness in Adorna's voice, and said bracingly, "She found your father instead, and made him very happy."

"Of course she made *him* happy." Taking a breath, Adorna said, "She had to marry quickly, and for money."

Astonished, Jane asked, "What do you know about your mother's marriage?"

"I guessed it by myself." Adorna pressed her finger into the indent created by the dimple on her dainty chin. "You sisters were orphaned by your wastrel father when you were ten and she was seventeen. Mama charmed the merchants into giving her the gowns she needed to make a show, and before they caught up with her and demanded payment, she nabbed Papa."

Jane had matured slowly, and at the death of their father she had withdrawn into herself. She hadn't wondered how Melba had provided for them before her whirlwind marriage to Eleazer. Now her niece had explained it, and Jane conjectured every word was true. "You remember your mother very well."

"Of course." Adorna's smile trembled. "She was pretty even when she was sick."

"Like an angel." *Like you.*

Adorna gave Jane her most angelic smile, but it faded as she looked over Jane's shoulder. "Oh, no, what's Monsieur Chasseur doing here?"

Jane was surprised to see the gangly young tutor walking alone along the ridge. He was a gentleman, of course, but in much the same position as a woman of good family who sold herself into servitude as a governess—no longer acceptable among the finer ranks. "Lord Blackburn extended an open invitation, so I suppose Monsieur Chasseur has every right to be here."

"He'll spot us soon, and he wants to start French lessons every day." Adorna rose to her feet. "Aunt Jane, you won't let him?"

Surprised again, Jane said, "You didn't tell me he wanted that."

"I hoped he would forget. But here he is, and he'll make me study. Oh, Aunt Jane . . ." Adorna shifted from foot to foot, impatient to be off.

Jane took pity on her. Today was not a day for lessons, or even for sitting with your maiden aunt. "Go on. Find your companions, but remember, stay in a group and check back with me periodically."

"Yes, Aunt Jane." Adorna hurried away.

"No going off with young men to view sundials," Jane called.

"No, Aunt Jane."

The wind blew her answer back, and Jane was alone. It felt rather odd, to be within sight of so many people and yet apart, with no friends to greet her. No one would come near Jane; disaster followed too closely on her heels.

The arrival of Monsieur Chasseur did nothing to ease her awkwardness.

"Mademoiselle Higgenbothem." He bowed, his face solemn. "Was that Mademoiselle Morant I saw hurrying away?"

Jane almost groaned in distress. She would never grow used to the more distasteful duties of a chaperone—such as breaking the news that Adorna wished to take French lessons only twice a week. A brave woman—Lady Goodridge, for instance—would tell Monsieur Chasseur in a forthright manner. Jane found herself smiling kindly. "She will be desolated she missed you."

His solemn face lightened. "She will?"

"Indeed, for she told me of your proposal to teach her every day, and much to her disappointment, her father wrote and refused to allow it."

His heavy brows lowered again. "He is a *rustre*, a boor, a barbarian."

"Nevertheless, Adorna has promised to study between her lessons."

"Mademoiselle Morant said this?" he asked, faintly incredulous.

"Amazing, isn't it?" Jane hoped lightning did not strike her where she sat.

"I think I must . . . *oui*, I must . . . offer to teach Mademoiselle Morant without pay."

Jane's relief turned to consternation. "No. That's impossible!"

"But when a lady wishes so much to speak *le français*, it is my duty—no, my pleasure—to teach her." Young Chasseur appeared enraptured by the idea.

Jane realized she hadn't been tactful; she had been encouraging. "Really. We can't permit you—"

"I will go now and speak to her. Discreetly, mademoiselle, I promise. I know what the English gentlepeople think of *émigrants* like me."

"Nothing so bad, surely."

"*Mais oui*, they think me ungrateful and beneath them. I know this." His eyes flashed with fire. "But I will tell Mademoiselle Morant of my plan, and I will teach her a phrase for the day . . . Did she tell you of the phrase I would teach?"

"Yes, but—"

"*Merci, mademoiselle.*" He bowed from the waist. "I will not disappoint you."

He strode off, leaving her protest to die on her lips. She had managed to mangle a simple situation; no wonder everyone left her alone.

Yet she had her own entertainment, if she dared. Violet had made a point of tucking Jane's paper-filled portfolio, with a collection of sharpened pencils, into her satchel. Sketching was a ladylike endeavor, like playing the pianoforte or arranging flowers. Other ladies had taken out their sketch pads. Why shouldn't Jane?

For no one wanted to sketch the scene more.

One last time, Jane checked to make sure she was solitary, then keeping her spine rigidly erect and her eyes on the Thames, she stripped off her gloves. No matter how improper a display of bare hands might be, she could never draw in gloves, and so she laid the thin kid daintily in her lap.

Without removing her eyes from the rolling river,

she leaned forward until her fingers found the bristly woolen bag, and slid her fingers inside. The portfolio's leather cover pricked at her; she grasped it and, still alert, she pulled it out.

No one had noticed. Over the years she had smothered these inclinations, yet now the need to perfect her art had returned with the force of deep waters too long dammed.

Seeing Blackburn had made it worse.

By taking pencil in hand, she embraced possible catastrophe, yet she couldn't resist this compulsion.

Stretching forward again, Jane fumbled until she found the wooden box and furtively opened it. Testing the points with her finger, she chose the sharpest.

What should she sketch?

Involuntarily her mind went to Blackburn, and she glanced around.

Her thoughts must have summoned him. Informally dressed in riding clothes and fingering his quizzing glass, he strolled among the blankets and chatted with his visitors with a geniality Jane considered nothing less than outlandish.

He seemed not to see her, and she studied him, her artistic instincts yearning. Blackburn looked like a man who could be sketched as the symbol of British courage, or painted as a god of nature's forces, or sculpted in clay and cast in bronze and kept to weep over when this fantasy had ended.

But no. Not him. Not again.

She wrenched her attention away.

She could add to her collection of portraits—quick sketches of Monsieur Chasseur, of the girl who swept the street, of Lady Goodridge and Eleazer and Athowe.

Instead, she should re-create the day in a way that would forever capture this sensation of sinking doubt, sharp interest, and unwilling hope.

What would she reveal? The gathering itself? No, the people were too many and too mobile. The background of rolling hills and tumbling river? No. It was Lady Goodridge's home. Blackburn's sister's home. Someone might think her covetous. No, she had to draw something different, something . . .

A flotilla of ships rounded the point of the Thames and headed for the open sea. In these dark days of Napoleon's continental blockade, when Britain hovered on the edge of disaster, they were the only thing that kept these innocent people safe from invasion. Yes, she would sketch the ships as a symbol of hope.

She went to work. On a loose sheet of paper, an outline of the scene took shape before her. Gray clouds loomed on the horizon, but the vessels' sails flapped in the brisk wind, and the dark frigates themselves almost seemed to fly like seabirds seeking their abode.

Involved in swiftly capturing the outline of the ships, she didn't hear the crunch of footsteps. When a shadow fell across her pad, she looked up in annoyance.

"Pardon, mademoiselle!" Still blocking her sun, Lord de Sainte-Amand smiled down at her. "You have the look of a very strict teacher just now."

"My lord de Sainte-Amand, how good to see you."

"And so soon."

He mocked her, insinuating intimacy, but Jane was not amused. She had been ruined once before in such a situation; she wouldn't let it happen because of one inconsiderate man's words. "I won't come to your house again if you tease me."

He sobered quickly. "That would be a tragedy, and I would be in trouble. May I see?"

Leaning over, he looked down at the maroon portfolio, then up at the ships, then down at the portfolio again. Jane could not define the expression on his face—excitement, or disbelief.

"*Magnifique!* You have captured *les navires* perfectly."

"Thank you, but it's not done. I'll have to fill it in later."

"You protest, but the ships, they are very beautiful. I would love to have this *tirage*." He stretched his hand out, and his fingers were quivering. "You will permit?"

Jane felt a pang. The sketch was good, a representation of the day, just as she wished.

De Sainte-Amand withdrew his hand. "But I am too bold. I can see you want to keep the drawing. As a memento, no?"

"Yes." She felt rather silly, and far too emotional if this man, a virtual stranger, could read her thoughts so easily.

"Ah, you are *la femme*, and *les femmes* are sentimental. This is sweet. But please, don't tell anyone that I, too, am sentimental." He winked at her. "These stiff Englishmen would laugh at me."

Inspired, she said, "I could create a sketch for you, too."

''You are too good.'' He glanced out to the river. Under full sail, the ships were clipping along at a good rate. ''That is a handsome one.''

She looked where his finger pointed on the page, then to the river where the ship, the *Virginia Belle*, plain and brown as far as she could see, raced past the current. ''Yes,'' she said politely. ''It's a lively specimen of good English shipbuilding.''

''Exactly. You have such an eye!'' Lord de Sainte-Amand flattered her. ''If you would draw this ship for me, then I would have a memento, too.''

With a clean sheet before her, she used quick strokes to outline the *Virginia Belle* while de Sainte-Amand squatted beside her, praised her artistry, and pointed out details she might have missed.

When the flotilla had disappeared over the horizon, she said, ''There. That's the best I can do. I'll take it home and finish it—''

''No, no! I wish to take it just as it is. The quickness of the work somehow shows the swiftness of *le navire*.''

''Nonsense. It is not my best work.''

''But it's finished. It's good enough. This *tirage*, my people will treasure *toujours*.'' He put his hand on her portfolio and tugged.

She tugged back, confused and a little angry. De Sainte-Amand had done her a favor, true, but *he* was not her art teacher. He had no right to tell her when she was finished. ''No.''

''*Mademoiselle, s'il vous plaît*. You will do as I say.'' He grabbed her fingers and began to twist, like a bully intent on enforcing his will.

"Lord de Sainte-Amand." Her voice rose in exasperation and disbelief. "What are you doing?"

"Sh." He glanced around to see if her cry had brought attention on them. *"Mon dieu!"* He let her and the portfolio go as if they had burned him. "Who am I to tell an *artiste* what to do? You take *le tirage* home and finish it." Standing, he backed away from her. "We will meet later and you can give it to me then. In the meantime—perhaps you should hide this."

Thoroughly confused, she said, "I beg your pardon?"

"Lord Blackburn is headed this way."

Chapter 16

As de Sainte-Amand hurried away, Blackburn saw Jane place her drawing in her portfolio and shut it hurriedly. Then, looking for all the world like a puppy caught shredding her master's slippers, she tilted her head up and stared straight at him.

The pained anticipation in her wide eyes squeezed his heart, and his first instinct was to allay her worries. His second was to carry her away and lock her up at Tourbillon until he'd taught her some sense.

Thus his manner was rather crisp when he said, "Miss Higgenbothem."

She smiled with patently false enthusiasm, and answered just as crisply. "Yes?"

Not at all the mood he sought. Lowering his tone to a more intimate level, he murmured, "Jane."

Her smile faded.

"I'm pleased you accepted my invitation to visit my sister's home."

"I found myself unable to decline." She blinked at him with false innocence.

The sarcasm was new, but he deserved it, and . . . she amused him.

To his surprise, much about the day had amused him. Since his return from the Peninsula, he had dreaded going out in public. But today he had spoken with many people he had never spoken with before. He had eavesdropped on conversations and led women to confide secrets about their husbands—dastardly deeds by a gentleman's code, but necessary to Blackburn's duty. And even spying, he discovered, gained relish with the prospect of seeing Jane, of being impaled by her sharp tongue, and of courting her—no, use the correct term—of *chasing* her while she fled in disarray.

If only his suspicions of her did not disturb him so. "May I sit?"

"As you wish." She managed to look disinterested.

She was the only one in the vicinity to succeed. All around them heads craned to watch the entertainment of the season. They were silly people, oblivious to the fighting on the Peninsula, pretending not to see the scars Blackburn bore for their sake.

When he had first come back, battle-scarred and cynical, he had wanted to shake each and every one of the ton until they comprehended how precariously close Napoleon was to cutting off England's livelihood. Napoleon would subject them to every indignity in the name of France. He would strip them of their wealth and use it to feed his armies. And the ton paid no heed, but complained about the quality of their tea.

Today . . . well, today he looked at these people,

frivolous and languid, and resolved no tyrant would ever strip their innocence away.

He was like Jane now, he realized—no longer a dilettante, but a laborer.

And he was thankful for the ton's preoccupation with gossip, for that made them perfect pawns. He had hoped his courtship would distract attention from his objective of searching for a traitor; as he glanced around at the interested faces, he recognized he had prevailed beyond all reason.

And as he looked at Jane, he decided this was not such a difficult duty.

The edges of the blanket fluttered in the breeze. A picnic basket held one forward corner down. Her outstretched feet held the other. The wind flirted with her hem, tugging it from beneath her ankles and displaying her legs and their slender length.

Lucky wind.

"What did you say?" Jane stared at him as if he were mad.

"I said, what were you drawing?" Settling himself on the blanket's opposite corner, he sat discreetly apart, yet half turned to face her.

"I believe you have forcefully expressed your disinterest in my art, my lord."

She looked at him as if he were a cretin, unable to appreciate the finer things in life, and he remembered Jane not only amused him, but annoyed him. Lifting his silver quizzing glass, he surveyed her. "Too forcefully, if we cannot have a simple conversation about it."

"Are we again making conversation and squelching any gossip?"

She was insolent beyond bearing, but he knew how to thwart her. "No, Jane." He allowed his gaze to travel down her body, lingering at the places that most interested him. When he looked at her face again, her chin jutted out and she glared belligerently. He almost meant it when he said, "I am making conversation to woo you."

She clearly meant it when she answered, "I wish you wouldn't."

"It seems the least I could do."

Leaning forward, she said fiercely, "And when you have had enough, and drop me once more into the grease, I will fry in hell while you go your merry way."

Dropping the quizzing glass, he allowed it to dangle from its chain as he propped his arm on his upraised knee. "My dear Jane, if I drop you in the grease and leave you to fry in hell, it will be for a damned good reason." *Like treason.*

"The drawing, my lord, was not of you."

He spoke of treachery. She spoke of art. And if her earnest expression was anything to go by, she thought of nothing else. But she was an accomplished actress, and he was not misled by her. After all, he had Wiggens and the report on her activities. "I'm crushed by your lack of interest. Has my form lost its allure, then?"

"Yes." Her bald answer didn't match the look she gave him, all over and quickly, as if she couldn't resist.

More acting? He preferred to think not. "You'll go to hell for lying faster than you'll go to hell for having discourse with me."

She still clutched the portfolio, and one of the papers stuck out and flapped in the steady wind. "What do you want to talk about?"

He'd won the first skirmish, and he could afford to be generous. "I wanted to apologize for dismissing your worries at Susan's ball. I didn't realize Miss Morant had such a penchant for trouble."

Sitting straight, shoulders back, Jane searched until she found Adorna with her gaze. She relaxed infinitesimally. "She has little sense, and men, when they are around her, have even less."

The girl held the string of a kite, and she watched it and laughed as she ran. The breeze molded her gown to her, and even Blackburn, unimpressed as he was, had to admit she was the image of the youthful Aphrodite. "It's been difficult for you."

"She's too sweet to be difficult, but ever since—" Jane glanced at him briefly, as if she just remembered to whom she spoke.

"Since?" He strove to look interested, and it wasn't hard. That sentence dangled before him, waiting to impart information about Jane's lost years.

"You are too easy to talk to, my lord."

Most people did not find him so, but he didn't doubt Jane. Of all the women in the world, she held him in the least respect. Probably because with her, he had behaved like a spoiled child. "I am remarkably discreet," he assured her.

"I'm sure you are." Folding her hands in her lap,

she stared at the toes of her shoes. "At fourteen, she looked much as she does now, and a young gentleman in our neighborhood took a fancy to her." She thought, then corrected herself. "Actually, he fell violently in love with her. Mr. Livermere was the son of a Methodist, of all things, sober and hardworking, and I never suspected he would kidnap her."

Intent, he scooted closer. "Kidnap her?"

"She and her maid were running an errand for me, and the maid came home, fearful and excited, saying the youth had forced Adorna into a cab and declared they would go to Gretna Green and there wed. I was frantic for hours, when she appeared at home no worse for the experience." She peeked at him. "She convinced her gentleman she could not in all conscience leave me alone with Eleazer, and they came back for me."

"Good God." Blackburn looked at Adorna with new eyes.

"Yes. His father took the young man in hand, and he is now studying in Rome—although he still writes Adorna every week."

"Good God," Blackburn repeated. Lifting his quizzing glass, he squinted toward Adorna, and found her talking to a tall, gangly man. She gazed at him as if he fascinated her, and spoke seemingly on his command. "Who's that?"

Jane sighed. "Oh, dear, it is her French tutor. Poor Adorna."

"She doesn't like him? But she appears fascinated."

"She looks at every man that way. I'm sure it's the

reason Monsieur Chasseur has so faithfully clung to the hope he can teach her.'' Humor warmed Jane's voice. ''She believes the way a woman looks at a man takes him from one fascinated by her to one who worships at her shrine.''

''How shallow,'' he murmured. And how true. Jane had gazed at him that way once, and because he had been a vain youth who valued only beauty and the social graces, he had disdained her regard. Now he thought it would be rather pleasant. Instead, she seemed more captivated by the river, her niece, and even her own toes. ''What will you do when she marries? Will you live with her?''

''Perhaps.'' In her lap, Jane's fists clenched briefly. ''Perhaps I shall just do as I've longed to do since my early years—go out into the world and seek my fortune.''

''Doing what?'' He knew he sounded sharp, but he couldn't help himself.

She glanced down at the portfolio in her hand. ''Teaching young ladies their art.''

She didn't appear to be teasing, and a picture formed in his mind of a procession of young women, all working in clay and creating nude statues of the men they admired. ''How appalling.''

She glared. ''I would be good at it.'' The faintly salty breeze caught her wide-faced bonnet and tugged it back, and she caught it with one hand on her head, revealing her body's profile to Blackburn's greedy gaze.

Her gown covered her bosom; not a bit of flesh could be seen. But seeing her breasts clothed made him remember how she had responded when he touched them. She'd been a virgin then, surprised by passion yet glorying in it.

She was a virgin still, if his sister was to be believed, but he knew well Jane would no longer glory in the passion. Young Jane's every emotion had shown on her face. Today's Jane lived in her mind, shut off from the spontaneity that had caused her pain. His fault; he'd killed that which he did not admire.

The thought caught him by surprise, and it surprised him to realize he wanted that spontaneity resurrected. The young Blackburn, he grudgingly admitted, had not known everything there was to know.

"Miss Morant, when she weds, will welcome you, I am sure."

"I'm sure she would." She spoke coldly, with patent insincerity.

Or you could spy for the enemy. The thought sprang forth from the place where it lurked in his mind, waiting to sabotage any trust he might have in her. Jane had no future, no reason to love English society, and a regrettable tendency to hobnob with a known spy.

The evidence was inconclusive, but if Jane was part of the network the French had concocted from immigrants and rogues, he could trap and threaten her. He could learn who instructed her, whom she passed information to. Between him and Wiggens, Miss Jane Higgenbothem would be routed. And perhaps a little punishment would be in order . . .

Impatient to end this charade, he said, "De Sainte-Amand is an irresistible fellow, is he not?"

She had been looking at him steadily, the green of her eyes accentuated by her sage gown. How was it Wiggens had described them? Eyes as green as the color of moss in the gutters.

Now she dropped her gaze to her hands. A blush stained the skin over her cheekbones. "I hadn't really noticed."

Ashamed. Goose bumps prickled along his skin as he stared at her and wished he could wring her neck. She twisted uncomfortably under his stare, and glanced at him repeatedly from under lowered lashes. She wasn't an actress at all, only a remorseful woman driven by circumstances to spy for the enemy. That would be better than knowing she did it to spite the country that had so rejected her.

And what was he doing, looking for excuses for a damned traitor? "Then you're alone in that." He sounded quite normal, he thought, with only a hint of frost. "Most of the ladies who meet de Sainte-Amand think him quite charming."

"I'm sure he is." She worried her lower lip between her teeth, creating color with each sting of her white teeth. "He seemed very pleasant the night he rescued Adorna. And look, he's speaking to her now."

He was. De Sainte-Amand had caught Adorna as she hurried back to her group of young admirers, and she now gazed at him, and recited, with the same attention she had shown her French tutor.

"And you were speaking to him earlier."

She wiped her palm across her thigh. "Yes, he admired my sketch." The other hand kept tight grip on the incriminating papers. "The one that's not of you."

What is it of?

Her color deepened beneath the shadow cast by her bonnet, and she stared at him guiltily.

It was time to end the game. It was time to prove to himself she was no traitor, or to her he was no fool.

With awesome deliberation, he reached and grasped the edge of the portfolio. Her fingers tightened for a moment, then loosened, and she let him take it.

"It's nothing, really," she said. "Anyone could do as well."

Still watching her, he opened the pad and glanced down. His gut clenched, and his fingers tightened. Without volition, he crumpled the edge of the paper. "What is this?" he demanded. As if he couldn't tell.

"The ships." She sounded improbably earnest. "I tried to create a feeling of the day, and they seemed symbolic . . . The other ladies probably have drawn something similar."

"And this?" He held out the clear, detailed drawing of the *Virginia Belle*.

"Another ship. De Sainte-Amand suggested—"

His ire burned deep and cold. "You can't even take the blame yourself." Standing, he grasped her elbow and jerked her to her feet. Her gloves fluttered to the ground. She stepped on her skirt and stumbled. He didn't care. With the sketch pad held tight in one hand and Jane held tight in the other, he wheeled and marched her toward the manor.

"Where are we going?" She tried to twist her arm free.

"To teach you a lesson."

"You're going to teach me about art?"

"No." He didn't look at her. He didn't dare. "About life."

Chapter 17

"I don't know what you're so angry about." Attached to an incensed Lord Blackburn by his grip on her wrist, Jane stumbled over hummocks of grass. "It's only a sketch, no different from a hundred others I've done."

"A hundred? So you freely admit it, eh, *Jane*?"

She didn't care for his emphasis on her name. She didn't like his sneer, nor his attitude. "It's better than the others. Is that a crime?"

He whipped her around and stopped. Shaking the portfolio, he said, "I don't know. Is it?"

Blackburn, cold and enigmatic to most, now blazed with demonic fury. The westering sun slipped between jagged clouds to illuminate half his countenance, caressing the full lips, the indent formed above them by a simple press of God's thumb into the wet clay of His creation. Light caught this day's growth of beard which sprinkled his chin with brushed gold. His nose jutted out as proudly as Dover's cliffs. His brow was broad and noble as Apollo's, and the wind feathered a radiant lock of hair from his forehead.

Shadow captured the other half of his face and held it prisoner, darkening the blue of his eye to black, revealing diabolical determination.

On one side, the beauty, the light. On the other, the fury, the anguish, the dark side of his soul. Jane beheld it, and the picture she would create.

"No!" His hand slashed through the air, a blade of denial. "Get that look off your face. You will not paint me."

Stunned, she tried to step back from his unwanted insight, but he wouldn't let her go. Instead he shook her arm, and said, "What conceit made you think you were the only one to *see*?"

"Because I'm the only one who ever looks," she flashed.

"Not anymore, dear." His mouth tightened in a ruthless smile. "Not anymore. I swear I will teach you, Jane, not to assume I am a fool, and I'll give you one reason, at least, to love what you have in England."

Turning, he tugged her along as she fought him, but for all her height and strength, he was stronger yet. This wasn't just about the sketch now; something deeper worked in him, and in her.

He had looked at her, and seen enough to know what she thought, and for her that was an intolerable invasion of privacy.

She twisted toward the beach, anticipating rescue from that direction, but all she saw was a swarm of faces, watching her and Blackburn and buzzing with delight and amazement. Desperate, she waved at

Adorna. Adorna enthusiastically waved back, jumping up and down as if her aunt were off on a long-awaited voyage.

As wild grass changed to domesticated lawn, the distance between the beach, the company, and Jane widened, and she set her heels. One last clump of sedge tangled her leather boots, and only Blackburn's hand under her armpit saved her from a nasty sprawl.

Halting, he watched her steadily. "Scream, if you're going to."

She filled her lungs. She opened her mouth. And found that too many years of restraint and dignity had taken their toll. Slowly she released the air, and said, "I don't scream."

"I saw that in you, too," he said with unpretentious triumph.

Scooping her into the curve of his elbow, holding tight to the portfolio with the other, he marched them toward the nearest garden path. Held close against his side, she could feel the tendons of his arm straining to hold her, the muscles of his thigh cording as he hurried them along. The scent of his lemon soap mixed with the ocean's breeze. The first of the wind-sculpted trees surrounded them, plunging them into the shade. She experienced the sensation of being swallowed up, defeated, and rushed along toward some fate she could not deny.

The grass gave way to gravel. On either side of them, tall, trimmed bushes burgeoned with blossoms. A branch caught the wide brim of Jane's bonnet and twisted it half off.

"Wait!" She tried to stop, to rescue the headgear Violet had lent her.

But Blackburn snapped, "You and your hats are a menace!" With one hand, he untied the ribbons and knocked the bonnet to the ground.

"You can't do that!" Jane said.

He ignored her with the disdain of a man who already had. Dragging her back into his grasp, he propelled her forward once more.

The trees still shaded them and the hedges grew thick. One path wandered off toward a gazebo. Another led straight toward the open lawn and to the manor's wide steps.

He whisked her toward some destination only he knew. Jane had learned her way around Montague House, the national repository of art, without a qualm. But now she found her head spinning as she tried to distinguish one planting from another. They had wandered into a maze of tall, well-clipped hedges, she realized. If by chance Jane eluded Blackburn, she would roam in circles for hours under a sky increasingly obscured by clouds.

Glancing at the inflexible set of his jaw and the glitter of cold light in his eyes, she determined to take her chances with the garden.

Yet she had no chance. The path twisted and turned, leading them deeper and deeper toward some madness she didn't understand. She gasped for breath, wearying of the rapid pace, the ever-changing direction, but Lord Blackburn seemed indifferent. He had a goal in sight, and however long it might take them—

and she thought they'd been walking forever—he would pursue it.

As they rounded the corner, one that looked like all the rest, he gave an exclamation of satisfaction. They had reached the sweet, warm heart of the maze. Here perfectly groomed grass lay over curvaceous mounds of earth. A small, decorative tree clung to one edge. A lattice zigzagged from edge to edge, and roses climbed it in luscious profusion, blushing with pink, pure with white, and sun-kissed with yellow. The encircling hedges rebuffed all but the faintest breeze, and the rich scent of flowers was seduction itself. In the center, a fountain gurgled with softly flowing water, and bluebirds twittered as they bathed and preened.

This place was a sensual feast for the lucky lovers who could find it—and Lord Blackburn had walked to it without hesitation.

No doubt he had brought a woman here before.

Striking without notice, Jane jabbed his ribs with her elbow. As he doubled up he dropped the portfolio. She spun away from him, and caught one glance of red-eyed fury before he charged her. He reached for her; she grabbed his hand and pulled him along, allowing his own momentum to propel him. Then she let him go and listened to the slam of his body into the thorny tangle of stems and blossoms.

Birds squawked and took wing, and without even looking to see the damage, she lifted her skirts and ran. She rounded the hedge before his howl of pain stopped her.

"My eyes!"

His eyes. His beautiful, midnight blue eyes. Plucked by the thorns?

She took two more steps. Not really. Not possible. He was bluffing. He was trying to trick her.

But although Blackburn said nothing else, she could hear him blundering, pulling down rose branches, and uttering moans, all the more piteous for being muffled.

She straightened her skirt and walked briskly away. Blackburn was a god. Nothing could hurt him.

She slowed. But he was a man. Already war had scarred him. And on the eye—had the brambles reopened his wound?

Cursing herself for a fool, she sneaked back and peeked around the corner of the hedge.

He stood with his back to her. With one hand he fought the clinging thorns. The other he held to his face. She trod toward him, avoiding the graveled path, keeping to the grass to deaden each footstep, trying to position herself to view him from the side and knowing all along she was moving farther from safety, closer to the fountain and to him.

Then he took his hand away from his face, and she saw the smear of rusty red on his cheek, and a bright trickle of crimson dripping from his brow. ''Lord Blackburn! Let me help you.'' She hurried toward him.

She got no closer than three feet when his arm snapped out. His fingers closed on her wrist, still sore from his previous imprisonment. His face unmarked, he looked at her. ''No rose is well won without fighting the thorns.''

Yanking her hand free, she unwittingly lashed it into the lattice. Thorns pierced her palm. She cried out. He caught her again, restrained her when she would have torn the flesh more with her futile struggles to free herself.

"Hold still," he said. One by one he loosened the clawing brambles. Tears sprang to her eyes at the pain—or was it the humiliation of being trapped so easily?

Yet blood did slither off his chin from a long scratch across his jaw, staining his starched collar. His forehead had been punctured, and brambles had torn his flesh through his clothing until ruby dotted his white shirt.

What a pair they were, bloodstained and bruised from fighting the roses, one another, and the world. A tear slipped down her cheek, and she hastily pushed it off with her free hand.

He asked, "What are you crying for?"

"It hurts."

"I'll make it better." Lifting her hand, he brought the palm to his mouth and sucked on it, an act of cleansing so intimate she closed her eyes to hide from the sight of that distinguished head bent in service to her.

That didn't help. He sucked harder, she thought, trying to draw out her wit and good sense. His tongue and his lips pressed against the muscles and the tendons, then his teeth bit into her hard. She squealed and wriggled, but he wouldn't let her go. Lifting his head, he spat out the thorn he'd drawn forth, then held her hand down where she could see.

A trickle of blood slid along the lines. He placed his slashed hand beside hers. With the precision of a master, he fit their palms together. His chest rose and fell as he took massive breaths, and she found her own breath matching his. His heart beat so heavily, she could almost hear it, and her heart slipped into his rhythm. He watched her from beneath lids weighted with significance, and his deep voice rumbled. "When our blood mixes, we're joined."

She started, and the tendons on the back of his hand bulged as his fingers tightened over hers to hold her still. "Blood siblings," she said, trying to lessen the meaning of his action.

"No, darling. I have a sister, and I promise you, whatever I feel for you, Jane, is not brotherly. In fact"—with his other hand, he lifted her chin and smiled into her face—"what I feel for you is quite carnal. I will show you now."

Chapter 18

"What do you want?" Jane whispered, paralyzed with fear and desire.

"You. You and clear vision and an end to Napoleon and safe streets and . . . you. If I can have you, that'll be enough for the moment." Blackburn kept their bloody palms together, and with the other hand cupped the back of her neck and dragged her face to his.

His kiss. The same lips, the same tongue, the same touch as eleven years ago, yet it was different. Events had come between them, shaped them separately, and now circumstances and his determination had brought them together.

His kiss. No longer greedy. Hungry, instead, with an edgy anger he could not have displayed eleven years ago. Then he'd been infuriated because she'd made him a laughingstock. Now he was incensed because . . . because . . .

"Why?" she found herself murmuring against his lips. "Why?"

"Because someone needs to keep a leash on you."

Holding her close, he tumbled her backward, and she beheld a brief flurry of sky now packed with gray clouds, of hedges seen sideways and ground much too close. Then she came to rest against a hillock of grass that supported her back and head like a settee, and he sank to his knees beside her like a supplicant before his queen.

A foolish image, for this tyrant didn't beg. He leaned over and, without giving her a chance to regroup, kissed her again. The questions were still there, rampaging through her mind, along with a vast indignation. How dare he think she needed a leash, and what gave him the right to wield it?

But they had exchanged blood. Now they exchanged breath. She had freely given of this intimacy eleven years ago. This time she resisted it, no longer the ninny she had once been. But he exhibited none of the same impatience, either, wooing her with kisses so insubstantial they might have been no more than the breeze—except for his smooth lips, and his enveloping warmth, and her body's response.

She'd called him mad, but what madness cursed her that she would soften and yearn, and open her lips to him?

A kiss. Only a kiss.

As he slanted his mouth against hers, the taste and wetness made her breath catch, and catch again. He touched her. His fingers molded her shoulders and swept the sides of her body with an urgency that hadn't changed in eleven years. Now she understood better what it meant, for she had warned Adorna against succumbing. Jane was older, of course, and a woman; surely the passions of the flesh should have subsided.

One thumb, soft as a mink brush, grazed her nipple, and the provocation resonated through her chemise and light wool bodice.

Older women, it seemed, could want as desperately as any randy boy.

And for all his experience and world-weary manner, Lord Blackburn gave a passable imitation of a randy boy who frantically wanted her, Plain Jane Higgenbothem.

Jane didn't understand him. Not anything about him. At least eleven years before, she had been able to read him, to know what he was thinking . . . because he'd been so shallow.

She cut off that thought, new and treacherous, but it recurred.

He *had* been shallow. Shallow and careless and uncaring.

That had changed. Something had changed him. Now depths swirled within him, and if she strained, she could catch glimpses of his thoughts, of his soul. But nothing was clear in those murky depths. He did not welcome her there, and if she observed too much, she feared she might find pain and loneliness just like hers. Where their blood joined, so might their minds, and not only would she know him, but he would know her. Her dreams and ambitions . . . and then he'd laugh.

Everyone always laughed.

"Don't stiffen. I'm not going to hurt you. You

poker up when I'm not kissing you. I need to kiss you all the time.'' Fleetingly he smiled into her baffled, frustrated face. Punctuating his speech with light touches against her demure collar and along the length of her sleeves, he said, ''I like that sage color on you. Your eyes . . . so green. The color of the moss.''

He frowned as if displeased with himself, but she knew exactly what he meant. On Lord de Sainte-Amand's street, moss grew in the shade, and it was the kind of luscious green only Mother Nature could create. Jane itched to bring it forth from her palette, yet she envied it, and appreciated Lord Blackburn's compliment.

''This gown, however lovely, is in the way.'' His palms smoothed the cords in her neck, massaging as he might have gentled a cat. ''Let me unbutton you. Darling, just let me see . . .''

Far, far away the ocean surged, and the sound of it surged in her veins, and in her womb. Nature's rhythms existed in Lord Blackburn's caress.

Desperately she tried to call forth her resistance. Did he still hate her? Was he still intent on punishing her? Why had a simple sketch created this fervor?

Did she care?

This man with his magical blue eyes and resplendent physique had slept with her in her bed, walked beside her on the street, haunted her for eleven years.

Arching her neck, she allowed him easy access to the buttons right under her chin.

As he descended, he fumbled and said, ''I should be better at this, but it's been too long since the last time I touched you.''

She never considered Blackburn a delicate man. Arrogant, always. Beastly, on occasion. But although she knew he had loosened a myriad of buttons in his career, he didn't talk about that. He spoke only of her, as if he'd been as celibate as she for the past eleven years.

He acted like it, too. The grace that characterized his every movement had vanished, leaving him listing on one hand and a flush streaking across his cheekbones. "I desperately wanted to see you then. Did you know that?"

"I didn't know anything that day." She'd been a fool. Was she being a fool again? "But I know better now."

He opened her bodice and loosened her chemise, and he stared as if he couldn't look enough. "Beautiful," he whispered. "Just as I imagined."

Scalded with chagrin, she tried to bring her hands up to cover herself, but he caught them. Caught them, and kissed the fingertips, and placed them beside her head.

"I wish the sun were shining." Glancing up, he frowned at the dreary sky. Then he looked at her again, at the pliant rosy brown of her nipples. "But it's still warm enough, isn't it, darling?"

The edges of her bodice and the raised waist thrust her breasts toward him as he leaned over her. A tremor shook him. He wet his lips.

She found herself wetting hers.

"I will kiss you, here"—he dabbed a touch on her chest, on the underside of her breast, and almost, almost on her nipple—"and the pleasure of it will be so great, you'll beg me for more."

"No . . ." She wouldn't beg.

"Yes. I promise."

He was right. She knew he was. Each of his caresses rippled like a great work of art through her eternity. She would do anything to be his sculpture—even beg.

But he released her, and reached for one of the torn and dangling rose branches. From it he plucked a blossom flushed with the inner gloss of a rosy seashell. He snapped the thorns from the stem, then raised it to his nose and sampled the fragrance. His eyes closed in sensuous delight, his lashes spikes of amber against his golden skin.

Then his eyes opened, and he smiled whimsically. He held the flower to her nose, and she inhaled the scent, laden with the warmth of sunlit afternoons and intense with the threat of rain. As he withdrew the rose, she saw that each petal curled in a graceful curve.

"The colors remind me of you." He wet his finger, used it to caress the soft rouge of the outer petals, then probed the heart where they became a tender shade of apricot.

She watched his motion, comprehending as he wished, yet now beyond discomfiture, beyond anything but a wash of desire so vehement she trembled from the force of it. Pressing her thighs together, she tried to control passion, but she knew she grew damp, and she ached as if she were swollen.

He lowered the blossom again, but to her mouth

this time. The velvet petals barely brushed her, making her lips tingle. He followed each contour, the lush fragrance rising to her nostrils. "Such a pretty mouth," he said.

"It's too wide." She could barely move her lips, so enthralled was she with the velvet texture, the sensual play.

"No. A man likes that. He can speculate how it would feel, kissing his face, his chest, his hips . . . and anywhere else a woman might kiss a man."

She forgot to breathe. She forgot everything but his eyes, roguish and attentive. He knew too much, she knew too little, and she had never, ever imagined the things he was doing. The things he insinuated. Not even in her deepest dreams had she . . . or had she?

"You're blushing, darling, and not just on your cheek." With the rose, he swept her cheeks, her forehead, her chin. Like dabs of silk, each petal brushed only a tiny patch of flesh, yet response vibrated through Jane's every muscle.

Under Blackburn's expert guidance, the blossom lingered along her jawline. As if he commanded her, she arched her neck away and sighed, and the flower progressed irrevocably toward her ear. Still on his knees, he leaned close. The rose . . . no, his *tongue* slid slowly along the outer shell, probed the center. She brought her hands up to clutch his hair.

"Jane." He whispered so softly, his breath cooled her damp flesh. "Put your hands back."

She was almost beyond understanding. Almost. But when he remained unmoving at her side, she gradually perceived he wouldn't continue with this exquisite torture until she obeyed him. And although she quivered as if she suffered from the ague, she didn't want him to stop.

Unkinking one finger at a time, she opened her fists. Languidly she slid her hands through his hair, down his neck, down his arms, and finally, reluctantly, she took them away.

She hadn't known that touching him would make *her* want more, make *her* more pliable, and never would she have realized he was affected, but for the tiny moan she heard close against her ear. Compelled, she tried to return her hands to him, but he sat up.

"No."

She reached out to him.

Shaking his head, he brushed the rose across his own lips.

A velvet promise. His midnight eyes glittered with daytime stars as she lowered her hands again.

"Put your arms over your head." His lips moved against the petals, and she could imagine those lips against her skin. "I like to see your breasts thrusting up so proudly. Did I tell you how beautiful they are?"

Even his voice was an aphrodisiac, deep and quiet, as if the secrets between them were too important to share even with the frisking breeze. She brought her arms up alongside her head once more, and as a reward he stroked her inner palm with the blossom, then drew it out over each fingertip.

How did something as mundane as Jane's hand, callused and scarred, become a thing of delicate sensation? This voluptuous agony surely couldn't grow greater, or she would lose all restraint. She would cry out as great spasms of joy overtook her, and such an exhibition would reveal the most sensitive part of all.

Holding the rose by its stem, he swirled the blossom across the width of her collarbones, from one shoulder to another. "You're fine and strong. I had the good sense to admire that about you even long ago."

With a single sentence, he confirmed the confidence her stature gave her. With a single stroke, he brought her skin in contact with the plush rose petals. With elaborate care, he dragged the flower down her breastbone to the place where the high waist of her gown concealed her.

But he hadn't yet touched her where she wished most to be touched. He watched her breathe; his eyes widened, then narrowed, and he wanted to caress her, she felt sure. Instead, he played this waiting game, and tormented them both.

"Please," she whispered. "Won't you please . . . ?"

He laughed, melodious and sure. Then when she took a deeper breath, his amusement wavered and dipped. "Wait. Let me . . ." Plucking a petal, he allowed the wisp of a wind to take it. It fluttered in circles, then drifted to rest on her chest. Another followed the first, nestling in the hollow at the base of her throat. Another followed, and another, and another, each floating down on a current of air to land on a special place on her body. One decorated her lips, another settled in her hair. And at last, apparently deciding he dared not trust the errant wind, Lord Blackburn plucked the smallest, sweetest, firmest inner petal and deliberately placed it on her nipple.

He didn't touch her; only the petal did, and he said, "Watch."

Lifting her head, she stared down at herself, brazenly nude, clad only in rose petals. They rippled, almost weightless, unstable in the breeze and the movement of her chest as she inhaled. The one, perched on the peak of her breast, clung to her smooth skin.

"Velvet to velvet," he said. Then, by infinitesimal increments, he reached out and barely brushed her skin with his fingertips.

The petal wavered on the sudden peak as her nipples contracted.

She arched up, into his hand, wanting more, wanting now. She waited for him to touch her, really touch her, and it was time. Past time.

His diverted, absorbed expression disappeared, vanquished by a surge of masculine demand. Sliding down beside her, he lay on his side. Holding himself above her, he kissed her fiercely, demanding the response he previously demanded she subdue. She answered him gladly, openmouthed and questing, requiring current satisfaction in exchange for previous restraint.

Her hands tangled in his hair once more, taking pleasure in the clean locks, in the firm skull. She wanted to direct him, but he needed no direction. He had said he looked at her and knew what she thought; perhaps it was true, for he lifted a breast in each hand. Supporting them, he kissed them, too, smoothing his lips across flesh made receptive by the breeze, the rose, and the man. When he suckled her she could no longer keep her excitement to herself. She whimpered and moaned, twisting beneath him.

"Lift your skirt for me, darling," he murmured against her skin. "Show me you want me."

She did. She wanted him acutely. She wanted him now. Gathering a handful of skirt and petticoats, she tried to jerk them up.

He stopped her with his hand on hers. "Slowly. We have all the time in the world."

He was smiling, stroking her with leisurely, casual gestures that didn't fool her a bit. His bright eyes watched her with febrile fervor. His legs moved restlessly, and he took elaborate care not to touch her with any part of his body except his hands.

He wasn't teasing. Not anymore. He was as frantic as she was, but for some reason he kept himself under severe harness.

Well, he wasn't the only one who could tease. So could she.

With tormenting indolence, she inched her skirt up, and secretly smiled as he looked everywhere but there. He purposely didn't see her white silk stockings, nor the garters that held them, nor the ruffle of her drawers where they buttoned at the knee. Yet when she stopped short of her hip, too abashed to bare herself to the leaden sky, she found his gaze fixed on her face with an intensity that scalded.

"All the way, darling. Please."

She would do anything for him when he called her "darling" in that tone of voice. With a twitch of her fingers, she raised her hem to her waist.

This time he looked directly, and whatever virginal uncertainty she experienced died. The skin stretched taut over his perfect features, and only his eyes looked alive. But they burned with the fires of the heavens, enthralled and compelled by the sight and proximity of her.

Of Miss Jane Higgenbothem.

His hand stretched out as if irresistibly drawn, and with the flat of his palm he smoothed the thin cotton across her belly. The heat of him across her sensitive skin made her toes curl, and when he opened the slit of the garment and barely brushed the dark, curly hair hidden therein, she had to bite her lip to contain her exclamation. Such a light touch, but it promised more. He moved in one direction, toward the center of her body, and now his finger touched flesh.

The top of her cleft, nothing more, but she pressed her thighs together to stop their shaking.

He misunderstood. "Don't close me out. Not now."

She wanted to protest, but her voice would tremble if she spoke. So what could she do but raise one knee?

"Oh, Jane. Oh, darling."

She had lifted one knee, and he sounded excited as Zeus when he created his first thunderbolt. Blackburn *did* worship her, she realized. She *was* a goddess worthy of her god. She wanted to exalt, but when he opened her concealed femininity, and touched her, she forgot why. His fingers performed a slow slide up and down, each time almost entering her, then skimming away. Since the moment he'd thrust her full-length on the lawn, she'd remained almost motionless, transfixed by his demands, by her own amazement at the deluge of stimulus.

Now she couldn't. Her hips lifted, rotated, trying to tempt him inside.

He was smiling again, fiercely pleased and fiercely enraptured. ''Do you want me there, darling? Tell me. Do you want me?''

His fingers stopped moving. She stopped moving. She could hear nothing but the sweep of the wind outside the hedges, the rasp of his breath, and her own light, rapid gasps. Even in the warmth of the maze, goose bumps slid over her skin; warnings of danger or harbingers of pleasure, she didn't dare guess. Did she want him? Yes, too much, for too long. If she said so, admitted it, gave in to him, he would have a triumph greater than before, and her personal disaster would transcend any she'd experienced.

The question was, had he really changed? Did the new depths she perceived hide a previously un-plumbed passion . . . for her?

Or was she once again falling prey to Blackburn's endless ravaging need for revenge?

She didn't know. She only knew if she told a lie, if she said she did not want him and he withdrew, she would regret it for the rest of her life.

''Yes,'' she said. ''I want you.''

She thought he sighed with relief, but more important, his finger glided inside of her to assuage the torture.

She didn't expect to reject him now, but she stiffened. She hadn't realized he would feel so alien, and far too invading. Allowing him inside required more trust than she had.

Yet some sensitivity must have moved him, for in a lover's tone he murmured, "The heart of the maze." He stroked in and out of her. "I've wandered for too long, trying to find it." Another stroke.

Within her, passion began its slow climb again. Her body tightened around his finger, and when he used his thumb outside to press against what surely must be the most sensitive place of her soul, she lost those last, lingering, vexing inhibitions.

She moaned out loud, and her eyes closed. She concentrated on one place, and that place was where he had his hand.

"That's the girl." He sounded breathless. "A little further. A little higher."

He wasn't making sense, but she didn't care. She just wanted . . .

Then a vague discomfort slowed her, and she heard him say, "Can you take a little more, darling? Just one more finger."

She couldn't take it, and she wanted to tell him, but as the second intruder joined the first, his thumb pressed ever more firmly. She stretched. It hurt. Then it didn't.

Soothing her with an openmouthed kiss on the breast, he murmured something; it sounded like praise. Crazed by the rhythm of his finger and thumb, she moved, trying to get close to him and to whatever destination he urged her toward.

And she reached it. Her whole body quivered, then clenched, every muscle tight, every sense shut down except the newly discovered sense of pure ecstasy. She thrashed and moaned and *lived*, totally caught up in her own pleasure, and totally dependent on Blackburn for every drop of rapture he wrung from her body.

When at last she came to calm, she rested, panting, on the good earth, and saw Blackburn watching her face, unsmiling, sweat beading his upper lip. Slowly she extended one hand toward him, mutely pleading, and he came to his knees. Opening his trousers, he began to push them down. Here in the open air he would reveal himself at last, and she waited, enthralled to see what a man really looked like. To see what Blackburn really looked like.

But he paused, and scrutinized his two fingers, then scrutinized her. Whether he was in pain or pleased, she couldn't tell. She only knew his mouth twisted downward and his eyebrows shot up and he both laughed and groaned. Leaving his trousers open, but firmly around his waist, he finally, *finally*, separated her legs with his knee, making a place for himself. Holding himself up by his elbows, he thrust his hips against hers as impudently as a man with the right. If he had loosened himself from his trousers, he would even now be inside her, and she couldn't have stopped him. She was too damp, too soft, too ready for him, to offer resistance.

And besides, she didn't want to. Vaguely she told herself that this was heady stuff to a spinster aunt so firmly on the shelf, as if that explained why she lay in the grass in the open with her skirt up and bodice gaping. With shy anticipation, she clasped her thighs around his buttocks, urging him closer.

He closed his eyes in one final ecstatic struggle, then he lowered himself to her, all the way to her, chest to groin.

And as if that were a signal to the skies, they opened to release a cold and drenching rain.

Chapter 19

Jane looked as startled and horrified as Blackburn felt, slapped by Mother Nature for indulging in her greatest pleasure. Jane blinked, blinded by the wash of the heavens.

The rain flattened his hair against his scalp and dripped on her, but for one long moment he hovered over Jane, preserving the sensations of warmth and closeness and passion. Then he realized how stupid that was.

But he couldn't move. He was protecting her from the wet. From the distant lightning and the faint rumble of thunder, and any other danger he could perceive. And that instinct was even more stupid.

Standing, he pulled her to her feet, saying, ''Bloody hell damn wretched rain.''

Jane pulled her hand out of his and hunched her shoulders, wrapping her arms around her waist. With the rain sluicing through her straight, short hair and the wind plastering her wet gown against her body, she looked disconsolate and guilty.

"Damn stupid bloody rain," he said again. He wanted to kick something, anything, but his swearing and frustration only made Jane stare at her ruined leather boots with the intensity she usually reserved for him. It wasn't fair that she should have got so close, only to have it end in a bloody damned English downpour.

Needless to say, it wasn't fair to him, either. She stood there, drenched, her gown still unbuttoned, her nipples pointing at him, every curve of her body beneath that gown outlined for his delectation, and the rain wasn't nearly cold enough to dampen his frustration.

If he hadn't been so determined to make it good for this virgin, if he hadn't been so damned noble, he wouldn't be suffering now. With most women, he would have climaxed half an hour ago and started on another round. But no, he'd wanted to make her first time special.

Well, this was special, all right. Wet, cold rain tamping out a hot, well-kindled fire.

Damn it to hell! Worst of all, *he* was frustrated and all he could think of was *her*. He'd told this woman she was beautiful. Yet how insignificant! He'd told countless women they were beautiful. But that was before he'd gone to the Peninsula, before he'd fought in a war, back in a time when he thought the only important thing was maintaining his considerable consequence. And after the disgraceful incident of the statue, that consequence had involved making sure his bed partners adored him. Telling them lies about their beauty meant nothing.

But this woman—*this* woman—stood in the rain, turning blue with cold, too embarrassed or too dazed to button herself up, and she really *was* beautiful. He'd damned well lost his bloody mind, and he'd like to know where and why.

He wanted to snap at her to dress herself. Instead his voice came out warm and coaxing. "Here, darling, let me help you."

She looked up, and her green eyes, her only really striking feature, weren't even green. They were bland, colorless gray, matching the skies and the entire wretched day. "What are we going to d-do?" Her teeth chattered. "I can't g-go back to the beach like this."

He'd pleasured her so long, every bit of silly, female wit had abandoned her. "No beach." He barely trusted himself to speak pleasantly. "Everyone will be rained out. They've got into their carriages and fled."

"But they c-can't. Not Adorna and Violet and Tarlin. They wouldn't l-leave me."

Without a thought, and with the intention of this time forcing me to marry you. But he just couldn't say that. She was miserable enough. "They trust me to take care of you," he said gently. Stepping closer, he pulled the edges of her bodice together and tried to match the buttons to their holes. If he concentrated on this simple task, she couldn't utilize that discerning ability of hers to read his mind. As fragile as she was right now, she might not appreciate his sentiments.

But it was hard to fasten buttons over blue-veined breasts so beautiful his half-frozen palms grew slippery with sweat. Water slithered down her neck and gathered at the tip of each taut nipple, and if he leaned down just a little, he could catch it in his mouth, then suckle . . .

"Let me do it." Her hands hovered above his as if afraid to touch him.

She'd read his mind, all right, but not the irritation.

"Yes." He released her bodice and stepped back. "That would be wise."

She probably thought if she laid her hand on him, his desire would overwhelm his discomfort and he'd take her right here in the sopping grass. And his treacherous, bloody damned mind flung up a picture of the two of them gloriously naked in the rain.

"I wish you wouldn't look at me that way." She'd tied her chemise, but her fingers kept slipping off the buttons and her voice shook. "You're making me nervous."

The picture faded, his mind reluctant to release it. "Right." Turning his back on her, he glanced around, seeking shelter. They would have to find their way out of the maze. Jane was shivering, and he had no wish for her to catch the ague now. Not when he had come so close . . .

Catching sight of the portfolio, he scooped the wretched thing up. "We'll have to go to the manor house."

She had covered herself, had even managed to make herself look respectable except for the rivulets of water trickling down her face. "As you say, Lord Blackburn."

Turning on her before he could catch himself, he

snapped, "For God's sake, call me Ransom. Our association has gone that far, at least."

She didn't answer, but stared straight ahead, her jaw flexing.

She wasn't responding with her usual polite, society manners. Perhaps they were both a little tense. "This way." He plunged forward, finding the passage out of the maze. Mundane conversation would help ease their disquietude. "The rain is much needed for the crops."

"For the crops."

He strode on. "Yes, for the crops."

"Do you farm?" She had a funny little choke in her voice.

He didn't know if it was better that she laughed at him, or cried for herself. "Tourbillon is a rather large estate, and I pay close attention to my manager. I don't believe in abandoning all responsibility. It encourages theft and debauchery." He noted that he frequently sounded pompous when around Jane. Then he wondered if he always sounded that way, and only noticed it in her company.

"I found I had to be watchful with the servants when I lived with Eleazer, also." The narrowness of the maze kept her behind him, and when he tried to do the gentlemanly thing and let her walk ahead, she put her head down and pretended that she didn't see.

A silence fell, made awkward by her reference to the time she'd spent in virtual servitude. He suspected she utilized those years to point out the differences between them, and perhaps to feed the bitterness she must feel for her dear country.

He couldn't allow that. She needed to realize there was really no difference between them. She needed to realize how much she loved . . . England. "Susan and I grew up at Tourbillon." As they left the narrow maze, he took Jane's arm, brooking no disagreement, and drew her forward to walk at his side. "It's not a magnificent estate. Certainly not as grand as this." He was wealthy, but she needed to know he esteemed things for more than their munificence. "But the land is beautiful in a primitive way. Do you . . . like the ocean?"

"Very much. There's really nothing I like more than being drenched by cold water."

Startled by her tart tone, he glanced down at her. "You're jesting."

"I suppose I am."

She sounded biting, a little more like the Jane he'd come to anticipate matching wits with. "Good. Yes, with this weather today, it's good you like a drenching. It's good, too, that you like the ocean. You did mean that when you said it, didn't you?"

Her voice softened. "I do like the ocean."

He experienced an odd kind of triumph. She really did, he could tell, and that was important. He thought it important, too, that she know his plans. "When this war is over, I'll go back to Tourbillon and live there."

"Do you visit often?" She sounded interested, almost normal, and she didn't struggle against his hold.

Both causes for jubilation. "Indeed I do. Brief visits only, for the Foreign Office requires my attention." He shouldn't have mentioned that! "Or it used to before I got bored and quit going there."

"You get bored easily, don't you?"

"Just last month," he said hurriedly, "I returned for the funeral of my neighbor's daughter. Dreadful occasion. Selma was only nineteen, a pretty ninny-hammer and out only one year, and she wandered off and fell from the cliffs."

Jane's arm jerked. "How awful!"

"Mr. Cunningham said the fog must be at fault, but Mrs. Cunningham said Selma knew her way around the grounds. She insists—"

"Cunningham?" Jane stopped short, and he lost his grip on her arm. "Did you say Cunningham?"

He turned back to her, wondering what had brought that distraught expression to her face. "Yes."

She swallowed, looked him in the eyes, then swallowed again. "I heard that Miss Cunningham was murdered."

Chapter 20

"*Murdered?*" *Blackburn stopped beneath a large oak* tree, which provided inadequate coverage from the rain. "Don't be ridiculous."

"I'm not being ridiculous." Jane looked up at him, a wood nymph indignant at being drenched and stung by his disbelief. "Miss Cunningham, and I'm sure there can't be more than one young woman of gentle birth who died last month, was Monsieur Chasseur's student, and he was quite desolated by both her death and the fact he had been summoned by the constable."

"Oh, that. Selma wasn't murdered. Her mother, a rather hysterical woman, insisted on an investigation, that's all. She said Selma knew her way around the grounds. She insisted the girl would never have lost her way." Yet even as Blackburn dismissed Mrs. Cunningham's suspicions, his mind raced. "Why was Chasseur summoned to face the constable?"

"He was there to tutor Miss Cunningham that day, and he's French. Those are good enough reasons for the skeptical, country mentality.'' Jane apparently read his thoughts in his face, for she added, "Like yours.''

An innocuous French tutor, one who had access to all the best houses, one who followed his students to London during the Season and back into the countryside when they left. It seemed unlikely that there was a connection between him and the French spy network, yet Blackburn couldn't forget the story of the Davises' French parlormaid. The girl had stolen kisses and state secrets from Mr. Davis, and family secrets and jewels from Mrs. Davis, and had escaped to the continent where she thumbed her nose at English Intelligence.

Had Miss Cunningham discovered Chasseur was a spy and been murdered to silence her?

Then he remembered Selma, as silly a girl as he'd ever met. Dryly, he said, "If Selma stumbled on the entire French army marching onto the beach, she'd have applauded the parade. I cannot imagine what a French spy could have learned from her, or even that she was aware of the conflict between our countries.''

Jane nodded, satisfied, but Blackburn would allow a doubt to linger in the back of his mind—he doubted everyone these days—and he would bring Chasseur's name up to Mr. Smith. Chasseur would be watched.

Blackburn watched Jane. Surely she wouldn't be involved in anything as gruesome as murder . . .

Lightning split the sky and thunder rumbled, and he realized the danger they were in, standing beneath a tall tree and inviting a bolt to strike.

Quite enough bolts had struck them today.

Hurrying her away from the oak, he said, "I'm sure you're right. Come on. Only one good run, and you'll be in the manor and we can get you dry."

She didn't want to go. He could tell by the way she tried to lag behind, and he understood completely. His sister, Susan, could be discerningly blunt in a formal social situation. God knew what she would say about them in private.

But they had no choice. It was late afternoon, dark with clouds, so he urged Jane up the steps and hammered on the great wooden door. The butler who answered had been at Goodridge Manor for as long as Blackburn could remember, and bowed them into the grand entry as calmly as if dripping people regularly took shelter there.

"Greetings, my lord. We've been expecting you and, I believe, Miss Higgenbothem?" Jane nodded, and Ilford bowed.

"Expecting us?" Blackburn lifted his brows inquiringly.

"Lord and Lady Tarlin and that extremely charming Miss Morant arrived after the start of the storm."

"Where are they?" Jane clasped her hands. "Are we going back to London tonight?"

Her glowing eyes and hopeful expression infuriated Blackburn. Handing Ilford the portfolio, he instructed, "Dry this and put it in Miss Higgenbothem's bedchamber, please."

Ilford took it and managed to look regretful at the same time. "I'm sorry, miss, but no. Lady Goodridge sent them on with assurances we would care for you on your coming." He handed the portfolio to a hovering maid. She hurried upstairs with it while Jane watched with an expression of such desolation, Ilford hurried to reassure her. "We *will* care for you, miss, and for your . . . uh . . . book. We have tea and towels waiting for you in the library."

His trousers dripped noisily on the marble floor, Blackburn noticed, and the draft coming down the curved staircase turned Jane's lips blue. He had to get her to the nearest source of warmth. He needed to remedy the lamentable mess he'd made of what should have been a spectacular seduction. He started to hustle Jane toward the open, lighted door.

Then he remembered what waited within, in an alcove behind the door. "Ilford, is that *thing* still in there?"

Ilford knew exactly which "thing" Blackburn referred to, and his eyes twinkled sympathetically. "Yes, my lord."

"Isn't there any place we can go except the library?"

"My lady Goodridge is in there, my lord, and if I may presume to say so, she asked that you greet her at once."

Jane's teeth chattered, and a frown of puzzlement puckered her forehead. "At once? Perhaps I should dr-dry first."

"Ransom?" Lady Goodridge's voice called from the library. "Is that you?"

Between his sister and the pursuing furies, there could be no escape from this moment. Blackburn didn't even know why he tried. "Yes, Susan," he called. But he wasn't resigned. He led Jane through the door and into the large, comfortable room lined with books, carefully keeping his body between her and that damnable alcove. The fire was surrounded by commodious settles and comfortable chairs, one containing his formidable sister, seated with her legs tucked under her and a rug and a book in her lap.

Lady Goodridge was alone, her mouth a little pinched and her expression more severe than usual.

Where was Fitz?

"Come close," she said bracingly. "Don't *hover*, Miss Higgenbothem, you'll not get dry that way."

"I don't want to drip on your rug," Jane protested.

She already was. Blackburn had positioned her in the warmest place, with her back to the alcove.

"Nonsense. It's only broadloom."

Jane stared at Lady Goodridge as if she were speaking a foreign language. "A guest is a poor guest indeed who ruins her hostess's home."

"And a *hostess* is a poor hostess indeed who allows her *guest* to *freeze*." Lady Goodridge gestured impatiently. "Really, Miss Higgenbothem, if the rug is *ruined*, then I will buy a *new one*. The maids have towels and blankets. Dry yourself and wrap up immediately."

Jane snatched up the largest towel from the pile deposited on the settle and put it under her feet while Blackburn and Susan exchanged exasperated glances. Jane's brother-in-law had caused this plebeian concern with possessions, Blackburn realized, and taking the next towel, he wrapped it around Jane's shoulders. Taking another, he placed it on her head and dried vigorously.

Muffled by the absorbent cotton, she said, "My lord—"

"Ransom," he corrected.

Her face poked out, shining with embarrassment. "My lord, I can't call you that!"

"No, I suppose not." He discarded that towel and took another. "Not in front of my sister, anyway."

She opened her mouth to deny she could ever call him by his first name, and he held the towel in readiness. If she refused, he would use that towel in such a way that Ilford, the maids, and Lady Goodridge would be in no doubt about his familiarity with her body.

And Jane knew it. He almost sympathized with her dilemma, and almost cheered for his victory when she said calmly, "My lord, you should dry yourself."

"It's more fun to dry you," he murmured.

"What?" his sister demanded. "What did you say, Ransom?"

Blackburn plucked up a towel. "I agreed that, as usual, Jane was right."

Under Ilford's supervision, one maid placed a tea tray loaded with a steaming pot of tea and three cups on the table at Lady Goodridge's elbow. Another placed a plate of cakes beside the tea tray. At Ilford's nod, they curtsied and hurried from the room. When Ilford was satisfied his mistress would want for nothing, he said, "The bedchambers are prepared for your guests, my lady. Is there any other service I can render?"

"None at all," Lady Goodridge said. "Thank you, Ilford. You may go."

As Ilford shut the door behind him, Ransom saw

that Jane had hurried to get the worst of the deluge wiped away and herself wrapped in a blanket. She probably thought, and rightly, that he would again attack her with a towel if she did not freely indulge herself in the blessed state of warmth. She was improperly independent and had too little concern for her own well-being.

Lady Goodridge handed her a cup of tea and gestured her to a settle facing the fire.

Jane had her back to the alcove.

"Seat yourself, Miss Higgenbothem."

Jane spread a towel on the seat and did as she was instructed.

Lady Goodridge watched enigmatically. "I find myself *curious* as to how you got in this *state*."

"I drew a picture," Jane said flatly. "Lord Blackburn objected."

Lifting an eyebrow, Lady Goodridge handed Blackburn his cup of tea. "A picture of what?" She looked significantly at his groin.

"A ship," he snapped. "An English ship going out to sea."

"I never knew you were such a philistine, Ransom." A smile played around his sister's mouth. "Will you next break the violins of the court musicians?"

Leaning against the mantel, he sipped the hot liquid and watched Jane. Damn her. She could have drawn any of the ships that had sailed that day. But she had picked the *Virginia Belle,* the one ship out of the whole flotilla carrying secret dispatches to Wellington. It couldn't be coincidence, not when she'd had de Sainte-Amand hovering at her shoulder directing her. "Miss Higgenbothem lacks the maturity to know that negotiating the shoals of . . . art . . . can be treacherous."

Jane's teacup rattled in her saucer, and she set it hastily on the table at her elbow. "I am quite mature, my lord. I doubt you could find among your acquaintances any woman as mature as I am."

Straightening, he said, "You are still a maiden—"

"Is she?" Lady Goodridge asked.

Blackburn ignored his sister, and locked his gaze with Jane's. "You are unproven in the experiences which mature a woman. If, for instance, you were married and properly supported by a man, I'm sure you would not be reduced to performing such immature acts as—"

"As drawing?" Jane leaned forward. "Your ignorance is showing, my lord. My drawing is not a ladylike occupation, it is an act of nature."

"It is an act of desperation. You cannot in all conscience do what you are doing!" He fervently wanted to believe that.

Obviously confused, Susan interposed, "Do you *think*, Ransom, that you might be *overreacting* to Miss Higgenbothem's *talent*?"

"I wasn't referring only to her art." He hesitated to confide in Susan. For some reason, he didn't want his sister to think less of Jane for succumbing to the Frenchman's temptation.

"No, Lord Blackburn believes he knows all." Jane's sarcastic tone informed him she was not of the same opinion. "To him, I am the same unformed lump of clay I was eleven years ago. He assumes that a woman is nothing without the maturing experience of marriage—''

He put his cup down with a clink. ''I did not say that.''

''—while a man matures on his own. If he ever does.'' Jane's eyes glittered when she rounded on him. ''I assure you, my lord, I am an adult. It began that moment in the ballroom when Melba collapsed. Do you remember, my lord, or were you too busy running from my art?''

With a start, he realized this was the emotion he'd seen in the depths of Jane's spirit. Anger. Deep, furious anger, the kind of anger that thrived on loneliness and frustrated longing. And that, perhaps, brought forth treason as its fruit.

''For a year, I watched my sister die, doing little more than hold her hand, for there was nothing else to do. I made a deathbed promise to care for Adorna, and I have lived in the house of a miserly merchant, reviled and unvalued.''

''Oh, my dear.'' Lady Goodridge took Jane's hand and patted it.

''No, don't pity me, my lady. My travails made me strong.'' Jane squeezed his sister's hand in return, offering more comfort than she received.

In that moment Blackburn realized just how mature Jane truly was. What could he say that would change her from her course? She would not be guided by a man. In her experience, men were spiteful, foolish, and untrustworthy.

As he had been, reacting to a statue she had sculpted in innocence and secrecy.

As if she'd read his mind, she said, "Even you, my lord, contributed to my maturity."

Hand against the mantel, he braced himself.

"Because of you, I never held on to fatuous hope. I knew no man would come to rescue me from my misery, for what man wants a fallen woman?"

"You are not fallen."

"Only you and I know that, my lord." She pressed her hand to her chest. "But I have triumphed. I have survived, I have my dignity, and if my dreams have withered—well, that is a woman's destiny, isn't it?"

He wanted to dismiss her as melodramatic. He wanted to tell himself her ranting was nothing but a virgin's frustration. But not even he, the Marquess of Blackburn, could patronize Jane now. As she looked into his eyes, she allowed him a brief glimpse of her soul, full of anguish and honest pain.

And, by God, he did feel guilty. He *was* guilty.

Then his sister, prosaic as always, said, "Miss Higgenbothem, while this is all *fascinating*, none of it explains how you got a *rose petal* stuck in your *hair*."

Running her fingers through her hair, Jane stared, quite dumb, at the sodden petal that fell in her lap.

"And, Miss Higgenbothem, correct me if I'm *wrong*, but I believe your *bodice* is buttoned *crooked*."

"Should have let me do it," Blackburn said, sotto voce.

Jane covered herself with her towel, and she looked suddenly tired, as if the day and its events—and him, with his constant demands—had drained her.

Blackburn wanted to go to her, to promise he would never hurt her, or let anyone else hurt her. He wanted to protect her from plunging ever deeper into treason, and at the same time shake her for ever indulging in such criminal behavior.

In short, when he was around Jane, he was torn between his duty and his instincts. Despite knowing what she must see as she left the library, his instincts spoke now. "She needs a tray and her bed. Which chamber is hers, Susan?"

"I don't need to be put to bed like a child. Or to create a great deal of trouble with my meal." Straightening her spine, Jane took on the aspect of the proper chaperone and perfect guest. "I am capable of dining with Lady Goodridge."

He hated it when she looked so much like a spinster aunt. "No, you're not."

"Or I can dine with the servants, if you prefer."

He pointed his finger at her. "Jane, I can be pushed too far."

She looked mutinous.

Lady Goodridge rescued the situation. In her stuffiest voice—and Blackburn thought she did stuffy better than anyone because it came so naturally to her—she said, "Indeed, Miss Higgenbothem, I am *insulted* you would think me such a *snob* I must send a *lady of your background* to dine in the *kitchen.*"

"No, oh no!" With very real distress, Jane laid a hand on his sister's arm. "I never meant to insult *you.*"

"Of course not, but I find one must *think* before

one *speaks*." Lady Goodridge rose, and Jane rose with her. "One of the maids will take you to your room, and Ilford will see to it you get a tray. *You* see to it you *eat* what is on it. There will be a nightgown for you, and I'll *personally* see to it you're not *disturbed*." Lady Goodridge glared at Blackburn meaningfully.

Eleven years ago, Lady Goodridge had told him he would be sorry for failing to do as he should and marry Miss Jane Higgenbothem. Now it appeared the fruits of his impropriety were frustration, heartbreak, and treason.

How he hated to admit his sister was right.

"In the morning," Lady Goodridge said, "Ransom will *return* you to the *Tarlins*, and I will see you at my *tea* next week."

Jane crumpled under the weight of his sister's self-importance. "Yes, my lady."

They were walking toward the door to the entry, and Blackburn lagged behind, dreading the moment she would see it.

The statue.

Surrounded by bookshelves, it stood in an arched nook like every other piece of art Lady Goodridge had placed in her library. Jane hadn't seen the bare, unvarnished embarrassment coming in. She couldn't avoid it going out, for, like a damned stage light, a branch of candles sat on the pedestal with the wretched source of all his youthful anguish.

She stopped abruptly, one foot in the air and her back stiff. She stared.

Blackburn averted his eyes. He hadn't looked at the

damned thing since that first, humiliating moment eleven years ago.

"I had it *bronzed*," Lady Goodridge said in a conversational tone. "Good, isn't it? Not a *master's* work, of course. You needed *professional* instruction, and you were *young*, but that statue is a *fine* likeness of Ransom."

With a swift glance, Blackburn took in the face. His sister was right. It looked just like him, or rather, like the boy he had been. Unscarred. Arrogant. He glanced again. The chest and arms and stomach were good likenesses, too. Amazingly like, considering that at that time, Jane had viewed only his countenance.

"It is good." Jane couldn't keep the note of pride out of her voice.

Taking courage, Blackburn glanced one last time— and covered his eyes with his hand. That was as bad—worse—than he remembered. Good God, the girl had insulted him as no one, man or woman, had dared before or since.

And she still didn't even know it.

With an attempt at civility and composure, he uncovered his face. "You don't keep that here because of any familial affection, Susan. Don't try and gull the lady into thinking such a thing."

Placing a hand on her bosom, Lady Goodridge backed from his admonition with mocking respect. "I'm not! The truth is, I keep the statue here for the moments—quite *frequent*, Miss Higgenbothem— when he is insufferably *arrogant*."

He'd heard this before, and all he could think was, *Don't say it. Don't say it!*

She said it. "Then I remind Figgy that *all of us* have our *shortcomings*."

Stiff with pride at her accomplishment, Jane looked between the two of them. "I don't understand, my lady. How could anyone who gazes on this statue, created by a stupid, worshipful girl, think Lord Blackburn has any shortcomings?"

Blackburn adored her. He adored Miss Jane Higgenbothem. She was the only woman he had ever met who left his sister with nothing to say. She was the only woman he knew he wished to spend the rest of his life with.

Moreover, he owed her reparation.

"Jane, there's no remedy for it." Stepping to her side, he enveloped her rigid form in a hug. "I shall have to marry you."

Wrenching herself free, Jane said, "My lord, I don't find that amusing."

Taking her cold fingers in his, he said gently, "I wasn't jesting."

Obviously, she didn't know whether to believe him. More obviously, she didn't care. Her chest rose and fell in deep, baleful breaths. Her eyes glowed green as a spitting cat's. "In that case, I must respectfully decline. I don't think I could bear to become any more mature."

Striding to the door, she opened it so hard it banged against the wall.

Miss Jane Higgenbothem, the woman who'd made him a laughingstock—the woman who could be a French spy—had refused his suit.

Chapter 21

"Stiff upper lip, my dear." Lady Goodridge pressed her cheek to Jane's as they stood beside the open carriage door. "You've got him *trapped* now."

Jane didn't even pretend not to know who Lady Goodridge referred to. "I don't want to have him trapped." The object of their discussion, Lord Blackburn—for Jane would call him Lord Blackburn, regardless of how far their association had gone—stood speaking to the coachman, looking revoltingly calm and not at all discomposed.

Yet last night he had proposed to her. That rude, miserable, rich, handsome, and wholly desirable lord of England had proposed to her.

"I don't want to have him at all."

"Don't be silly, girl." Lady Goodridge took Jane by the shoulders and shook her. "He's *rich*, he's a *Quincy*, and he's *in need of a wife*. You cannot do better than that."

Folding her hands at her waist, Jane looked down

at the gravel drive beneath her feet. "I can remain a spinster. *That* would be better."

"No need to be *truculent*. He is doing what is *proper* this time. You will do the same."

Jane pressed her lips together and fought to maintain her composure. She had lost her temper last night. She would not do it again, she had vowed, regardless of the provocation.

"There, there." Lady Goodridge adjusted the new bonnet she'd insisted on giving Jane. "I know this isn't easy—a Quincy has never been born who easily submitted to the *yoke* of matrimony—but I would be *derelict* in my duty if I didn't remind you that your dear sister Melba would have wanted this for you."

That was true, of course, but Jane couldn't keep herself from retorting, "My sister wished me to be happy."

"As you will be. You're of the same social class, you're strong enough to stand up to him, and you have *repeatedly* proved your compatibility for the marriage bed." Lady Goodridge examined her fingernails. "That is very important, Miss Higgenbothem, and I *do* speak from experience."

Jane struggled to contain the blush that stained her cheeks in what she knew must be unattractive blotches.

Not even when she and Blackburn had been compromised eleven years before had she felt so awkward.

And of course not. Eleven years ago she hadn't been forced to face him after being in his arms and kissing him and allowing him—nay, encouraging him—to kiss her mouth and parts of her that were exposed only in her bath. Now she had the memory of not only a vast intimacy between them, but also of her wanton behavior and of that dreadful scene she'd made in the library.

Mature indeed. A mature woman wouldn't have lost her temper over something so trivial as a man's pigheaded, incredibly large, thoughtless, and ignorant stupidity. His proposal had been nothing more.

"He's comely, too, as are most Quincys, and I feel I can safely predict that your *children* will be well set up, strong, and handsome." Lady Goodridge beamed benevolently at her brother as he strolled toward them. "It's a *beautiful* morning for the drive back to London, Ransom," she said in her ringing tones. "You'll be riding inside *with* Miss Higgenbothem, of course."

"Of course." He answered smoothly, hiding his nefarious plans, whatever they were, beneath a veneer of civility.

But Jane could scheme, too. Jane could hide the turmoil of her emotions beneath a simulated courtesy, too. Jane could be better than any toplofty lordship— and was. "It would be better if you rode, I think," she said. "Such a noted horseman would soon be stifled in the confines of a carriage."

Arrogant and insolent, with a confidence that made her grind her teeth, he lifted his quizzing glass and looked her over from head to toe.

Jane wore the clothing she'd been almost seduced and severely drenched in the day before. Everything had been dried and pressed by Lady Goodridge's servants, of course, but the gown was marked with stains and tears.

Blackburn, on the other hand, wore the clean clothing he left at his sister's home for just such an emergency.

The contrast between his good grooming and her own slatternly appearance made her hate him more.

"I'll take that chance," he replied.

With Lady Goodridge, Jane confined herself to tact. With Blackburn, she felt no such compunction. "I don't want you."

"You made that abundantly clear last night." His half smile ironed a cleft in his cheek. "After such a crushing setdown, you may be sure I can keep my hands off of you."

He didn't look crushed, blast him. Nor did he look inflamed with passion. He looked predatory, like a wolf on the trail of a dove.

But she was no dove, no helpless, chirping, gray chick. She was more of a phoenix, rising from the flames of scandal. "See that you do," she said.

"That's the girl." Lady Goodridge clenched her fist and nodded. "You'll set the *hook* with your defiance."

Which had the effect of withering Jane's bravado and making her wish, desperately, that she were anywhere but here, getting into this luxurious carriage for another ordeal by Blackburn.

The cleft in his cheek deepened. "Susan, you're incorrigible." He dropped a kiss on his sister's cheek. "You'll be back in London soon?"

"I don't know." For the first time in Jane's experience, Lady Goodridge looked uncertain. "There is much to be done here."

Blackburn looked at her sharply. "You're not feeling well."

Lady Goodridge straightened her already rigid shoulders. "I am fine."

"Nothing less than ague has kept you from the season before."

"I'm getting too old for such frivolity."

"Too old to meddle in my affairs?" Blackburn pulled a skeptical face. "I shall need your help with my courtship."

"Courtship?" Jane couldn't believe his gall. "Don't you take *no* for an answer?"

"No."

"No? You would dare to once again assault my—"

"Spinsterhood?" He bowed. "Indeed, yes. I'm not so enfeebled I would allow a mere refusal to thwart me."

"Miss Higgenbothem, you look much like a *fish* out of *water*." Lady Goodridge made shooing gestures. "We Quincys have that effect on people, but as you become a *part* of the *family*, you will settle *nicely*."

"And speaking of family," Blackburn said, "if you're gone from London as Jane's disappearance yesterday becomes fodder for gossip, she will be ostracized."

"Oh, damn." With uncharacteristic rawness, Lady Goodridge swore and put her palm to her forehead.

"So if you're not back in town by tomorrow night, I'll send my own physician to bleed you."

''Ransom, you're *insufferable*,'' Lady Goodridge snapped.

''I learned from the best.'' He dropped a kiss on her cheek. ''Tomorrow.''

Taking the footman's hand, Jane stepped into the cramped quarters of the carriage. A lemon scent pervaded the coach, inviting her memories, resurrecting the sensation of being close to Blackburn.

His coach, brought to Lady Goodridge's while last night's storm raged. His coachman had been frantic to find him, desperate that the great Blackburn not be troubled by the discomfort of a ride in a strange vehicle. Everyone groveled before Blackburn. Everyone gave him his way.

No wonder he didn't believe she had the audacity to reject his suit.

She stared resentfully as he squeezed himself through the door. He sat opposite from her, tapped the ceiling, and they were off.

He smiled.

She turned her head to look out the window.

He said, ''Actually, riding backward makes me queasy. You won't mind if I join you?''

Before she could protest, he'd scooted her aside and settled beside her on the well-cushioned seat.

''This is silly,'' she said. ''Two such large people cramped together in such a small space. *I'll* sit backward.''

''And be queasy in your turn?''

She didn't answer. She *would* be queasy.

''Quite the quandary, eh? To sit next to me and

suffer my closeness, or dare the threat of nausea and know I would hold your head.''

She half rose, furious at the mockery in his tone, but his fingers clamped on her thigh and pushed her back down again.

''Enough of that. Two such *large* people fit quite comfortably on this seat, although 'large,' I fancy, is not the correct term.''

She scraped his hand off her leg. ''What is, then?''

''Tall. We are tall. Which is one of the things I most admire about you. You're not some little dab of a thing.'' He turned his head and looked at her. ''When I kiss you, I don't have to bend until I have a crick in my back.''

She stared straight ahead. She *was* tall. If she faced him, their mouths would be close. She had no doubt he would take her movement as an invitation.

She would douse his fire. ''I had wondered which of my beauties attracted you most, and why. It is good to know for certain.''

''There are a good many of your beauties which attract me, Jane.'' His voice deepened with amusement, and his breath touched her cheek. ''Not the least of which is your independence. You never cling to me.''

''Why would I? You seem an unlikely candidate for any clinging at all, much less mine.''

''On the contrary, most women believe that clinging gives them a feminine allure that provokes my protectiveness.''

Jane snorted. ''You? Protective?''

''Yes, protective. I am probably also possessive,

although that has never been put to the test. But I choose my women, I am not chosen by them.''

''How very manly of you,'' she muttered.

He ignored that. ''And I find clinging tedious. I have discovered, however, my protectiveness is definitely aroused by a woman who knows her strength, yet is overmatched by circumstances or—''

She couldn't bear it anymore. She looked directly at him to deliver her rebuke. ''Brute force?''

''Yes.'' His smooth-as-butter lips caressed the word.

She swallowed and found herself pressed against the sidewall of the carriage. Not by him, but by her own apprehension.

Blast him for making her act like a quivering idiot with a simple ''yes.'' Just when she'd been steeling herself to be totally autonomous, he made her imagine how it would be to have him protecting her, possessing her, making her his own. His wife.

She thought she had gained possession of her wayward emotions, but no. The threat of passion, the lure of security that she knew to be false, they conspired against her. She wanted those things, and at the same time, it infuriated her that he could so easily manipulate her.

And did he really think he could conceal his deception from her? She didn't know what it was, she didn't know why he was lying, but she had studied him too long not to recognize the signs. Yes, he had proposed to her, but for what reason? What was he hiding?

Leaning toward him, she draped herself over his

arm. "But I can cling, too, Lord Blackburn." She smiled a siren's smile and in a breathy, helpless tone, so much like Melba's, she said, "Oh, Lord Blackburn, won't you rescue me from the dreadful straits I'm in?"

Now he leaned back against the wall, studying her in surprise. "What are you blathering about?"

"I'm accepting your marriage proposal, of course. You haven't withdrawn it, have you?" She batted her eyelashes in an exaggerated flutter. "That would be the act of a cad, and you haven't been a cad for . . . oh . . . at least the last minute."

"Jane, tell me at once what you mean," he snapped.

She sensed the urgency in him, and dropped the enticing facade. "I mean I've been turned out of my home. I have nowhere to go, and if I were the kind of woman you disdain, I would indeed accept your proposal. It is, after all, preferable to the streets."

Chapter 22

"*Am I mad, sir? Do I see conspiracies where there are none?*" Blackburn had rushed to the Foreign Office as soon as he'd dropped Jane at Tarlin House, hoping that his recitation of the events of the week and his conclusions would bring a bout of mockery from the insightful old man.

But Mr. Smith did not mock him. He didn't insist Blackburn give the name of his mysterious lady. Instead, the man behind the desk stroked his palsied hand over his chin and said, "No, you're not mad. You say this lady visits de Sainte-Amand, that at first she acted guilty, and now she is simply gleeful."

"So my watchers tell me."

"You said that in her youth her reputation was ruined by a cad who refused to marry her."

"Yes." *Blackburn* had been a cad. "Yes."

"She has labored for years in obscurity and poverty, and now, when her youthful bloom has fled and the disintegration of old age awaits her, she has been ejected from her home and has nowhere to go."

"She's not old!" Blackburn instinctively protested.

"Unimportant." Mr. Smith dismissed that with a wave. "From among the flotilla of English ships, she chose to sketch the one carrying commands to Wellington on the Peninsula, and she tried to give it to de Sainte-Amand."

"I stopped her."

"I expected no less of you, Lord Blackburn," Mr. Smith snapped.

"I always do my duty, sir." Except last night, when he had forgotten Jane could be a spy, and had proposed to her. And this morning, when he had told her he wouldn't give up.

"Of course you do," Mr. Smith said bracingly. "The weight of evidence is heavy against this lady."

"What about the Monsieur Chasseur I told you about?" Blackburn offered the young French tutor as a distracting bone.

"I'll have someone investigate him at once, of course, but I've had no reports of the man. Even if he was the one who murdered the Cunningham girl, he could have done it for reasons other than espionage." Mr. Smith snickered. "Lover's quarrel, perhaps."

"Oh, definitely." What a horrible word—*love*. Could it be that he himself . . . ? Blackburn shook himself. No. Impossible. No.

Mr. Smith continued, "Someone is getting information out of the Foreign Office and into France. De Sainte-Amand is a link in the chain, and it makes sense he would have recruited a woman disenchanted both with England and with society."

"She has reason to be disenchanted," Blackburn said glumly.

"Of course she does. I was not born a gentleman, and I have myself been known to indulge in bitter moments when one of those idiotic noblemen fancies himself above me because of the cut of his coat or the blue tinge in his blood." Mr. Smith's sharp gaze raked Blackburn. "Present company excepted."

"Yes, sir."

"Other . . . contacts have made it clear that the messages are being passed through the ton. There are a lot of links to this chain, but with your help we are close to finding them all, especially the traitor within the Foreign Office."

"If the traitor is part of the ton, can't we question those who work here?"

"Oh, do think a little more clearly, Lord Blackburn," Mr. Smith said. "How do we find out which one? Any lord or gentleman who wishes may take a desk. Not to mention the younger sons who work as secretaries in hopes they'll get ahead in politics. I can't stop them, or their silly conceit that they're making a contribution to the war effort."

"Do any of them have too much money?"

"Several, but they inherited it. The others—well, they're wise enough not to flaunt any extra blunt." Mr. Smith leaned back in his chair and tapped his fingertips together. "Is this certain lady dressing rather better than she should?"

Blackburn remembered the silk ball gown, then the dull wool of yesterday. "She does wear some fine pieces she can't afford."

"Very suspicious."

"I spoke to her. She's putting up a good front, but she's desperate." Damn Jane. Because of her, he'd been angry, baffled, ruthless, and worst of all, insightful. Yes, when he'd looked at her as she taunted him in the coach, declaring she would wed him for security, he had seen the panic beneath. "Perhaps she can see no other recourse."

"Than treason? A woman of that class can always go live with a relative. Failing that, she can work as a governess. Or a scullery maid, or a prostitute, or she can go to the workhouse for all I care." Mr. Smith's faded gaze blazed with contempt. "Young man, there is no excuse for treason!"

"You're right, of course." Jane. Blackburn had seen her watching Adorna with affection. Frowning at him in censure. Smiling . . . only rarely.

Yet now another picture superseded those in his mind.

Jane, thin and threadbare, the typical English governess. Jane, toiling in the workhouse. Jane, walking the streets.

He swallowed painfully.

"The lack of support, the visits to de Sainte-Amand, combined with the drawing of the ship, does not bode well for this unnamed lady." Mr. Smith nodded. "Good work. You're on the verge of exposing another rat, and in only three days. I knew I was right to send you."

Dismissed, Blackburn stood and walked slowly toward the door.

Mr. Smith must have seen his aversion, for as

Blackburn stepped over the threshold, he said, "Lord Blackburn, I assume by your reluctance to name this woman that you are feeling queasy about betraying one of your own, and a lady at that."

Betraying one of his own? More than that, if he declared Jane a spy, he would be betraying the woman he declared he would marry. The protection of his name might keep her from the gallows, but was he so lost in lust he would break faith with his country for a lifetime between Jane's thighs? Or was this awful, gut-wrenching sense of wrongness all the proof he needed of her innocence?

He had to be wrong about something. About Jane's character. Or about his own conclusions.

Wrong. What an awful concept.

"I would be very suspicious of any attempt on her part to contact you. She, or her French superiors, may realize how she has jeopardized her cover by allowing you to see that drawing. She may try to seduce you out of your suspicions, or even seduce you to her side."

Mr. Smith's insight infuriated Blackburn. "That is not likely, sir."

"I've seen men do stranger things for a woman they desired."

"Not a Quincy."

"As you say." Mr. Smith's faded gaze pumped iron into Blackburn's veins. "Remember, if you would, that young man from Tourbillon who followed you into battle and died so slowly with a chunk of metal in his gut. Remember the drummer boy who today lives on your estate, his drumming days gone with the loss of both his arms. Remember, Lord Blackburn, why you started this.''

No matter how Blackburn wished it, Mr. Smith's reminders could not be ignored. He grasped the door-frame in his hand and pressed until the sharp edges of the wood dug into his palm. ''I remember. I can never forget.''

Chapter 23

Jane missed the step off the curb. A grubby hand caught her arm before she could fall, and the child who swept the crossing said, "Careful, miss."

"Thank you," Jane said. "I must watch where I am going." Before she was crushed beneath a carriage's wheels for remembering yesterday's events, last night's insulting proposal, and her own mocking acceptance today.

She waited while the girl—Jane thought she was a girl, although who could tell beneath those rags—used her broom on the gritty cobblestones.

Two days ago the child had positioned herself on this corner of Cavendish Square. Patiently she waited to sweep the street for any noble pedestrians who wandered by. Jane didn't understand how she earned enough in tips in a place where almost everyone rode in a carriage or on a horse, but the girl seemed pleased enough with her station, and swung the worn broom vigorously every time Jane chose to walk out.

Which Jane had done twice since returning from

Goodridge Manor this morning. Once to visit Lord de Sainte-Amand's home with its secret source of satisfaction, and once for a walk to escape Violet and Adorna and their endless questions.

And because every time she sat down to do needlework—not to sketch!—memories of the long ride back to London overwhelmed her.

After her flaming announcement of homelessness, Blackburn had—oh, dash it, she *would* call him Ransom. After all, their relationship had certainly gone that far.

Jane took her breath and closed her eyes against the admission.

But it was true. She knew him too well, and not at all. She knew his scent, his breath, his touch.

She didn't know his mind. Not at all. Never.

She had said marriage to him was preferable to the streets, and meant it . . . but not really. In some secret, unacknowledged place in her mind, she had hoped he would snatch her to his bosom and overwhelm her objections. He would force her to take his name and accept his protection, and she wouldn't have this horrible uncertainty dogging her every footstep.

Instead, when she said, ''I have no home,'' he had looked at her with such intense revulsion, she thought he had truly been overwhelmed by nausea.

Covering her trembling mouth with her gloved hand, Jane wished she could erase his expression from memory.

For she had thought he knew better than to judge a person, especially a woman, by her circumstances.

''Miss?''

Jane opened her eyes and jumped.

The child had stuck her face close to Jane's and now examined her anxiously. "It's swept, miss. Did yer little mishap shake ye more than ye realized? I can 'elp ye across."

"Thank you. I'm fine." Digging a copper out of her handbag, Jane presented it to her.

The girl took the coin, then gave the gap-toothed grin of a seven-year-old who had lost her two front teeth. "Welcome, miss. Watch where ye're goin'!"

"I will." Where she was going, not where she had been.

When Jane reached the top of the steps to Tarlin House and glanced wistfully back, the sweeper tipped her hat. Nice child, Jane thought absently.

She lifted her fist to knock on the bottle green door.

Blackburn had worn a waistcoat of just that color this morning. Before her announcement, he'd looked at her with such heat that his gaze could fire clay.

After, he had moved back to the front-facing seat.

What was he feeling? How could she know, when she herself pivoted like a pendulum between every emotion?

The door swung away from her hovering fist.

"Miss, did you wish to come in?" Springall the butler waited, his expression perfectly composed, as though houseguests routinely stood immobile on his doorstep.

Jane's hand dropped. "Yes. Thank you."

She noted that the footman grinned as he took her redingote and bonnet, and she stared at him curiously.

Springall did not normally allow such freedom of expression among his minions.

"Miss, you have a letter from Mr. Morant." Springall held out the sealed sheet on a silver salver.

Jane took it with a secret, ironic smile. That was that she needed to finish off a simply dreadful day—another letter from Eleazer. Stripping off her gloves, she broke the seal and quickly scanned the words. It appeared to be more of the usual: how much money had they spent? How soon could Adorna contract a wealthy marriage?

But today there was a new fillip to add to Jane's tribulations—a message from Dame Olten written in Eleazer's hand.

There was no subtlety to the missive. She and Eleazer would marry by summer, and Dame Olten did not look forward to having a stepdaughter live with her in her new home, nor did she expect to see Jane begging for sanctuary at her new doorstep. So if Jane knew what was good for her, she would make her plans for a new residence now.

Jane imagined how much Eleazer must have enjoyed penning those lines, and she laughed softly at the picture that formed in her mind. Two people, reveling in cruelty and crude boorishness, imagining themselves clever and proving themselves the opposite.

"Good news, then, miss?" Springall asked.

"Not news," she answered. "But always amusing."

Springall's austere expression appeared almost benevolent. "That's lovely. Lady Tarlin and Miss

Morant have requested your presence. If you would be so good?''

''Certainly.'' She would have to explain what had happened yesterday sometime, she supposed. ''Where might I find them?''

''In the garret.''

Jane blinked. ''The garret?''

''Yes, miss.'' He bowed her up the stairs.

She went, but skeptically. She couldn't dismiss her suspicions of Violet and Adorna. She knew them too well. If they found out about the proposal, they would have her wed to Blackburn by any trickery they could devise. Yet rationally she doubted they had stunned him and dragged him into the attic with any base objective. There had to be another reason why they summoned her to the dusty garret of Tarlin House— although Jane's imagination could not supply it.

''This way, miss.'' A smiling housemaid curtsied, then led her up the final, narrow, creaking flight of stairs to a bare wooden door, and swung it open.

The chamber was bright with the afternoon sunshine, full of large, dustcloth-covered objects, and lit by the beaming faces of the two women Jane loved most.

''Surprise!'' Adorna clapped her hands together. ''Surprise, Aunt Jane. Aren't you surprised?''

''Very surprised.'' Jane moved into the room and looked cautiously around. The room measured half the width of the town house, twenty feet across, and was about fourteen feet wide. The dormer windows all faced north, and were open to the fresh air. No dust or mildew tainted any corner of the garret, and except for the covered objects, one rather worn couch, and a dressing screen, it held no furniture.

No long, man-shaped forms lay trussed up on the bare wooden floor.

Jane relaxed marginally. "What is this?"

Adorna took the corner of one of the dustcloths. Violet took the corner of another. Together they pulled them off to reveal a simple wooden modeling stand, complete with turntable, and a large, sturdy table covered with modeling instruments.

Jane stared dumbly.

"Aunt Jane, you don't look happy. Aren't you happy?"

Jane didn't move, didn't breathe.

"It's your studio, Jane," Violet said.

"Studio." Jane blinked, sure she had imagined the chisel, the wood blades, the wire-end tools.

"For you to do your sculptures." Adorna sounded a little tearful.

"It is Adorna's special surprise for you." Violet was prompting her, wanting her to say something, to do something besides stand and stare in vast disbelief.

"It's . . . very nice." More than nice. It was a miracle. If it was true, it would give Jane back the greatest pleasure of her life. "It's . . . I . . . I don't know what to say." Funny. Her voice trembled and her vision blurred.

Violet relaxed, the strained frown disappearing from between her brows.

"But you like it?" Adorna still needed to be reassured.

"Like it? Like it?" Jane tasted the phrase, giving

it incredulous intonations. '' 'Like' is insufficient to describe my . . .'' She faltered, holding her fist to her chest.

Adorna laughed joyously. ''It *was* my idea. After I heard about the statue, I knew what you'd been needing all these years and I wanted to get it for you because you've been so wonderful to me, but it was Lord Tarlin who suggested the garret, and Lady Tarlin who ordered the art supplies, and the maids who bustled around to get the room scrubbed because it was nothing but an old storage room, and everybody's worked so hard to make you happy because we love you, Aunt Jane.''

Everyone smiled at her. Violet, Adorna, the maids gathered in the doorway, Springall and the footmen behind. Jane knew of Violet's and Adorna's affection, but to think of such an elaborate gift! And for Lord Tarlin to take time from his day to concern himself with a place for her to practice her art! And the servants! All she'd done was to try and be a pleasant and unobtrusive houseguest, to help Violet if she could, to guide Adorna through the treacherous shoals of London society.

And done a lamentably poor job because of one idiotic, irrational, handsome, and appealing Blackburn.

But she couldn't think of him now. She couldn't allow him to intrude on this moment, as he had intruded on so many others.

''This is so kind. I don't know what to . . . how to thank you.'' She dabbed at her eyes. ''All of you.''

Springall didn't approve of aristocrats having emotion. He clapped his hands, two smart smacks that brought the lesser servants to attention. "All right. Back to work."

"Thank you," Jane called to the departing servants. She needed a handkerchief.

Violet handed her one.

"Look, Aunt Jane. Here's the clay, here in the bucket. Here are some work clothes hanging behind the screen. There's a jug of water and a basin so you can wash up after you get done, and Lord Tarlin said the light was just right for an artist." Adorna behaved like a street peddler selling chips to a potential client.

Jane shared a smile with Violet. "It's perfect."

Throwing her arms around Jane's neck, Adorna asked, "Do you really like it?"

"Very much." Jane hugged her back, this little girl she raised when she was so inadequately prepared for such a responsibility. She'd always been afraid that the lack of a real mother would display itself in some horrible quirk of Adorna's personality, but no. The only lack showed now, here in London, in herself.

Yet Adorna loved her, despite her shortcomings. Again Jane blinked against the tears.

"Don't worry, Aunt Jane." Adorna patted her back. "We're well on the way to conquering London. When we're done, nothing will be the same."

Jane gave a watery chuckle. No wonder the child had had a dozen proposals. "With that I must agree." Her gaze strayed toward the covered bucket beside the modeling stand.

"We thought you might have something you wanted to sculpt." Violet moved toward the door.

"Or someone." Adorna followed Violet.

Jane didn't need the unsubtle suggestion. Already her palms could almost feel the sensation of cool clay as she shaped the jut of *his* jaw. "You're inviting disaster," she warned.

Jane could have sworn she heard Violet mutter, "Yes, and I hope he accepts."

Then they were gone. She was alone, shut in with a bucket of clay, a plethora of tools, and her thoughts of Blackburn. Handsome, maddening, faithless Blackburn whose form had been almost completely revealed to her yesterday.

She slipped behind the screen. With trembling hands she struggled to remove her intricately fastened gown. She replaced it with a simple gray work gown, loose and comfortable, with buttons up the front. She covered that with an unadorned black apron. Sitting on the sofa, she removed her boots and her socks— she could only work barefooted—then slowly walked toward the modeling stand.

She laid her hand on the flat surface. It turned. She twirled it and laughed a quiet, exultant laugh. A turntable, just like a real artist. Gently she touched each of the tools, shining-new and crying out to be used. Lifting the cover on the bucket, she gazed at the clay. It smelled rich and moist, and its gray exterior gave no hint of the beauty, and the treachery, hiding within.

But she knew it was there. She reached out and sank her hands into the cool depths of her beloved clay.

* * *

As Blackburn drove to Cavendish Square, he handled the ribbons with more than his usual care. The busy streets of London required all his attention, especially with the high-perch phaeton and his best pair of matched grays, and he was distracted by worry and speculation.

Who wouldn't be? After that distressing interview with Mr. Smith, he had arrived home to find an invitation to call on Jane.

To call on her. After the things she'd said to him, after the contempt she'd heaped on his head! Disjointedly he had noted that Jane's handwriting looked remarkably childlike, with letters that were large and open and with each *i* dotted by a heart. That surprised him, but not nearly as much as the cloyingly sweet tone of the note. If he didn't know better, he would have thought someone else had sent it.

But no. He had to face facts. Just as Mr. Smith had warned, Jane wanted something from him.

She had arrived back in London, reported to her French superiors, and undoubtedly they had scolded her for allowing her emotions to divert her from her mission. Probably she had been instructed to cajole the sketch of the ship from him. Perhaps to try and discover what he knew about the workings of the Foreign Office. And maybe, just maybe, she had been told to apologize and beg him to take her as his wife.

That apology would only double his suspicion of her, but he found himself wanting it very badly. Worse, he found himself contemplating accepting it. After all, if he wed her, he would control her.

She was only a woman. He *could* control her.

"Damn!" Rounding the corner, he saw the line of carriages and horses before Tarlin House. "Damn." He pulled the phaeton to a standstill. Every bachelor in society was there, paying court to Miss Morant, and there was no chance his coming would escape anyone's notice. He'd already made it clear that he was courting Miss Jane Higgenbothem. He had used it as a diversion to cover his activities. He should want the ton to buzz about his attentions . . . yet somewhere along the line Jane had become the most important matter of his life. To once more expose her to the swooping vultures, even for the good of England, gave him a vague, crawling sense of disgust.

He was, as Mr. Smith accused, feeling queasy about betraying her.

Stopping his phaeton at the corner, he said to the child who swept the street, "Excuse me. Can you tell me if Miss Higgenbothem is at home?"

The saucy urchin grinned and winked at him. "Aye, m'lord, she is. Been out fer two walks today, but she's back now."

"Really." Blackburn considered the situation. "Would you happen to know if she went to that very special destination?"

The girl glanced around, and seeing no one eavesdropped, she nodded.

Blackburn nodded back. "Thank you, Wiggens."

"Nice 'orses, m'lord," Wiggens said.

"The best in my stables." And appropriate for a man who wished to impress a woman.

At an impatient shout from behind him, he drove away from his little spy to join the line at the Tarlins'.

He noted a swift round of grins as he swung himself down and made his way to the door. Handing his beaver hat to Springall, he asked, "Is Miss Higgenbothem at home?"

"The ladies are in the morning chamber," Springall said.

Blackburn started toward the door.

"But Miss Higgenbothem is not there."

Blackburn paused. "Where is she?"

"You'll have to inquire of Lady Tarlin." Springall sniffed. "She's in the morning chamber."

Blackburn reflected that the butler matched his mistress—irritating and condescending. But he was in no mood for Violet's mechanisms, and so he told her when he found her, surrounded by low-toned matrons. "I want to speak to Miss Higgenbothem, and I want to speak to her now."

Violet appeared singularly unimpressed by his impatience. "I'm afraid Jane is . . . busy at the moment. I'll tell her you called, shall I?"

"Busy." Blackburn remembered Wiggens's confirmation. Jane had walked to de Sainte-Amand's today, possibly to deliver a sketch done from memory of the *Virginia Belle* and receive further instructions. "Doing what?"

Violet's gaze slid away from his. "I couldn't say."

"You'd better say, or I'll tell Tarlin about the time you drove his team through Hyde Park on a wager."

One of the eavesdropping matrons giggled, then subsided as Violet glared, first at her, then at him. "You are detestable, Ransom."

"Yes, and you're guilty about something." B'God,

he was seeing treason everywhere he looked. He had to be going mad—or else the ladies of London had made treachery into a grand new entertainment. He wouldn't put it past them, frivolous and silly as they were, but neither could he allow Violet to become entangled. "You'd best not be involved in Jane's activities, Violet. This is not a game."

"No one knows that better than I, Ransom." She tossed her head. "Very well. She's upstairs in the garret."

"In the garret? What's she doing there?"

"What people do in a garret," she replied coolly. "Go up and see."

He bowed, turned on his heel, and left, barely noting the satisfied smiles Violet and Adorna exchanged.

Springall pointed him upward, and a wandering chambermaid nodded toward a narrow stairway. "Miss Higgenbothem's up there, m'lord. Ye can tell which door—she's singing."

And not well, if the maid's puckered lips were anything to go by. He bounded up the stairs, his heels clattering on the wood, and heard Jane warbling in high, wavering tones of unqualified pleasure.

Whatever she was doing, she was enjoying. He started to rap sharply at the door with his mahogany cane, then stopped in loathsome self-awareness. He was trying to warn her, to give her time to hide whatever contemptible project enthralled her. Surely he was tougher than that. If he found her drawing pictures of every ship and admiral in the navy, he would do his duty and send her to hang.

Taking hold of the knob, he twisted and flung the

door open—and saw Jane, dressed in work clothes and working on a rough, man-sized clay statue. A noble brow, a proud nose, a muscled chest . . . and . . . he squinted. Yes, every detail was just as before.

Including a damned tiny, baby fig leaf.

Chapter 24

Treason? Treachery? Disloyalty to England? All these thoughts flew out of Blackburn's mind.

Frustration and rage sprang to the fore. Once again she had created a statue whose likeness could not be mistaken for someone else, yet that insulted him in the most basic way. No man could hide his equipment behind such a small leaf.

Especially not a Quincy.

Just as he had been so many years ago, he was reduced to primal humiliation and fury. "You still don't have it right!" Stepping inside, he slammed the door behind him. "Damn it, Jane." He ripped off his cravat and starched collar. He wrestled his way out of his coat and waistcoat and tossed them on the floor. He opened his shirt so abruptly that the neck string tore. "This! This is what I look like!"

She stood posed, her hands gray with clay, staring with a kind of wonder, and for a brief moment, sanity overruled his rage. Did she think him a madman?

But no. She stared with wonder blended with an

abstract regard. Her work had cast a spell on her, removing the virginal shyness and replacing it with avid curiosity. Deliberately she put down her tools. She wiped her hands on her apron. She walked toward him, and circled him, slowly, looking at his bareness as if it were a marvel of aesthetic delight. Without shyness, her hands reached out and pushed the fine linen shirt off his shoulders. "Beautiful," she murmured. "Better than I'd imagined."

She laid hands on him.

She didn't mean anything by it. He knew that. Her art held her in thrall; the conventions of society held no place in her thoughts.

But he was here. He lived in the now. He was aware of his surroundings, of the proprieties, of himself, of her, of their previous eagerness and their future passion.

Rage cooled. Fire smoldered.

Her fingers molded the column of his neck.

He swallowed, trying to ease the tightness of his throat. She followed the movement with nothing less than adoration, touching his Adam's apple, caressing the muscles as they tensed and released.

She pulled his shirt loose from his trousers, then touched each rib as she lifted the garment.

He strove for breath.

"Let me . . ." She struggled to pull the fine linen over his head.

He ducked his head, lifted his arms, and the shirt slithered to the floor.

She looked at his nipples, her eyes round. She

glanced back at the statue. "I've almost got them right. Don't you think so?"

She didn't wait for him to formulate an answer, but with her fingers circled the small disk, rode over the little bump in the middle. "Yes. They're not so different from my own."

He hoped she felt his touch as acutely as he felt hers.

She looked at him, studied him, pushed him around to view his back. With insatiable interest, she formed his shoulder blades, ran a fingertip over each vertebra of his spine, explored the juncture of skin over biceps.

She was an artist. He had given her what she wanted—a living model.

His heart thumped hard and languorous. His blood rushed to the surface. That part of him in which he held such pride and which she had so insulted stirred and grew in a sudden, adolescent rush of anticipation. She wanted to see him. She adored him, not for his money or his mind or his title, but for his body.

It was a heady notion.

Her hands guided him again to face her. She stroked his arms, noting the direction of each hair, the color of each vein. With her gaze and her touch, she explored each tendon in his hands. She manipulated him as if each part were precious to her. "Look. You have a scar here." She touched the old, whitish proof of a childish folly. "What did you do?"

"Fitz dared me to—"

She stared at his lips. *She* was watching the movement.

He was contemplating yesterday's kiss. "He dared

me to climb out the dormitory window. Jane?''

"You were hurt!''

"Broken bone. Some blood. Jane?''

"So perfect, and yet so human.''

"Jane!''

His desperation penetrated her absorption. "What?''

He took her wrists and guided her fingers to the flap of his trousers. "Here.''

Frowning, she looked into his eyes. No embarrassment flickered there. No doubt, no self-consciousness, hindered her. She didn't know what she would see, but she was vitally, vibrantly interested. "Yes,'' she said. "This is what I want.''

He had never desired a woman like this in his life.

With sure, easy strokes, she unbuttoned him, then slid her hands along his hips and pushed his trousers down.

"Jane, untie the drawers.'' Expectation left him hoarse.

He prompted her, but she didn't need his advice. She thought no more of viewing him than she thought of viewing a marble statue.

But marble was not so hard as he. She was already freeing him from his last scrap of clothing. Except for his boots, and he didn't give a damn about his boots right now.

He just wanted her to see him. Really *see* him, as he was, not as she imagined him to be.

Then she did.

"Oh!''

Just "oh," but that one word made him grow when he thought he could grow no more.

"I've had the proportions wrong." She put her hands on her hips, and she tilted her head to the side as she studied him. "How stupid of me. Of course." She moved around to view him from the side, then walked to the other side and stared as if enthralled. Slowly her hand extended and she touched him with the tip of one finger.

She might have been burning him with a branding iron. His balls twisted tight, his diaphragm clenched. Without thought or pride, he groaned.

She started and snapped her hand back. "Did I hurt you?"

She sounded so anxious, he had to chuckle. Pain could not describe the sensation. "Remember when I touched you yesterday?"

"Yes."

"It hurts . . . like that."

Her eyes, beautiful, green, grew brighter. She looked at him again, her artistic abstraction suspended by the memory of that oh-so-real encounter. "Really. So you like this." Gently she wrapped her palm around the head, and slowly she slid it down to the base.

"Far too much." Putting his hands on her waist, he looked at her, alive, bright with curiosity, and ready to live the life he had denied her. He would not deny her ever again. "Jane, let's finish this."

"I can be who I want to be." She gestured to the statue. "I can live where I want to live. I've been stifled, shut in, cut off from sunlight. But I can grow once more.''

''Me, too.'' He sounded a little too fervent, but she didn't understand.

''I want your boots off.''

She wanted him totally naked.

''I want to see your feet.''

He was bribing her to copulate with him by allowing her to see his body.

Did he care?

Sitting down on the wooden floor, he grasped the heel of his boot.

Kneeling at his feet, she pushed his hands away. ''I'll do it.''

A man's boots were made to fit tight, and normally it took both Blackburn and his valet to get them off. But Jane was strong. As she tugged, each muscle in her upper arms was delineated, clean and pure in its beauty. She was no useless bit of fluff, his Jane. She was a woman, capable and healthy, and he luxuriated in both her ingenious regard and her quiet confidence.

The boots came off, one at a time, and Jane tossed them aside. Each skidded and clattered, contact with the floor no doubt marring their perfect finish.

His valet would be crushed.

Blackburn exulted.

She didn't pretend to be coy. She was unblushingly eager, and his conceit expanded as rapidly as his manhood.

She tugged at the hem of his trousers, stripping them away, then untied his garters and removed his stockings.

He was nude, without a stitch on, sitting with one knee raised and the other extended, in a garret with the westering sun streaming through the windows and a woman kneeling at his feet. It should feel odd.

With Jane, it felt just right.

She laid her hand across his toes. "I never sculpted feet because I didn't think them attractive, but yours are quite handsome."

If it were anyone but Jane, he would suspect seduction.

She was too direct for that. He was not. "Are yours?" he asked with the intention of easing her out of her clothing, and found, to his surprise, he was truly inquisitive.

He wanted to know about her feet. Had his interest grown to obsession?

"My feet are large for a woman's."

"You're large for a woman." He stroked her hand. He touched the knuckles, noting how the clay clung in the creases. Clay filled the cuticles and under her fingernails, too. It stained the skin and flaked off in small patches. It itched, he knew, for she'd touched him when the clay was wet and now he itched, but the discomfort was minor compared to the miracle of her hand, and the delicate, pale skin that belied the power beneath. "I like knowing I don't overwhelm you."

"No." She said it, but her gaze fell to his organ.

"Jane, I promise . . ." What would he promise? That he wouldn't hurt her? He probably would, but his need had grown to such proportions he couldn't deny himself.

She might have been reading his mind. "I want to do this. I may have to flee to the continent afterward, and be scandalous, and live by my art, but I will have some satisfaction out of England." Her hand stroked his calf, massaging and seeking after each thread of muscle. "And out of you." She probed his knee, seemingly insatiable about each bone and ligament that formed him.

Ever so subtly, she ran her palm up the inside of his thigh.

Torment. Or bliss. He didn't know which. A red fog formed before his eyes.

Her thumb traced the cord back to his knee.

The fog cleared slightly, and he said, "You've been studying this."

She leaned forward, closer to him, and her hand dallied on its trip back up. "Art?"

"No. How to make me demented."

"I'm only doing what you did to me."

Disappointment twisted inside him. "Revenge, then."

She paused. She lifted her hand so it hovered over the sensitive skin at the junction of his thigh and his belly. "Is that what it was yesterday?"

He'd said the wrong thing, he realized. She gave the appearance of having forgiven him everything— all the insults, the public compromise, his insulting abandonment. He couldn't have done it, and he assumed she could not, either. But she had never given him reason to doubt her; in this matter, at least, he insulted with his distrust.

"Never." Taking her wrist, he lifted it to his lips

and kissed it. Looking into her eyes, he tried to gratify her with the truths of his soul. "Yesterday was not revenge, Jane. Yesterday was pure pleasure."

Her white teeth bit into her lower lip as she tried to subdue the blossoming of her smile.

With his thumb he touched that lip, and when she released it, he smiled back.

Now happiness shone from her, and he fed on it, bathed in it, absorbed it as his own. "Come, sit on me," he commanded.

"No. You come." She rose and extended her hand to him.

He stared at it, steady as the earth. Then, knowing the significance yet believing in paying his debts, he put his hand in hers and stood.

"There's a sofa back here." She led him behind the screen.

It removed them from direct sight of the door, and in some vague, still functioning corner of his mind he thought that a good thing.

Dropping his hand, she dragged at the long seat cushion until it lay on the ground. "There." She pointed.

He felt odd, almost as if he were the virgin, not knowing for sure what she wanted. He sat down, then stretched out to full length. She just stood there and looked at him. "Jane?" This time he extended his hand.

She took it. Sinking down on her knees beside him, she touched him once more. This time neither art nor respectability distanced her from this reality. Eagerly she ran her hands over his chest, and followed the path of hair down his belly. Again she clasped his rod, then slid to the base. She weighed him in her hands and squeezed.

He grabbed at her. "Softly!"

"Of course." Her touch gentled as she explored the contents inquisitively. "This is so fascinating. I never imagined—"

"Obviously." Rolling onto his side, he clamped his hand over her wrist and lifted it to her buttons. "Disrobe."

She stripped off her apron to reveal a gown even uglier than the previous day's sage monstrosity, and streaked with clay.

"Hurry." She moved efficiently, but not efficiently enough, and he attacked the buttons, too, dragging them free and pushing at the gown. He'd used up all his patience the day before, and he wanted her now.

"I'll do it." She took the gown off over her head.

While her arms were up, he tangled his fingers in the ties of her chemise. "I'll help."

Tossing the gown, she shoved at him. "No!"

He jerked her toward him. She landed on top, and suddenly they were wrestling, fighting for control. He didn't want to hurt her, but she wasn't easy to subdue. He wanted control, but she wouldn't cede him that. They rolled, and he thumped off the cushion onto the floor. While he gasped for breath, she straddled him, and laughed, low and deep.

Leaning down so her face was close to his, she said, "You do as I say."

"Yes." He realized the slit of her pantalettes gaped, and her loins pressed against his. "Whatever you say.'' He grabbed the back of her head and pulled her the rest of the way. Their open mouths met. They fought for the kiss. She sucked his tongue. He surged upward in agonized carnality.

Everything was sharper, fresher, newer, with Jane. He wanted her with all his youthful vigor, and he held her face in his hands. ''Jane, I can't bear to wait.''

''You will.'' She nipped his chin.

Her chemise hung half open, tantalizing him with the sway of her breasts in the shadows. He reached for them. ''Let me—''

''My turn.'' She slipped down him and flattened herself against his body. Her flesh pressed against his, absorbing him in every way but one. Taking his nipple into her mouth, she sucked at it, and blind with lust, he found the bow of her petticoats. He ripped at it, and something tore, the distinct sound of fragile cloth separating thread by thread.

She bit him.

Grabbing her head, he jerked it back. ''Brazen!'' It was a compliment.

He rolled with her, putting her under him, and rose on his knees above her. He grabbed handfuls of petticoat and pantalettes and pulled, bringing everything down around her ankles, and she let him. She even helped him, using her feet to shove the material all the way off.

Such long legs. His hand skimmed her thigh, came to rest on the cleft between her thighs. How many women had he had since that first time he'd touched her? It didn't matter. Jane's scent, her taste, and the sight of her flesh had marked him then, and it marked him now.

With her hands, she pushed her hair out of her eyes, then lifted herself until she was sitting. Then until she had her knees under her. Then she rose until she faced him, both of them kneeling, both of them naked. Sliding her capable, long-fingered hands on his shoulders, she said, "Show me now."

"Like this." He sat on his heels, and with his hands he spread her thighs wider. With his thumb he touched her the way she liked. The way he'd touched her the day before. She gasped, and her fingers tightened on his shoulders. She was deep, mysterious, damp. She was ready; heaven knew he was, too. But the day before he'd touched inside her, and she'd been so tight . . . He took just one moment to prepare her more.

"Now!" But her voice shook.

Smoothly he tilted her onto the cushion and hooked his arms under her knees.

She sat up on her elbows. "What are you doing?"

"Do you think I don't know?" His weight still rested on the attic floor. Her back lay crooked across the soft cushion, and no matter what happened, he was in charge. She just didn't know it.

He slid her toward him, lifted her to him. His penis touched the heat and moisture of her; then nothing mattered but the drive to be inside her. He pressed firmly; she cried out as she sank into the pillows and he sank into her. She closed in around him, almost too tight for comfort. She struggled, fighting to pull him into her.

He used precious breath to chuckle, and maintained his slow, steady pace. "Patience," he whispered. "I'll give you what you want soon enough." Briefly her maidenhead challenged him; contrary, she tried to push him away.

With the strength of his arms, he pulled her legs to their full extension and half lifted her from the cushion; he broke through. He slid home, touching the deepest part of her, and he was done with fortitude. Drawing himself back full length, he thrust again. She fought her legs free. He flattened each hand in the cushion beside her, imprisoning her between his arms and his body. He thrust again. Putting her feet on the floor, she thrust back. This was war. This was strife. This was primitive and basic.

This was mating.

Groans broke from her throat, small at first, then growing to a crescendo. They filled his ears as he filled her body, and he took savage, supreme satisfaction in hearing them, in knowing pleasure had overwhelmed all other sensations.

And he . . . only one thing absorbed him, commanded him, and that was the place where they met and mingled. He had to have her; he *was* having her, but it wasn't enough.

He leaned over her, called her name. "Jane. Look at me, Jane."

Her eyes fluttered open; she stared at him.

Crude eloquence drove him. "See the face of your lover. Not a statue. Not an art object. Your lover."

"Yes." Reaching out, she caressed his cheeks, his neck, his chest. "My lover."

Her touch magnified his sense of triumph, and he increased the pace. Her fingers clenched at his waist, and he increased the pace. She lifted her hips to take all of him—and froze. Her eyes rounded. She trembled, and every muscle deep within her spasmed around him.

Frantic, he crushed her into the cushion. She clawed at his back. He hammered into her. He reached his peak—all motion halted. Arrested in the supreme moment of pleasure, they stared at each other.

This was it. They were mated.

Shuddering, he pumped his seed into her while she held him with all the strength of a woman possessed. And as the frenzy slowly ended and he sank down to cover her with his body, he thought she was possessed. By him.

As he was possessed by her.

Half on, half off the cushion, they lay there as their breathing slowed, as individual consciousness returned. He ought to say something meaningful, he thought. Something that would let her know this had been no random encounter, no throwaway moment. Something had happened here today, something that had never happened to him before, and while he didn't understand it, he at least knew it was significant.

First he had to lift himself off of her. A gentleman always leans on his elbows, and he had proved he was no gentleman. Yet he was oddly reluctant to rise. He had claimed Jane. She comprehended that, he was sure. At the same time, he was reluctant to relinquish any bit of his control, almost as if he thought she would flee at the first chance.

Absurd. Slowly he raised his chest off hers. Her head was turned away, her eyes fixed on the screen, and alarm stabbed at him. With gentle fingers he brushed the wisps of hair off her forehead. "Jane."

Her head turned, and in clear, precise tones, she said, "You need a leaf corresponding to the size of the trunk."

It took a moment to collect himself and perceive her thoughts. "The . . . statue. Yes."

She frowned. "*That's* why you've been so angry?"

This was not going as he'd planned. "Jane, you don't want to talk about this now."

"I want to understand. Is that why everyone laughed?"

She sounded faintly scornful, and annoyance made his voice rough. "Don't dismiss it as a small thing." The pun made him wince.

She didn't even catch it. "Men are odd creatures."

"Men?" She dared say that? When instead of loving murmurs and sweet caresses, she talked about a statue?

"Don't worry. I'll get the proportions right from now on." She struggled to sit up.

He didn't let her. He was still inside her, and with very little provocation he could teach her the proper way to end a love scene.

"Get off." She pushed at him.

"No." He caught her hands.

She tried to free them. He clung grimly. She kicked at his legs. He seated himself firmly. If she wanted a fight, he'd give her one, and show her what the Marquess of Blackburn was truly made of. They struggled silently, only the occasional thump of a foot against the wood floor punctuating the conflict. He was winning, naturally, although she stubbornly refused to concede, when she stopped.

"Yes." He pinned her to the cushion. "You've got to realize I'm stronger and—"

"Sh!" She shushed him forcefully.

"Jane?"

Then he heard it, too. The creak of the stairs. A rap on the door. And Adorna's bright voice as she opened it, saying, "Reverend Rydings, Mr. Southwick, Lord Mallery, Mr. Brockway. I had no idea you gentlemen were so interested in art!"

Beneath Ransom, Jane whimpered.

"This is my aunt's new studio. Aunt Jane is supposed to be in here somewhere . . ." Adorna's footsteps moved into the chamber. "I don't know where she went. Oh, look. A gentleman's boot."

Beyond the screen, silence reigned.

Then Mr. Brockway said, "*Blackburn's* boot."

"Do you really think so?" Adorna asked. "Yes, how silly of me. I recognize the tassels."

Horror etched Jane's face in stark lines.

"There's another boot." Adorna might have been an explorer on an expedition of discovery. "And his coat, and waistcoat, and shirt, and . . ." She paused.

"Trousers." Blackburn recognized Lord Mallery's voice, witty as ever. "Miss Morant, those are called trousers."

"Oh." Adorna sounded surprised. "What do you suppose this means?"

Chapter 25

Marriage. That horrific scene in the studio garret had meant marriage, and as quickly as possible by special license. Between Adorna and Violet, they had made sure of it. Jane had been in an artistic daze that day, but she was no fool. She recognized a well-planned feminine scheme when she saw one.

And Lord Blackburn—Ransom—had gone along willingly. If she hadn't personally seen his dismay, Jane would have thought that he had been in on that disgraceful arrangement.

Blast them. On the very day, almost at the very moment, when she resolved once more to live for her art, to seek her fortune abroad, those conniving women had sent her nemesis to vanquish her.

She looked into the mirror in her new bedchamber, at the half-dressed woman framed there.

Vanquish her, he had since their wedding a week ago. Repeatedly, and with great vigor. With all her will she had resisted. She had ignored him. She had pretended to be elsewhere. She had silently recited poetry.

She hadn't won. Not once. With charm and grace and a devastating knowledge of her body, he had forced pleasure on her. Each time a little of her resentment had been chipped away. Each time she had responded.

Her response apparently did not satisfy him. He knew she hid within the sanctuary of her mind, and he wanted her, all of her, in his arms.

"My lady."

Jane paid no attention.

"Lady Blackburn." The aging maid spoke a little more firmly.

Startled, Jane realized she was being addressed. Looking away from the reflection, she stared at the gown Moira held up.

"Will you wear the gold dimity?"

Jane scarcely refrained from shrugging. "As you wish."

"Yes, the gold dimity." Blackburn leaned against the doorjamb, smiling at her with odious confidence.

What was he doing here, looking so at ease and so completely clad in austere black and white? Always he made her uncomfortable with his proprietary air and his everlasting watchfulness.

"The gold gives a warm cast to your skin, and you must look your best this afternoon. Susan would be insulted with anything less."

Her clothing, or lack of it, put her at a disadvantage. "I am not dressed, my lord."

"So I see." His gaze flirted with the lacy top of her chemise, then slipped across her shoulders, down the slender line of her petticoats, and tickled her stockinged feet. "Most enchantingly undressed."

"If you would leave, I would endeavor to finish."

"My dear Lady Blackburn. It's not necessary that I leave. We are wed, remember?"

He was being charming.

Charm was not a trait she trusted from Ransom Quincy, Marquess of Blackburn. "I can hardly forget."

"Besides, it's not what you think."

"What do I think?"

"You imagine I am an insatiable libertine, intruding into your bedchamber because I am always lusting after you."

Moira twittered.

Jane uttered a soft, shocked sound of protest.

"But that's only half the truth."

"And the other half?"

"I come to help you because, unless you are properly gowned, you will slip in the tricky shoals of society."

Her skin prickled as she watched him in the mirror. She had that uncomfortable sensation again—the one that said he was chasing her, even though he had not moved from his station at the door. And why? He already had her trapped in every way possible. "Your nobility overwhelms me."

"So I should hope." He sighed with extravagant weariness. "The sacrifices one must make . . ."

Jane refused to respond to his bantering. She refused to acknowledge it at all. "It is kind of Lady Goodridge to turn her planned tea into a wedding reception." And indicate her approval of their hurried nuptials.

"It will be a crush." A smile played around Blackburn's mouth as he strolled toward Jane. "Everyone in the ton wants to see if I truly have fallen for Miss Jane Higgenbothem at last."

Stepping behind her, he bent and with his lips softly brushed the nape of her neck. "I will make my adoration clear."

Moira stirred restlessly, clearly unsure whether to go or stay. It was a dilemma she had faced several times in the last week.

"It would not do for us to be late," Jane said.

His hands settled on her shoulders, cupping them gently. "Again."

Heat swept her from the tips of her breasts to her forehead, and he watched the colorful display with satisfaction.

But she answered him tartly enough. "Yes. If we arrive late and leave early *again*, the disgrace will never completely fade."

He started. His fingers tightened, and his smile became nothing more than clenched teeth. "Which disgrace?"

"They found us in my studio a fortnight ago, my lord, and we were married a week later. That is the latest scandal in a long line of scandals involving us, is it not?"

"Oh." He relaxed, easing from his previous tension so quickly she might have imagined it, and tossed that ignominy away with a flick of his finger. "You're a Quincy now. What the ton thinks is of no consequence to us."

He sounded sincerely scornful, yet she hadn't studied him so thoroughly without knowing when something disturbed him. Not passion, but some emotion had indeed held him in its grip—and it involved her.

Sliding out from under his grasp, she turned to face him. "Why did you look concerned when I mentioned the scandal?"

"Did I?" He looked past her into the mirror and adjusted his cravat. "You'd think I was used to scandal by now." Briefly he smiled at her as if to ease the sting. "But we do need to hurry."

"I thought we were Quincys and had no need to fret about such common things."

"True, but we do have to fret about Susan. She would not take our tardiness with equanimity." He snapped his fingers at the maid.

Moira came forward with the gown and would have dressed Jane right there, in front of Blackburn, but Jane led the way behind the screen.

"And we have Adorna to steer through the season." Blackburn's voice sounded closer, as though he would not allow even so simple a thing as the screen to separate them.

Adorna had been thrilled with the wedding, and more than willing to stay with Violet during the brief four-day honeymoon to Tourbillon. But Jane couldn't leave her niece with the Tarlins indefinitely, and in her new position as Lady Blackburn, she could shepherd her through society with as much influence as any society maven. Moira placed the gown over her head, and Jane hurriedly yanked it into place. "Do you mind dealing with Adorna?"

"Not at all. She's a charming girl, but we can't have her growing impatient." Blackburn stepped into view. "She might take it into her head to go on without us."

Jane faced him, holding the neckline up while Moira hurriedly fastened the back. "She wouldn't do that."

"Of course not." He pulled a droll face. "Since her arrival here, I have been much struck by her good sense."

Adorna had moved into Blackburn's household three days ago.

She had been creating havoc ever since.

Not that she meant to. But the marriage of her aunt to the Marquess of Blackburn made an already acceptable maiden positively desirable, even to the most critical of mamas. The gentlemen's morning visits had doubled, the crowd at the balls could not be penetrated, and Jane recognized that expression of wild infatuation on several suitors' faces. She feared another abduction attempt loomed.

Or something worse, for Adorna had been rather pensive and quiet, as if she were deep in thought—an unusual place for her.

"I am almost ready," Jane said.

As they descended the stairs arm in arm, Blackburn glanced down toward the study. "What's he doing here so late in the day?"

Monsieur Chasseur stood in the entry, his fists

clenched and his head down. "I don't know." When they reached the entry, Jane called, "Is there a problem, monsieur?"

The French tutor's head snapped up. "Lady Blackburn. Ah. *Non.* I simply came by to assure myself Mademoiselle had learned her French phrase perfectly."

"How dedicated," Blackburn drawled. "Had she?"

Monsieur Chasseur's tight smile fairly radiated frustration. "Miss Morant is a challenge, as always, my lord, but we proceed *néanmoins.*" He bowed. "You are ready for the reception, and I must go."

"*Au revoir*, Monsieur Chasseur." Adorna stood in the doorway of the study and waved at him limply. "Until tomorrow."

"*A demain,*" he said.

"A . . . what?" Adorna wrinkled her nose.

"*A demain.* That means, 'Until tomorrow.' I have told you before, *a demain* means—" Monsieur Chasseur halted, finger lifted, a ruddy flush on his pale face. "*Pas importe, mademoiselle.* Never mind."

Blackburn coughed as the tutor stormed out of the house, and Jane knew he did it to cover his mirth. "It's not courteous to laugh," she said.

"But you want to, too," he answered.

It was true. She did. But if she gave in and laughed with him, it would undermine her justifiable resentment. And if she lost even a smidgen of her rage, that irrepressible hope would burst forth. She'd start to remember . . . remember how much she worshiped Blackburn, how a mere glance from his somber eyes thrilled her, how his conversation always fascinated her.

How she loved him.

If she let those memories loose, and gave in to the hope and the love, she would be vulnerable once more. And if he spurned her once again, she didn't know how—or if—she would recover from the blow.

"I never know what Monsieur Chasseur is talking about," Adorna said, clearly suffering from a frustration of her own. "He's so intense. He never smiles. And he teaches me the stupidest things to say."

"Like what?" Blackburn took Jane's redingote from his butler and helped her into it.

One of the footmen rushed to help Adorna into her fashionable cropped jacket. "Today I am to say, *Une maison bleu de près le pain de miche a beaucoup les habits rouge.*"

Blackburn took Jane's hand.

She took it back to put on her gloves.

He translated, "The blue house near the round loaf of bread has many scarlet coats."

Jane looked up at him sharply. He had once claimed not to speak French, yet he interpreted like a native.

"Are you finished?" he asked her.

"With what?"

"Your gloves."

"Yes."

He took her hand again, and said to Adorna, "That does sound odd. Are all the phrases he teaches you so unusual?"

"Yes! If I must take French, I want to be able to

say, 'I need that silk gown' or 'You're such a big, strong man.' " The last was accompanied by a flutter of lashes and a practiced coo. Then Adorna's eyes flashed indignation. "Something useful. Not this nonsense."

Recalling Adorna's ineptitude with the language, Jane suggested, "Perhaps you're simply not remembering your daily phrase correctly."

Adorna stomped her dainty foot. "I am! Besides, when the gentlemen ask me what I learned, no one corrects me."

Blackburn's hand tightened painfully on Jane's. "Gentlemen?"

"Yes. They ask me, and I tell them."

"Who asks you?" Blackburn insisted.

"Everyone. It's the style to ask me." Adorna shrugged as she tied her bonnet under her chin. "I don't know why. I think it makes them feel superior because no matter how bad they are, I'm worse."

"It can't be that!" Jane protested.

"Can you think of a different reason?" Adorna asked.

Jane couldn't.

"The carriage is at the door, my lord," Blackburn's butler announced.

Whent wasn't the same butler Blackburn had engaged eleven years ago. Indeed, none of the servants, regardless of the length of their employment, seemed to remember Jane's first visit. She had been treated with the greatest of respect and the first glimmerings of affection, and that added to the burden of hope within her bosom.

Wretched, undying hope.

Blackburn kissed Jane's gloved palm, then released it to offer his arm. She didn't hesitate, but laid her hand on it at once. To hesitate might indicate apprehension, and she would not have him think she was aware of him in any but the most superficial way.

He then offered his arm to Adorna. With a pretty smile, Adorna accepted, and he led them onto the street and assisted them into the carriage. When the horses were under way, he said, "Adorna, I'll teach you a new phrase, and you can use it instead of that absurd one Monsieur Chasseur taught you. Would you like that?"

"Oh, yes." Adorna leaned forward.

Blackburn turned his attention to Jane. "Do you have any objection?"

"Not at all. If it helps her learn French, I would be glad. I only wish I had thought of it. Starting tomorrow, I will instruct Monsieur Chasseur to teach her phrases she wants to learn," Jane said. Blackburn looked so very stern; what was he thinking?

"You are a very intelligent woman, Jane." With a hint of his old brooding, he said, "I don't know if I admire that or not."

No, he wouldn't. Men didn't admire intelligent women, and Jane stifled an indecorous sigh.

Adorna missed the undertones, and chimed right in. "She *is* smart. She's smarter than anyone I know. My mother used to say Aunt Jane was so smart it was going to get her into trouble one day."

Adorna's praise seemed to deepen Blackburn's cynicism. "So it has."

"Yes, but you married her anyway." Adorna beamed impartially at both of them.

"So kind of him," Jane said astringently.

Blackburn studied her with that nerve-racking concentration. He was looking for something, Jane couldn't say what, but she stared back at him with a haughty lift of the chin. Let him make of her as he wished. She didn't care.

"Very well, then," he said. "I will speak to Monsieur Chasseur. Leave him to me."

"As you wish." Turning to Adorna, she said, " 'I want to buy a gown for me' is *Je voudrais acheter une robe pour moi.*"

"How about *Une maison bleu de près le pain de miche a quelque-uns les habits rouge,*" Ransom suggested.

Adorna frowned in suspicion.

Jane took a breath, then let it out. She felt as if she were missing some vital clue that would tell her his intent. " 'The blue house near the round loaf of bread has *few* scarlet coats'? How will *that* interest Adorna?"

"We have so little time before we reach the reception." Blackburn contemplated Adorna intensely, seeming to compel her with his conviction. "Such a small change will be easy for her to remember."

That didn't make sense to Jane, but Adorna nodded. *"Une maison bleu de près le pain de miche a quelque-uns les habits rouge,"* she repeated. "I can remember that."

Chapter 26

"*You're a good friend of Blackburn's. You were his* best man. How long do you really think she can hold him?" Lady Kinnard asked, sotto voce, then leaned forward to hear Fitz's answer.

Fitz indicated Blackburn, standing at the far end of the receiving line and accepting congratulations with an air of smug complacency. "I don't know. Why don't you ask him?"

Lady Kinnard drew back with a hiss, then rearranged her face into a smile and stepped on to Miss Morant. "So lucky for you that your aunt married well," Fitz heard her say.

"Lucky for Lord Blackburn to have found her again." Miss Morant turned to Lady Goodridge. "Isn't that right, my lady?"

"Absolutely," Lady Goodridge proclaimed. "I have schemed for this moment since I realized Jane's good breeding marched hand in hand with her great artistic talent. She's worthy to be a Quincy"—her gaze bored into Lady Kinnard's daughter who followed close to her mother—"which is more than I can say for other unmarried young ladies who made their curtsy this year."

As the offended and effectively silenced Lady Kinnard moved on to Lord and Lady Tarlin, Fitz looked toward the last arrivals in the line that, at its height, had stretched across the main floor of the hideously pink ballroom, up the stairs, and, as far as he knew, out the door. Now they hurried to the tables, anxious to quench their thirst, eat, and gossip with their friends over this most curious of unions.

Yet none of the guests, Fitz knew, could compete with the approaching couple for sheer oddness. The Vicomte de Sainte-Amand, always so well dressed, always so scornful, stood with his arm around an enfeebled man of indeterminate years. The man, whoever he was, had the waxen complexion of one who faced a not-too-far-off death, and he leaned on a cane with the dedication of one who would fall without its support.

Fitz had never seen the chap before, nor did he understand why he came here, to this celebration, but his heart went out to both de Sainte-Amand, struggling to support him, and to the fellow who looked so anxiously toward the newlyweds. "May I help you? Could I fetch you a chair?" Fitz asked.

The stranger didn't even look at him, as if his lids were too heavy to lift.

"We can manage," de Sainte-Amand said. "He should not be out. He came only to honor Miss Higgenbothem. Or, shall I say, Lady Blackburn."

The stranger murmured something in French too

low and rapid for Fitz to follow, and de Sainte-Amand led him past Miss Morant as if she weren't there— something Fitz had never seen any man do. Clearly the stranger was very ill.

Miss Morant shrugged her shoulders at Fitz's questioning glance, and only de Sainte-Amand returned Lady Goodridge's greeting. By now the Frenchmen had everyone's attention as they hobbled past Lord and Lady Tarlin and stopped directly in front of the new Lady Blackburn.

Her countenance was a mixture of stark horror and amazed gladness. "Monsieur Bonvivant, I never expected . . . I'm honored."

"I had to come . . . to congratulate you on the occasion . . . of your marriage." His English was accented, his delivery interrupted by painful breaths.

"Thank you." Lady Blackburn stepped forward. De Sainte-Amand released him, and she wrapped the stranger in her arms. *"Merci beaucoup."*

His cane dangled from his hand as he returned her hug, touching his cheek to hers, first one, then the other.

Blackburn didn't like that, and Fitz could almost understand why. Jane had been coolly stoic during the hours in the receiving line, the picture of a proper English marchioness, projecting emotion to no one . . . not even to her bridegroom. Now this foreigner elicted an uninhibited display of sympathy, kindness, pleasure, reverence, even . . . love.

"Dear wife." Blackburn stepped forward and loomed over them. "Introduce me to our guest."

Jane tucked her arm into the stranger's, and together they faced Ransom. "This is Monsieur Bonvivant." She said it so proudly, so defiantly, Fitz had the impression they were all supposed to know who this Bonvivant was.

Fitz, at least, had never heard of him.

"He is one of the foremost art teachers in Europe," she said. "He is . . . my art teacher."

"Ah." Blackburn looked to Lady Tarlin, who shook her head in bewilderment. "What an honor to meet you, sir. You have . . . helped my wife with her . . . sketching?"

Bonvivant swelled like a toad in mating season. "It is not sketching!" He waved his cane, and de Sainte-Amand grabbed for him as he swayed. "Sketching is for *ladies*. What Mademoiselle Higgenbothem does—it is painting. It is life. Your wife, she has a wonderful talent, especially with the clay, and you will surely foster it."

Jane patted his hand. "Don't disturb yourself, monsieur. I couldn't bear it if you made yourself ill over this."

"Over you." He smiled on her, a painful smirk that exposed yellow teeth bared almost to the bone by receding gums. "You have the talent. You are worth everything."

Fitz couldn't remember a time when he had seen Blackburn so nonplussed. "She had a studio at Lady Tarlin's."

"But will she have a studio at your home?" Bonvivant fixed his sunken gaze on Ransom. "You have married her, and you have a responsibility to future generations to allow her artistic freedom."

"Future generations." Blackburn fingered his cravat. "Yes. I must think of the future generations."

Not the same future generations Bonvivant was thinking about, Fitz suspected. No, Blackburn was thinking about the future generations of Quincys, and the pleasure of begetting them.

But Bonvivant seemed satisfied. "Good." He sighed heavily, and the brief flare of personality and fire faded. "Then I have done my duty. Come, de Sainte-Amand, I am ready to go home."

Silence fell as they watched the two odd companions walk away, de Sainte-Amand staggering under Bonvivant's rapidly collapsing weight. Lady Goodridge summoned a footman, who hurried to help, and everyone tried not to look at Jane, who wiped a tear off her cheek with one gloved finger.

Miss Morant broke the silence. "Aunt Jane, is that where you were always disappearing to? To go to your art lessons?"

"Not always, dear." Jane's voice sounded husky. "I only had a few lessons before . . . all the other events interrupted."

Blackburn placed his fingers on his forehead. "At de Sainte-Amand's home?" he asked.

"Yes."

Fitz thought Blackburn would say more, but he laughed, a staccato burst of swiftly contained amusement, and turned to the others. "Any other guests are too late for a receiving line," he said. "Jane and I will greet them, of course, but the rest of you should go and enjoy yourselves."

"Thank goodness," Adorna said. "My curtsy knee has almost given out."

"One does not discuss one's *knees* in a mixed group, Miss Morant." Lady Goodridge admonished her almost absently. "It is *unseemly*."

Fitz snorted expressively.

Lady Goodridge ignored him with all the majesty of an Amazon queen.

He ignored her right back. He was Gerald Fitzgerald, last of the Irish Fitzgeralds and as important a sort as any man jack here—in his own opinion, at least. Some might not agree, but she didn't matter. Fitz looked sideways at her. She didn't matter at all.

If she wouldn't cooperate with his plans to support himself through his attractiveness and virility, there was always that offer from the French to consider.

And he would do so. See if he didn't.

"If you wish, Miss Morant," Lady Goodridge said with awful decorum, "and if you have your aunt's consent, you may go and find your *friends*, provided you follow *all rules of propriety* without *exception*."

"Will you go with her, Violet, and supervise?" Jane asked with understandable caution.

"Yes, dear." Lady Tarlin touched cheeks with Jane. "Although I keep telling you, Adorna never gave us a moment's trouble when she stayed with us."

"Except for that time she disappeared with that old Viscount of Ruskin—oof." Lord Tarlin held his mistreated ribs while his lady smiled fixedly and rubbed her elbow. "Never a moment's trouble," he said hastily. "But we'll both go with her just to be sure."

Adorna bobbed another curtsy, as graceful as her first of the evening, and the little party decamped as rapidly as possible. Fitz thought that the former Miss Higgenbothem watched after them wistfully, and Blackburn seemed unusually intent on Miss Morant. But as if his thoughts were too fantastic, he shook his head and returned his concentration to the group before him.

Moving to face Blackburn, Fitz offered his hand. "Marriage has changed you."

Blackburn took it, and the men shook heartily. "For the better, I hope."

"You could only change for the better," Fitz quipped, and squeezed hard.

Blackburn pulled back his hand, flexed it with a wince of pain. "You win, both in strength and in wit."

"No." Fitz bowed to the new Lady Blackburn as she stood beside her husband. Taking Jane's fingers, he brushed a kiss across them and in his deepest voice roughened by his best brogue, he said, "You've won all that's important, for you have taken to wife the loveliest woman in the land."

Jane, Fitz thought, didn't seem taken in by his balderdash.

In fact, she looked as if she wished to roll her eyes, although she replied politely. "Thank you, Mr. Fitzgerald. That is a charming compliment."

"I'm known for them," Fitz said. "But for you, I can do better. How about if I say—only Blackburn deserves you, for although it took a decade he was the only one smart enough to see the wit and talent which you embrace in your very person.''

Obviously she didn't like that compliment, either. In fact, Fitz thought for a moment she was going to spout a very frank expletive—or cry. But she gathered her composure and turned to her new sister-in-law. To Lady Goodridge, with her upright morals and her snobbish opinion of herself and her fabulous fortune languishing in need of spending.

"I can see why you like Mr. Fitzgerald," Jane said. "He feeds a woman's conceit very skillfully."

"Yes. *Any* woman's conceit," Lady Goodridge said acidly. "If you would *excuse* me, I have my duties as *hostess*."

She stalked away, and against his will, Fitz found himself watching and admiring. She was a magnificent figure of a woman, even if she was older and less nubile than . . . say . . . Adorna. Or Jane. Still, Lady Goodridge had something about her . . . "An obnoxious conceit," Fitz said, more to himself than to Blackburn. "Quincys have an insufferably superior opinion of themselves."

Blackburn answered, echoing his sister all unknowing. "Superiority is not an opinion. It is a fact."

Delighted in this consistent manifestation of arrogance in his friend, Fitz asked Jane, "How do you bear him?"

"He is very easy to bear." The words were correct, but Jane sounded extraordinarily composed for a woman in the throes of love.

Still, Fitz knew how long she'd cherished a tendre for Blackburn. Surely there couldn't be trouble among the roses already—although Ransom's gloved hand clenched.

Then Fitz thought he saw the reason for that. "Oh, blast. Here are our latecomers. Athowe and his Frederica."

Blackburn glanced toward the top of the stairs where the earl and his lady stood, waiting to be announced. "Such a pleasure," he drawled in deadly sarcasm.

He sounded just like the Blackburn Fitz had always known, and Fitz was glad. In his opinion, Blackburn had been a little more wounded by the war than he admitted. Instead, marriage had returned him to his former self.

"Shall I leave you to greet your friends in peace?" Fitz savored the chance to tease.

Blackburn clamped a hand on his wrist. "At your own risk."

"Lord and Lady Athowe." Jane was the picture of the social lioness as she greeted the pair. "How good of you to come."

"Wouldn't miss it!" Athowe said heartily, taking Jane's hand and kissing it fervently. "Talk of the town. Incredible coup, Miss Higgenbothem."

"Lady Blackburn." Ransom took her hand back and tucked it into his own. "She is Lady Blackburn now."

"He's hardly likely to want to admit that." Frederica aptly wore sour-apple green. "He still worships at her shrine."

An awkward silence struck, and Fitz interposed hastily, "As do we all."

"But it's so touching!" Frederica laid her hand on Jane's arm. "All these years I've heard, 'If only you were like Miss Higgenbothem, Frederica, we wouldn't be in financial straits.' And 'Miss Higgenbothem wouldn't have gambled away all her allowance, Frederica.' "

"Frederica," Athowe said so lamely, Fitz wanted to smash his fist into his face. "That's enough."

"You wouldn't have liked being wed to him, you know, Jane." Frederica cast him a venomous glance. "He's a pinch-purse."

"This is a ludicrous conversation," Blackburn snapped.

"Athowe was courting her all those years ago," Frederica said. "Don't you recall, Blackburn?"

At the back of Fitz's mind, a memory stirred. B'God, Athowe *had* been dancing attendance on Miss Higgenbothem; he'd created quite a stir by abandoning Frederica for her. Then, after the scandal, Frederica had soothed his wounded feelings with generous applications of split-tail, and they'd married. At least, that was the story as Fitz remembered it.

And from Blackburn's expression, he remembered, too.

Yet with remarkable composure, Jane said, "My being married to Lord Athowe was never a question."

Fitz's admiration for the woman deepened.

"That's not what Athowe says," Frederica taunted. "Is it, Athowe? He always reminisces about those moments in the secluded alcove. Why don't you tell us about them, Jane? I've only heard Athowe's version, repeated over and over again."

Jane glanced from Frederica to Athowe, perplexed but not dismayed. "I'm afraid I don't remember."

And she didn't. Fitz would have wagered his deceitful soul on it. Her countenance exhibited no pucker of guilt, her color didn't change, and she stood quietly, waiting for the next round to be fired.

Blackburn still held her hand, and Fitz saw the flex of his fingers as he gripped her tighter. "That's that, then. We'll hear no more about this."

Frederica seemed taken aback, and Athowe positively apoplectic. Then a slow, catlike smile spread across Frederica's face. "You really don't remember, do you?" she asked Jane. She turned to Athowe. "She doesn't remember. Your most holy moment, the apex of your wretched life, and the lady doesn't remember!" Throwing back her head, she laughed long and shrill. "This is too good."

Red-faced and humiliated, Athowe never once looked at Jane as he mumbled an apology. Grabbing Frederica's arm, he yanked her away. The laughter trailed back toward them, still shrill and with an edge of recklessness that made Fitz want to swear off women for at least . . . well, for a while.

Narrowed-eyed, Blackburn looked after them. "I wonder why Susan invited them."

"I wonder *if* Susan invited them," Fitz responded.

Blackburn considered Fitz. "I hadn't thought of that." Without hesitation, he turned to his wife. Lifting their linked hands, he kissed the back of hers. "May I offer you refreshments?"

If a moment of suspicion had crossed his mind, he gave no indication of it. Fitz hid a grin. Trust Blackburn to treat Frederica's accusations with the disdain they deserved.

"I am thirsty," Jane answered. "And at the risk of offending Lady Goodridge in absentia, my curtsy knee also hurts."

Fitz noted that Jane didn't even excuse herself or offer an explanation for her behavior eleven years ago. And remembering the former Miss Higgenbothem's attachment to Ransom, he suspected she had always had the good sense to ignore Athowe's attentions.

As he was being ignored.

The comparison hurt, as did the knowledge he would soon be forced to make a decision.

De Sainte-Amand was pressing for an answer, his mother's health was worsening yet again, and Fitz had no options. None at all.

"If Fitz would procure you a chair," Blackburn said, "I would procure you a drink, and something to eat."

"Gladly," Fitz agreed.

"I'm not hungry," she said.

Blackburn again kissed her hand, this time with a little more fervor. "I'll tempt you."

Fitz waited until Blackburn had walked away before he located a chair, then offered his arm. "I must tell you, Lady Blackburn, that I stood in line here for two hours, and waited the better part of twenty years, for this moment."

"What moment is that, Mr. Fitzgerald?" She let him lead her to her seat, than sank down with a weary sigh.

"To see my best friend married, and have the cynical bastard—beg pardon, my lady—stand guard before his new wife like a man convinced someone would steal her away. He's fallen, and fallen hard." Fitz rubbed his palms together.

She appeared politely incredulous. "Has he?"

"Everyone can see that. Look at them watching him and you. Look at them buzzing about his infatuation."

She smiled without warmth. "Look at them wondering how long it will last before he banishes me to the country."

Her reply halted his celebration and shook his delight. She sounded as if she wondered the same thing.

But she was in love. Of course, she had to be.

"Marriage is not so bad, heh? Not even to that old man."

"Not at all." Jane smiled stiffly. "In one fell swoop, marriage has elevated me twice as far as scandal had dropped me, and solved my worries about the future."

He looked at her, beautifully dressed, attractively coifed, sitting so upright and composed in her chair. He wouldn't have thought it of her, but she must be suffering bridal nerves. Pulling up a chair, he sat close beside her and leaned forward, his elbows on his knees and his hands clasped together. "I know Blackburn well, and while he is many things, not all of them admirable, I assure you he is steadfast. He has taken his vows, and he will cleave to them."

"Whether he wishes to or not. How flattering."

Nerves? This was more of a full-blown trauma! ''He wouldn't have wed you if he didn't want to. At the risk of being impertinent, I would remind you he didn't before.''

Her color rose, but she answered steadily, ''It hadn't gone as far before.''

''I don't know much about what happened''—except what every one of the witnesses had said—''but it wouldn't have gone as far this time if he hadn't ultimately been willing to wed.''

She didn't answer, but began a slow, systematic twisting of her handkerchief.

''Look, what other reason can you give for his pursuit of you?''

''I don't know, but he's not telling all the truth.''

That jolted Fitz a little. He'd suspected the same thing. But what had Blackburn to hide? ''Who ever tells all the truth?'' he asked, adroitly turning the question. ''Have you told him every secret you hold?''

''I don't have any . . . oh.'' She remembered something, for she stopped in midsentence. ''No, I suppose I haven't.''

''There, you see.'' Fitz cranked his head around to the front of her until she was forced to look at him. ''Blackburn is chained fast, and you have done it.''

''He is not a dog to be kept on a leash.''

''No.'' Fitz chuckled with relish. ''He's a stallion and you—'' Abruptly he realized the inappropriateness of repeating Blackburn's analogy. ''My lady, you won't be sorry you wed him.''

She thought about his assurances, and her troubled expression lightened. "Call me Jane."

B'God, he had missed his calling. He should have been a reverend who counseled the newlywed. "Jane. And you call me Fitz."

"Fitz . . . you think I can trust him?"

"With your life."

She pressed her flattened palms to her heart. "I was more worried about his fidelity."

"You can trust him with that, too."

Chapter 27

Blackburn filled a plate for Jane and started back across the ballroom, watching the throng around Adorna the entire time. All those gentlemen—all those suspects—hung on her every word as if they were coined in gold. Perhaps one of them would ask to hear a particular French phrase, and rather than hearing the passage Monsieur Chasseur had selected, he would take note of Blackburn's abridged version.

Blackburn avoided a tipsy matron.

And perhaps not. Since working for Mr. Smith, Blackburn found himself imagining plots at every turn, but this one seemed a little outlandish even to him. It was surely a mediocre way to pass messages.

Yet using Adorna's poor French as code might be only one of the methods used to relay information, and if Blackburn had broken the first link of the French Intelligence chain, perhaps the remaining links could be deduced.

He glanced again at Adorna. If what he hoped was

true, he should leave her alone to speak to whoever desired it.

And he would go back to court his wife.

Jane held herself rigidly erect as the carriage lurched through the dark London streets on the way from the reception. She didn't want to fall against Blackburn. She hadn't voluntarily touched him since their hurried wedding. Yet Fitz's assurances clung to her mind, and she didn't know what to think. Fitz admired Blackburn, that much was clear, and it was also clear he did so without illusion. After vouching for Blackburn's good character, he had then regaled her with tales of their early life together, laughing at every manifestation of Blackburn's insufferably superior attitude.

She'd laughed, too, for the first time in a fortnight, and laughed harder when she'd looked up to see Blackburn, holding a plate and cup, glowering down at her.

So now she was in a quandary. Give up her grudge against Blackburn and admit that maybe, just maybe, he had married her because he wanted to do the right thing, because he desired her, and because he . . . liked her.

Or remain disgruntled. And how long could she keep that up? She was a practical woman with a basically pleasant nature. She knew she couldn't continue forever with this coldness to her husband . . . especially when she loved him so.

She stared into the darkness pooling at her feet.

Yes, she loved him with all her wretchedly consistent heart.

So she would allow herself to let go of her anger, and if that little bit of hope crept in, that hope that he would someday love her back . . . well, she wouldn't encourage it. But she wouldn't deny it, either.

"Jane, you never told me you were taking art lessons." His voice sounded smooth and warm, like syrup heated before the fire.

Automatically she went on the defensive. "I only took a few."

"Monsieur Bonvivant seemed impressed with your talent." Blackburn didn't *sound* revolted by her gift.

"Yes. Well . . . yes, so he said."

"How did you find this foremost art teacher from France?"

"When de Sainte-Amand met me, he recognized me from an early painting I'd done." She didn't mean to brag about her early work; Blackburn might take it badly. "You remember."

"In Susan's garden."

"Yes. De Sainte-Amand invited me to his home to meet Monsieur Bonvivant." The excitement she'd felt! The fear and anticipation! "I couldn't resist. When he said he'd seen and admired my work, I was so flattered." She realized she was burbling, remembering that moment when Monsieur had fixed her with his large, long-suffering eyes and uttered the first official words of praise she'd ever heard.

Embarrassed, she stopped talking.

Blackburn turned toward her and slid his arm behind her on the seat. "Tell me more."

He seemed almost encouraging, but Jane knew better. All proper English gentlemen were uncomfortable with her talent, Blackburn with more reason than most. "I went when I could, and he taught me so much in just a few hours. I was excited, I wanted to tell everyone, but I've never been encouraged . . ." *To revel in my talent.* No, she couldn't say that. That sounded like whining, and it wasn't that she pitied herself. Only that she'd been practical and accepted what had to be done, just as generations of women had done before her. "That's all."

His hand rubbed her arm through her sleeve. "So you will continue."

Straining her eyes through the obscurity of night, she tried to read his expression, but she could see only the faint glisten of his eyes. He sounded carefully neutral, and she used the same tone when she answered. "I would like to, but I understand if it's not possible."

He shifted her toward him. "We have those future generations to think about."

"I don't expect to be a master, but—"

Lowering his head, he spoke softly in her ear. "I was talking about the future generations of Quincys."

"Oh." Air swirled along the sensitive whorls, and goose bumps rose on her skin. "You mean children."

"Our children." His lips touched the tender spot on her neck just along her hairline. "You wouldn't neglect them."

"Neglect?" Disappointment quivered through her. He didn't want her to paint. He didn't want her to sculpt. She knew that; the man had been subjected to

ridicule because of her work. This came as no surprise.

He wanted her to be his wife, to bear his babies, to
devote herself to the family to the exclusion of all
else. She wanted that, too, and yet . . .

"I couldn't neglect children."

"Good." He almost purred as he tilted her chin
with his thumb and followed the cord from her neck
down to her collarbone. "I knew you wouldn't."

Two dreams. One to create a masterpiece of humanity that would resonate with passion for all to see.
The other . . . just to marry Blackburn, and be happy.

For so many years, she would have done anything
to achieve those dreams. Now she had to sacrifice one
to obtain the other.

Two dreams. Only one could triumph.

Turning to Blackburn, she wrapped her arms
around his neck and pressed close to his chest.
"When we get home, do you think we could work on
those future generations?"

"You've lost him already."

Jane jumped, but didn't turn. She recognized the
voice. Frederica, Countess of Athowe, had sought her
out to say what everyone was thinking.

"He's following your niece like a stallion scenting
a mare."

Clenching the balcony's balustrade, Jane stared
down at the crowd around Adorna. Blackburn's head
lingered close. He didn't interfere with the other gentlemen; indeed, he seemed to encourage them. But
these actions were not the behavior of an infatuated

husband. They were the actions of a disgruntled lover.

And why? Jane didn't know. Since their reconciliation in the carriage five nights ago, they had spent every moment together, either passionately entwined, resting after being passionately entwined, or preparing to be passionately entwined. Oh, they had slept occasionally. They even ate once in a while. But for the most they had been creating the kind of unbreakable bond one seldom saw but always dreamed about.

Or so Jane thought.

Until today, when his valet had brought a message to their bedchamber. Blackburn had risen, and read it, and in a voice absent of inflection, he'd said, "We're going to attend the ball at the Manwins'."

Now those who marveled at Blackburn's dedication to his plain new wife were having a laugh, and at Jane's expense.

"How humiliating for you." Frederica's tone grew in depth and viciousness. "But you must have known it could never have lasted."

Turning, Jane stared down at Frederica. "I would like to paint you."

Frederica lifted her brows and smirked.

"Not as a human, but as a badger, all teeth and bristling fur." Indeed, Jane could almost see the sketch in her mind, and imagined adding it to her portrait portfolio.

Leaning forward, Frederica bristled and bared those teeth. "You are a bitch. You come to London and steal the man I've chosen—"

"You chose Blackburn?"

"No, Athowe. He was mine until you showed up."

Jane's head reeled. This business with Athowe was puzzling. She had been nothing but an interlude for him, and he had fled her willingly enough when scandal hit. "He was yours after I left, too. You mistake a brief infatuation on his part for something more."

"Really?" Frederica put her hands on her hips. "When all I've heard for the past ten years is *Jane*. I'm sick of it."

"I don't want Athowe. I never wanted him."

"That's the worst of it, isn't it? He wanted you. You wanted Blackburn. I wanted Athowe. And no one wanted me." Frederica drew back, her cheeks a ghastly pink beneath her lead powder. "That's why it's such a delight to see Blackburn betray you so quickly."

Jane stared over the rail again. Blackburn was still there at Adorna's side, and Jane was faint with jealousy.

Jealous of her own niece, when she didn't even really believe there was anything between them. Blackburn had never, ever indicated any interest in Adorna. Not even from the first moment he'd laid eyes on her.

Jane knew that, because she'd been so surprised. Most men were bug-eyed and slobbering at first sight of Adorna; Blackburn had been engrossed by *Jane*.

Although there was that one time in the carriage on the way to the reception, when Blackburn had taught Adorna a new French phrase. They'd seemed almost to communicate without words then, but Jane could have sworn the fascination had been purely academic.

"And now you don't even have your art," Frederica said with blatantly spurious sympathy.

Jane tore her gaze from the couple below. "What?"

"You've given up your art for your true love. Isn't that right?"

That got Jane's attention. Only yesterday she had sent a farewell message to Monsieur Bonvivant, trying with unsteady eloquence to explain that, out of practical considerations, she had given up her impossible dream. Bonvivant did not leave de Sainte-Amand's; his impairment made him reluctant to display himself. He had come to the reception only to honor her, and his seclusion, even within de Sainte-Amand's home, was complete. So how had word spread so quickly? "Why do you say that?"

"My French tutor told me today. What's his name? That earnest young man—"

"Monsieur Chasseur?"

"Yes, that's him." Frederica smoothed her charcoaled brows with one finger, and Jane noted that the nail was chewed to the quick. "He's such a bore, and so intense I can scarcely bear the lessons. So when he hands me a piece of interesting gossip, I would hardly forget it."

"Monsieur Chasseur says I have given up art." Jane leaned over the rail at the dance floor again. This time she looked carefully, searching for de Sainte-Amand. "How does he know that?"

"I don't know. I suppose he heard you say so when he was teaching your niece." Frederica leaned over the rail. "She's so pretty. How do you stand it?"

"It's not something we talk about."

"Yes, I would hate to talk about her, especially if she's already stolen your husband."

"No, I mean my art. We don't talk about it."

Jane found de Sainte-Amand. He stood alone, his gaze darting from one person to another. He started to walk around the ballroom but stopped, and stared longingly at the clump of men around Adorna.

That day at the beach, de Sainte-Amand had indicated that he knew Monsieur Chasseur only vaguely. Yet Monsieur Chasseur must have seen Monsieur Bonvivant or spoken intimately with de Sainte-Amand; there was no other explanation.

Fitz came up to him and spoke, and de Sainte-Amand answered with palpable agitation.

"I wonder what this means," Jane said absently. "De Sainte-Amand is acting oddly." As oddly as Ransom.

"So's Athowe," Frederica muttered. "As soon as the news came today, he went mad with fury."

"Athowe?" Jane said, surprised. "Fury?" Then, "News? What news?"

"Frederica," Athowe spoke from behind them. "Stop tormenting Miss Higgenbothem."

Jane twirled and saw Athowe standing a little too close for comfort.

Frederica jumped as guiltily as any woman caught gossiping about her husband.

"Go on, woman." He was smiling at Jane affably, one hand thrust into his waistcoat, and all the while talking to Frederica in a tone that made Jane want to cringe. "Miss Higgenbothem doesn't need to listen to your poison."

Frederica recovered her composure almost at once, and smiled her puckered, taunting smile. ''She's Lady Blackburn. She married her true love, remember?''

Athowe turned his head. He looked at his wife.

Whatever Frederica saw in his face frightened her, for she backed away rapidly. ''I'm leaving,'' she said. ''But remember, Athowe, what she said at the reception. There was never a chance that you two would marry.''

He took a step.

She ran.

Jane wished she could be anywhere else right now. Even facing Blackburn with his perfidy would be better than witnessing the ugly scene between husband and wife.

Yet Athowe spoke mildly as if the incident had never occurred. ''You'll have to excuse my wife.'' He came to stand beside Jane. ''She doesn't know when to stop talking.''

Uneasy in his presence, and not comfortable with any discussion of spouses, Jane shrugged. ''She doesn't bother me.''

''How fortunate you are. I wish I could say the same.'' Leaning his elbows against the balustrade, he watched the crowd below, taking special note of Blackburn and Adorna, Jane was sure. ''You can almost smell the jubilation in the air tonight.''

''Jubilation?'' Down on the floor, Blackburn never spoke to Adorna. He just watched and listened, and if anything, that made Jane more miserable. At least Adorna should have to coo at him to make him worship her. ''About what?''

''My dear Miss—''

She shot him a glare.

Smoothly he changed. ''Lady Blackburn, haven't you heard the report?''

Of course she hadn't heard any report. She'd been avoiding her friends all evening.

''A ship full of French soldiers came ashore at Breadloaf Rock near Dover.''

Athowe enunciated each word, and looked at her as if searching for something. Pleasure? Excitement?

Blackburn had abandoned her for Adorna. Did Athowe really think she cared about the French?

''They attacked the garrison there,'' Athowe said, ''and when they were captured, the commander confessed to receiving false information through the spy network. It seems they were told the garrison was poorly manned, and the idiot thought it would be a triumph to capture a few English soldiers right off English soil and carry them away to France.''

He recited without inflection, watching her all the while, and slowly the sense of what he said penetrated Jane's desolation. ''How curious. Does anyone know how this happened?''

''Apparently the French spy network has been infiltrated.'' He didn't sound as if he were repeating happy news.

''That's good, isn't it?''

''Inevitable, I would say.''

''Who infiltrated the network?''

''A very clever man.''

He spoke with such meaning, she jumped to conclusions. ''You?''

"Me?" He laughed. "No, not me. I'm not nearly clever enough to *catch* traitors." At the end of the gallery, something caught his eye, and he stared and muttered, "What is he doing here?"

Jane looked, too, and saw an elderly man, spry for his age, walking toward them. He wore a black jacket of cheap wool and breeches of a style at least twenty years old, and his thin white hair couldn't cover the variety of liver spots that shone off his scalp.

But he had an air of command about him, and Jane found her gaze caught by his.

"Lady Blackburn?" he said when he was in earshot.

"Yes," she acknowledged.

"Good. I had wanted to meet you. I'm Mr. Smith." He bowed, then looked beyond her. "Your companion couldn't wait to leave."

She glanced around. For the second time in her life, Athowe had disappeared, although she thought perhaps the circumstances were not quite as dire as the last time.

Mr. Smith's next words proved her wrong.

"I'm a director in the Foreign Office," he said. "Your husband reports to me, and he tells me he believes you're a French spy."

Chapter 28

A spy. Fitz couldn't believe it. He was a spy—for France. At the Manwins' ball, de Sainte-Amand had snatched on to him like a drowning man snatched on to a log. "*Oui, oui!* You will be our man. We will"— he glanced around at the press of nobles around them and lowered his voice—"we will have you go at once to the Foreign Office and offer your services. When you are established, you will be contacted by someone and told what to do."

His agitation gave Fitz a sinking sensation—or perhaps it was his own guilt. "What about you?"

"The network cannot remain static." De Sainte-Amand fidgeted with his snuffbox. "Others will come to take my place."

"You're leaving."

"It is time."

Fitz didn't like this. He didn't like it at all. The instincts he'd developed on the Peninsula stirred to life. Almost without thinking, he sought to draw out the Frenchman. "So it is true?"

Wiping a trickle of sweat off his brow, de Sainte-Amand asked absently, "What?"

"That the Foreign Office is preparing to arrest an English lord for traitorous activities."

De Sainte-Amand pulled out a handkerchief and dabbed it across his face. "Yes, I fear it is so."

"I can't believe it." As if in dismay, Fitz clutched his chest while he searched his brain for a name. "They're going to arrest . . . Lord Blackburn?"

De Sainte-Amand snapped to attention. "Lord Blackburn?"

Fitz could almost smell de Sainte-Amand's brain burning with excitement. "I have connections myself, and I've heard that they traced the leak of information to him." If one knew how, he knew, one could stretch out a lie for hours. "He used to work at the Foreign Office, you know, and apparently helped himself to all kinds of intelligence."

"Really?" de Sainte-Amand muttered. Then regained some degree of caution, and his gaze measured Fitz thoughtfully. "Who is your connection?"

Now Fitz threw discretion to the winds. "I spoke to Mr. Smith. I think he's in charge of something over there."

"Why did you leave, Jane?" Blackburn strode into Jane's bedchamber with so much arrogance, she wanted to fling her palette of colors right in his contemptuous, sneering, lecherous face. "We looked for you and we were told you were already gone."

Then he took in the rumpled counterpane, the broken crockery, the easel and canvas and the brilliant colors that smeared it, and she rejoiced in his appalled astonishment.

"Jane, what are you doing?"

"I'm painting." She pointed her cobalt-dipped brush toward his face. "Do you have any objection?"

To her gratification, he sensed a bit of her frenzy and took one step back. "No."

"Good. Because I wouldn't care if you did."

He stared at her feet. "You're dripping paint on an Aubusson rug."

"What difference does it make?" She gestured grandly, and drops flew from her brush. "I'm a Quincy now. I can do whatever I want and hurt whomever I like and no one can tell me I'm mistaken. Isn't that right, my lord Blackburn?"

His brow knit. "Jane, you're acting oddly."

"*I'm* acting oddly?" She tapped her chest. "I'm not the one romancing my niece!"

"Ah." He loosened his cravat as if it were too tight. "I was afraid you might have noticed that." His upper-crust accent stiffened. "I would like to explain, but I'm afraid it's not possible."

"Not possible?" She smiled with false affability. "You act as if it's a matter of national security."

He cleared his throat. "Well, actually—"

"I mean, the way you're acting, you might have been hanging near Adorna to hear who she told her newest French phrase to."

"I beg your pardon!" he snapped.

"Her newest French phrase," she prodded him relentlessly. "That was your intention, wasn't it?"

Striding over to her, he grabbed her wrist. "How do you know about that?"

"I'd love to tell you I figured it out on my own. Yes, I'd love to tell you that." She glowered at him. "But that wouldn't be true."

"Jane," he said warningly.

"The truth is, tonight I met someone I had never met before. Someone I didn't even know existed." Yanking her hand away from his, she dipped her brush in the carmine and smeared the canvas bloody red. "His name was Mr. Thomas Smith."

She enjoyed the great, exuberant pleasure of watching Blackburn's jaw drop.

"Yes," she said. "Mr. Thomas Smith. An interesting man. An almost frightening man. And very direct. Do you know what he told me?"

As if his head ached, Blackburn touched the spot between his eyes. "I can't imagine."

"He told me you thought I was a spy."

Wholly discomfited, Blackburn muddled along. "Well . . . yes. I'm sure if you think about it, you can see where I got that . . . that idea. Evidence pointed toward—"

"*You*"—she pointed at him—"thought *I*"—she pointed at herself—"was a spy."

"At the time—"

"It took me quite a bit of explaining before Mr. Smith was convinced I was *not* a spy."

"I wish he had not taken it upon himself—"

"He seemed to think he couldn't leave such a matter of grave national importance to you. He thought you were prejudiced in my favor."

''Well, yes, in that he was right, of—''

''Prejudiced in your wife's favor. What a novel idea! Prejudiced in your wife's favor.'' For a moment, words failed her, but Blackburn didn't again make the mistake of trying to speak. He just watched her cautiously, as if he thought she might ignite. Recovering her momentum, she repeated, ''You thought I was a spy.''

''We've established that.''

''You watched me, you kissed me . . . and all the while you thought I was drawing ships for the French!''

''You did try to give that one to—'' Blackburn halted.

''The Vicomte de Sainte-Amand—who really *is* a French spy.''

Appalled, Blackburn asked, ''How do you know *that*?''

''Oh, how stupid do you think I am?'' She flung out her arms in the grandest gesture she knew, and it wasn't nearly expressive enough. ''Very stupid, obviously. But once I started working on it, I knew *why* you thought I was a spy.''

''Did you?''

''Once Mr. Smith decided I definitely wasn't, he confirmed my suspicions.''

Blackburn's voice was not free from suspicion when he said, ''Mr. Smith is not usually so free with information.''

What did he think, that she'd tortured the old man until he confessed? ''In this case, it's old information. After all, the French network is unraveling at a rapid rate, and the only reason he came after me was to plug any bolt-holes before the rats could flee.''

''I see.''

Obviously he did see, for he had the good sense to look offended. She assumed it was with himself. ''So let me flip my tail, wipe my whiskers, and look at you through my beady little eyes while I say—yes. I drew a ship for de Sainte-Amand. He asked for it, and he'd been so sincerely admiring of my work, I thought he wanted it because it was good.'' A little of the hurt began to seep through her anger, but she hastily choked it back.

Blackburn apparently decided it was time to employ his least-used faculty—tact. ''De Sainte-Amand truly did admire your work. I think perhaps he simply saw an opportunity to get a clear rendering of an English ship and tried to take advantage of it.''

She hated that cajoling, reasoning tone of his. ''Shut up, Blackburn.'' She opened the pot and slapped yellow ocher onto her palate, then frowned. The vibrant color would do, she supposed, although it was a little too placid for her tastes.

''Why are you so upset?'' He sounded a little more frazzled now. ''The Foreign Office is the one with the problem. We don't know who the main culprit is.''

She'd always thought Blackburn an intelligent man. No, no; she'd thought him a god. Now she reeled from his feeblemindedness. Not only did he have the audacity to bring up the Foreign Office when her heart was breaking, but he didn't even know who his spy was. ''It's Athowe, of course.''

"Athowe?" Blackburn dared to chuckle indulgently. "That idiot?"

"Athowe," she mimicked. "Who has escaped your net how many times?"

His smile vanished.

"Who did you think your master spy would be? Some nefarious jackal who lurked in the shadows and came out only to feast on the hearts of English soldiers?" She splashed the yellow on the canvas. The drawing was beginning to take shape. "Of course it's Athowe."

"Why do you say that?" He dared to sound suspicious.

In her most mocking tone, she said, "Someone in the Foreign Office is collecting information. He is passing it to Monsieur Chasseur, and one or both of them are distilling the information into one or two key, coded phrases to be taught to one of Monsieur Chasseur's students."

"How did you know about Monsieur Chasseur?"

"Let me think." She put her finger to her cheek in mock concentration. "Adorna didn't like the odd French phrase Monsieur Chasseur had insisted on teaching her. Something about a loaf of bread, if I recall."

Blackburn winced.

"You taught her a new one, not significantly different from the old one—I surmise you were mildly suspicious at that point—and she repeated it to several people, including, I suppose, de Sainte-Amand."

"I suppose."

"And within a week, a French ship comes ashore

at Breadloaf Rock in a foolish attempt to capture the garrison.'' Baring all her teeth, she smiled at him. ''That surprised you, I know it did. You didn't really think Adorna could be passing messages. She's not clever enough. And that's why the chain was always so successful. Young English girls with nothing more on their minds than clothes and husbands have been utilized as a vital link in the French espionage.''

''And killed if they suspect anything.''

Jane squeezed her brush in her fist. ''Killed?''

''You remember. You're the one who told me. Miss Cunningham didn't fall from the cliff, she was pushed by Monsieur Chasseur. Why else would he have said she was murdered?''

That aspect hadn't occurred to Jane, and she gasped as if a giant vise gripped her lungs. ''Oh, my God.''

''That's why I stayed so close to Adorna tonight. I wanted to see who she spoke to, yes, but I wanted to protect her, too. She doesn't know she's passing messages, and she certainly doesn't know she passed one incorrectly—''

''She's not as stupid as you might think,'' Jane said, remembering Adorna's unusual concentration as she memorized that phrase.

''No, I guessed that. Maybe the others would, too, and if something happened to her, you'd—''

''Kill you.''

''I was going to say weep.'' He looked about the broken room. ''But perhaps you are right.''

''Adorna.'' She'd been angry at Adorna, and all the time the girl had been in danger.

In a tone of sweet reasonability, he said, ''So you

see, Jane, there's really no reason to be jealous. I don't love Adorna. You're my wife. You're the one I love."

Could he *be* any more stupid? "You think I'm angry because you chased after Adorna? No." She slashed paint onto the canvas. "I was hurt. I was humiliated. But angry? No. No, that came when I realized you compromised me and all the while you thought I was a spy!"

"You feel betrayed because—"

"*Feel* betrayed?" She mixed red and blue into an atrocious shade of purple. "I *was* betrayed. You told a complete stranger I was a suspect."

"I was going to say"—he was talking through his teeth now—"you feel betrayed because I was not completely honest with you."

Frustrated beyond control, she slapped her brush to the canvas and didn't flinch when paint splattered back. "You are such a . . . *man*. Completely honest? I'd say you weren't completely honest. I'd say you lied to me every way a man can lie. With words. With your gaze. With your body. I thought you trusted me."

"What are you talking about?"

"You married me. You took me into your family. I was going to bear your children. I was going to be their mother. And you thought me capable of the most despicable treachery imaginable. You married me thinking I was a spy. What were you going to do, watch my every move? Ship me off to Tourbillon? Imprison me?"

From his expression, she guessed he had considered all three.

"I *did* marry you." He said it as if that was supposed to make a difference.

"Oh. The great Ransom Quincy, Marquess of Blackburn, deigned to marry a woman who was not only compromised, not only on the shelf, not only poor, but a spy." She stood with her hands hanging at her sides, paint dripping on his precious rug, sarcasm dripping from her tone. "I am so honored."

A spark of hostility caught fire in him, and she saw him tamp it down. "All right, Jane. You're angry. But we are married and we'll talk about this when you're feeling a little more reasonable."

"I am not unreasonable."

"I'd have to disagree." Gently he reached out and caressed her cheek.

She slapped it away, furious that he dared retreat, glad that he was leaving her in peace.

As he turned to leave, he stopped, caught by the portrait she'd drawn. He stared, motionless, blank. "Me?" he asked.

"No one else," she answered.

Primitive and bold, the painting portrayed him with vivid acrimony. His hair was yellow ocher, his skin a disgusting shade of orange. His bulging purple eyes divulged mania, and each tooth was outlined in black, giving him a predatory air.

Worst of all, below the waist, there was nothing. Wavy lines trailed off the canvas in random order and colors. Her very indifference emasculated him.

She saw the moment the insult hit him. His ex-

pression flattened into emptiness, and his mouth
smiled without warmth.

''Very well, Jane. Sleep by yourself tonight. But
remember this.''

She was stepping back before he reached for her,
but she wasn't fast enough. He scooped her up, carried her to the bed. She twisted in his arms. He placed
her on the mattress and swept down atop her like an
avenging angel. Gripping her jaw, he held her still.
He looked into her eyes. And she saw the face of a
man who had killed for his country, who would die
for justice, who had grown beyond vanity and into a
hero.

And despite all that, he thought nothing of insulting
her in the basest manner.

The wretched blackguard.

Grabbing his hair in both her hands, she dragged
his lips to hers. She would always know him. His
taste, his aroma, his texture, had not changed in
eleven years.

But he had changed, and she had changed with him.
No longer would she grovel for any scraps he might
throw her. She was Jane. She was an artist. And she
was a mature and loving woman who deserved a man
who believed in her.

They strained together. Her fingers furrowed in his
hair. His hands gripped her as if he couldn't bear the
slightest separation. She savored him on her tongue,
through her pores, absorbing him like pure pleasure
into her veins.

Into her tender, adoring, broken heart.

Damn him. He didn't believe in her. He didn't love

her. She was nothing but an obligation successfully discharged, a wife adequate for breeding, a woman easily ignored.

Her body must have signaled her desolation, for he lifted his head and stared. ''Jane . . .''

Rebuffing him now was nothing but a feeble gesture, but she did it. She removed her hands from his body. She turned her head away.

''Jane . . .'' She heard something in his voice, something almost yearning.

But when she turned back to look, his expression was nothing but snow and stones.

Standing, he straightened his lapels in his fists, not knowing how the pigments that marked her had also marked him. Purple stained his cravat. Yellow streaked across his forehead. Carmine striped his hair.

But below the paint, his natural color shone with raw energy. His eyes flared with midnight blue, his cheeks were ruddy. And his sweet, damp lips moved as he said, ''Remember that, Jane.''

He moved stiffly away from the bed as if it hurt to walk, but it gave her time to collect herself. Time to push herself erect. Time to reach out and grope for something—anything—unbroken by her previous rage. The best she could do was a shard of a vase, and she hurled it after him.

It didn't even reach halfway across the chamber.

Flinging herself backward, she covered her eyes with her arm. Never in her life had she allowed herself such an awesome fit of temper, but even now she couldn't work up any remorse.

Remember this, he'd said.

Well, she would. No woman could ever forget that kiss.

Neither could she forget the betrayal.

Chapter 29

❦⟋

Had she slept? Jane didn't know. She only knew the canopy above her was dainty, ruffled, and not at all the masculine canopy she'd grown accustomed to seeing when she awoke in Blackburn's bed. Afternoon sunlight now greeted her, not Blackburn's hands groping for the hem of her nightgown. She missed his heat, the way he nuzzled her even in sleep. She even missed his snoring, that proof the man was just that— a man, and not a god.

She hated him so much. She loved him so much. She clenched her fists, gathering handfuls of bedclothes. And she would never settle for second place again.

Yet what could she do? She had married him. She hadn't had to. She could have run away. She could have protested until his desire had faded to humiliation. Instead she had married him, and he'd proved her rancor was but the foolish wavering of a woman unsure of her allure.

What an irony to discover it wasn't her charms he

doubted, but the character of which she was so proud.

Shoving the bedclothes away, she rose and stumbled to her feet. The floor did not move, and she didn't understand why. For her, the whole world was in upheaval.

A timid knock sounded, and she clutched the front of her nightgown and glared at the connecting door. Then she realized the knocking came from the outer door, the one that led into the hall.

Stupid. To want to see him, if only to fight with him.

"Aunt Jane?" Adorna stuck her head inside. "Can I talk to you?"

Jane stared at her, resentment sweeping through her. Gowned by the best modiste in London, washed and coifed, Adorna was the picture of health and youth. She was nubile, perfect, with no hidden depths, no burning ambitions.

"Aunt Jane?" Adorna's eyes were wide and pleading.

Yet Jane couldn't punish her niece for being what God had made her. "Come in, dear, and be careful of the crockery."

Adorna trod gingerly across the floor, her gaze darting from the broken vases to the hideous painting tossed on the floor. "I guess you were angry with me?"

Jane picked up her dressing gown. "No, dear."

"Oh." Adorna perched on the edge of the bed and pulled her feet up. "At Uncle Ransom, then?"

Jane thrust her hands into the sleeves. "Yes, dear."

Plucking at the lace on Jane's sheet, Adorna said,

"He wasn't really paying attention to me, you know."

"He wasn't really paying attention to *me*, either."

"No, that's not true!" Adorna said. "He'd been paying a lot of attention to you. He's always watching you and—"

"Watching me." Jane laughed bitterly. "Yes, he has been watching me."

Confusion puckered Adorna's forehead. "I don't understand. This is bad?"

"He was watching me for the wrong reasons," Jane explained.

"No." Adorna shook her head until her curls bounced. "I don't think so. When a man gets that sort of hot, scary look in his eyes all the time and the only thing that seems to relieve him is going off alone with his wife, I'm pretty sure that's good."

For the first time in Adorna's life, Jane wished she hadn't established such a strong bond with her niece. *Tell me anything*, Jane had always said. *Tell me what you think.* Now Adorna did, and Jane didn't want to hear it.

Adorna clapped her hands together. "But I didn't come to discuss you and Uncle Ransom. I came to tell you I've found the man I will marry."

That captured Jane's regard as nothing else could. "Have you? And why hasn't he applied for your hand?"

"He thinks you should be warned first."

Jane's well-developed intuition for Adorna-trouble quivered to life. "Warned? Why?"

"He thinks you might object because of his age."

"His age."

"He's older than I am."

"How much older?"

"A lot." Adorna fidgeted with a tendril of her hair. "About fifty years."

Jane sucked in a horrified breath.

Adorna hopped off the bed and took Jane's hand. "But don't worry! He's got everything I want."

"Money and a title," Jane guessed.

"Yes, but I could always get those." Adorna dismissed that with a shrug. "No, what Daniel has is kindness."

Her mind searched wildly. Daniel? Daniel . . .

"When I talk to him, he looks at my face. I mean, most men seem to think it's my bubbies that speak."

Daniel . . .

"He listens to me. If I say I like yellow roses with a sweet scent, he sends me yellow roses with a sweet scent, instead of those eternal red roses that indicate deep passion." Adorna sighed dramatically. "Deep passion. Most of the boys wouldn't know passion if it wet their legs."

The light slowly dawned in Jane's mind. "Daniel . . . McCausland?"

"Yes! Viscount Ruskin! You remember, we saw him at the beach!"

Jane did remember. That tottering old man? He wanted to wed her Adorna? Her beautiful young niece planned to marry *him*?

Adorna must have read Jane's thoughts, for she tumbled into speech. "He's nice, Aunt Jane. He's common, like me. He doesn't patronize me because my father's a merchant like the rest of them do. He won't go out and find another woman within a year of marriage just to prove his manhood, and I can keep him busy the second year. Aunt Jane''—Adorna looked up at Jane pleadingly—''he likes me. He . . . loves me.''

Jane took her hand out of Adorna's. Turning to the window, she stared out at the garden below. He loved her. Daniel McCausland loved her niece.

And who was Jane to say there should be more? Who was Jane to tell Adorna she was wrong? Maybe Adorna wasn't bright. Maybe she rushed to embrace life too impetuously. But give Adorna a few hours with a man and she knew him down to his tassels, and if she said Daniel McCausland was the man for her . . . indeed, he undoubtedly was. ''Well.'' Jane turned back to her niece and held out her hands. ''If this is what you want, you have my blessing.''

''Oh, Aunt Jane.'' Adorna disregarded the hands and impetuously hugged her. ''I'm so happy. I'll send Daniel over to talk to Uncle Ransom.''

''We'll have to get permission from your father.''

''Who will give it. Daniel is very rich.''

''Yes, I suppose he will.'' Eleazer had been jubilant about being so closely connected to Blackburn, never thinking that his treatment of Jane had been shameful and even now not realizing he would gain no advantage from her union. He would be equally happy to have a bond with Daniel McCausland, and equally surprised to find himself a pariah in his daughter's home.

"We'll be married in the autumn, and I'll give Daniel a child by the next year."

"The next year?"

"I told you he ought to marry and have children so he could pass on his title." Adorna let her go and grinned wickedly. "He says he's always done anything he puts his mind to, and he's more than willing to put his mind to this."

"I can imagine he is."

"I've got to go. He's going to be at the Fairchilds' today. I can't wait to tell him."

Vaguely surprised that the former commoner had been invited to such an elite gathering, Jane said, "He'll attend the Fairchilds' soirée?"

Adorna giggled. "They owe him money." She glanced over Jane's shoulder. "What time shall I be ready, Uncle Ransom?"

Jane twirled and saw him leaning against the doorframe, just as he had not too many nights ago. This time, however, he displayed none of the mockery and exhibited none of the charisma. Instead, his gaze rested speculatively on Jane, although he spoke to Adorna. "We will leave at two."

"Four?" Adorna covered her mouth in dismay. "That's so early."

"Four," he repeated.

Adorna rushed to the door, muttering, "I have to dress."

Blackburn looked ruefully at Jane. "That way, she'll be ready by three."

Adorna stuck her head back in. "I heard you," she said reproachfully. And to Jane, "I'll send the maid in to clean up this mess.'' She glanced at the man deliberately treading his way toward her aunt. ''After *he* leaves.''

She disappeared again, leaving Jane alone with a very thoughtful-looking husband.

Last night's passion had dissipated, leaving Jane feeling wan and skittish. But she didn't retreat. She was never going to retreat again as long as she lived. ''What is it, Ransom?''

''We should talk.'' A shard of porcelain crunched beneath his heel. ''With a little less heat than last night.''

''Go ahead.''

He halted two steps away. ''You're still irate.''

''I am not irate. 'Irate' is too small a word to describe my sensibilities.'' She considered her emotional state, and found the correct descriptive word. ''I am incensed.''

''You're making too much of what was nothing but a misunderstanding.''

She stared steadily into his eyes. ''Foolish of me. Of course, I can't help but wonder how a Quincy would react if he were accused of treason.''

''Your family cannot be compared to—'' In a rare flash of intuition, he must have realized she might take exception to his words, and caught himself.

Too late. ''My father was the tenth Viscount Bavridge, and you are the fourth Marquess of Blackburn. The Higgenbothems were nobles when the Quincys were grubbing in the dirt. My bloodlines are better than yours.''

''Not better, surely.'' Holding up one hand, he said,

"But I didn't come here to get in a slanging match with you. I came to ask that you go with us to the Fairchilds' tonight."

She laughed without humor. "You don't feel I've had my share of humiliation yet?"

"You won't be humiliated. You can stay beside Adorna and me—"

"The *ton* would crow out loud, my lord, to see your new wife guarding you from the wiles of her niece. No. I thank you, but I will stay home."

He groped for his quizzing glass, but he hadn't yet attached it and he fumbled fruitlessly. "I thought you might say that, and of course, you shall do as you wish, but I have to ask—why say Athowe is the traitor?"

Jane dropped her head into her hands for one brief moment. Blackburn hadn't come to mend fences. He had come for information. Naturally. How could she ever doubt it?

"Jane?"

Then another thought struck her, and she looked up. "Has Monsieur Chasseur arrived to teach Adorna her French lesson today?"

"No." After a brief hesitation, Blackburn said, "In fact, the watch found his body near the London docks this morning."

Shaken to the core, she said, "God rest his soul. Are you sure . . . ?"

"We had a man following him. Not a man, actually, but a child who could do nothing when Chasseur was attacked and shot."

Leaning against the nightstand, she whispered, "Murder."

"Yes, for failing the emperor. The spy trade is most unforgiving. However, Jane, before you feel too sorry for him, please remember—he most likely killed Miss Cunningham, and she was an innocent as surely as Adorna."

"Yes. Quite so." She took a shaky breath and recalled his original question. "Athowe is the traitor because Frederica is taking French lessons, which she seems not to enjoy. Because after telling me about the French ship which came ashore, and watching me very carefully for reaction, he literally ran to avoid your Mr. Smith."

Blackburn's face dropped with disappointment. "That's not conclusive evidence. A lot of men run when faced with Mr. Smith."

Elbows akimbo, she put her hands on the small of her back and wondered whether to tell him, and decided she might as well. He wouldn't believe her, but at least she would have tried. "I'm an artist. I studied him last night, and I assure you, he has the character and the morals to be an assassin. He is surely your spy."

Blackburn just stared. Why should he, a man who lived by facts and reality, believe in her powers of observation?

"Yes. Well. Thank you for your wisdom." He took a deep breath, then tried to soothe her vexation. "I wouldn't ask you about him if it weren't important."

Casting about on the floor, she found her night shoes. "I know."

"I wouldn't even go tonight if it weren't very important."

"Why not?" She pulled them on and brushed past him. Opening the door, she signaled to Moira, and when she turned back and saw Blackburn remained, she said, "Really, Ransom, go on. It's not as if we have anything to say to one another."

A more miserable afternoon, Jane had never spent. Her meal congealed on a tray at her elbow while she shifted in her chair. For some masochistic reason, she had chosen to sit in the same library where she had come to confront Blackburn eleven years ago.

The room had not significantly changed. Books still lined the walls, as well as paintings of the finest sort and cleverly placed statues. Beyond the open double doors lay the garden, small and well tended, and with the fragrance of carnations scenting the air.

The room should have soothed the artist in her. Instead she could scarcely stand to be here—but to be anywhere else in the house seemed dreadful. Nothing could make her happy. She had thought last night stripped her of all dignity, but no. Tonight was worse, for tonight she realized Blackburn's contempt for her didn't matter. She still wanted to see him and know what he was doing.

Was there anything more pathetic than a former spinster craving the affection of her disinterested husband?

The setting sun cast a warm light on her maroon leather portfolio as she dilatorily flipped through it, trying to find a face or a scene that could interest her.

If she could only make herself rise, go to the easel, and finish one of these drawings . . . She fingered the infamous sketch of the *Virginia Belle*. Even this one, the one that had caused her so much trouble, didn't appeal to her.

Taking a pencil and a plain piece of paper, she drew a quick picture of Frederica sprouting fangs and hair, then wadded it up and tossed it. The poor woman didn't deserve that; if Athowe had proved one thing last night, it was that he hid his true personality well. He bullied Frederica; from the jittery way she acted, Jane thought perhaps he even beat her.

Flipping through the portraits, she found the one she'd done of him after that first sighting at Lady Goodridge's ball.

Yes, cruelty rippled along his sagging jaw and his weak mouth, and the greed that consumed him shone in his eyes. Jane had just not noticed. Why should she? He wasn't Blackburn. He never had been.

The fangs and the hair went better on his face, and she sketched them in with quick strokes, then grinned at the result.

A soft knock sounded, and her heart leapt. Blackburn. It might be Blackburn. Standing, she settled her portfolio on her arm, brushed out her skirt, and called, "Yes?"

The butler opened the door. "Would my lady like a visitor?" Whent asked.

"A visitor?" Deflated, she could only stare.

"Come, Miss Higgenbothem, you'll see me." Athowe stepped around the butler as he spoke. "Go on, now." He waved a dismissive hand at Whent.

Impassive, Whent waited for her orders.

Hastily Jane considered the situation. Yes, Athowe was a spy, and yes, Blackburn would probably soon attempt to arrest him. But she didn't make the mistake of assuming Blackburn would do so on her recommendation. No, he'd poke and pry, trying to ascertain she was right while Athowe skipped the country.

The capture of that French ship had rattled Athowe, but really, even if he sensed the trap closing on him, he couldn't imagine that she had seen the truth in him, and maybe, just maybe, she could persuade him all was well. "Yes," she said to Whent. "You may go."

He lingered still. "My lady, will you require refreshments?"

She would serve Athowe refreshments if he wished. "My lord?"

"No, really." Athowe wiggled his hands in genial denial. "I can't stay."

She watched him cautiously as he moved into the room. He was dressed in his traveling clothes. Not a good sign.

"So you've got your dream," he said. "You're married to Blackburn, and happy as no woman has ever been before or will be again."

She didn't like his tone, and she glanced at the portrait she held. The petulance drawn there was echoed in Athowe's face right now. Something had disturbed him. "We *are* just married."

"But he's not here." He prowled close to her, and the smell of brandy came at her in a wave. "He's at the Fairchilds', romancing your niece."

"He's not really romancing her, he's—" Standing guard over her.

No, that would be a stupid thing to say.

But even if Athowe made the connection, he couldn't do anything to her in her own home, in such civilized surroundings.

Except that he was standing too close, and looking too earnest.

"You stare at me with those green eyes," he said, "and I see nothing but accusations."

She flinched back, then contained herself. He had no reason to believe she had charged him with treason. "What do you mean?"

"I abandoned you when that damned statue was revealed, and you've never forgiven me."

She moved the heavy portfolio from her arm to the front of her chest. He couldn't see his portrait that way, and besides, it protected her like a shield. "Truly, Lord Athowe, I have not dwelled on it."

"You never thought of it."

"Well . . . no."

He slammed his fist into the table. "It's Frederica's fault, and Blackburn's, that we never got together."

"I wouldn't say that." An offensive scene had developed. Her nerves crept beneath her skin, and she could scarcely maintain a civil expression.

But he *really* couldn't do anything to her. She would scream and— She glanced around for a weapon, and her gaze rested fondly on the fireplace implements. "Your consequence, as well as your fortune, were much greater than mine."

"But it would be right for us to be together now."

"Not possible." She spoke as firmly and as affably as possible while she moved toward the door. "Lord Athowe, we are both married."

"I didn't say anything about marriage." His voice sounded right in her ear. "Just togetherness."

She tried to turn to face him, but he took her wrist and twisted it up and behind her back. The sudden pain brought her up on her toes, and she cried out.

"Dear, dear Miss Higgenbothem." He spoke in a low, rapid tone. "I haven't been home since last night. The Foreign Office has officials searching my house. My wife is telling everything she knows. And I have to get out of the country. It seems fitting that Blackburn's wife accompany me, not only as a companion, but as a safeguard."

Her elbow throbbed as the joint stretched beyond the limits of endurance, and she whimpered as she realized how stupid she had been. She'd told herself he could do nothing to her in her own home, but what use was it to attribute civilized behavior to a man with no honor? "I don't want to go," she said.

"To Italy? Of course you do." Turning her in a circle, he headed her toward the open garden door. "It's your dream, remember?"

As she stumbled along, she dropped the portrait of Athowe and it wafted to the floor—the first of her markers to fall.

Chapter 30

Fitz had never seen Blackburn fidget like this. He stood next to Miss Morant while she wiggled, and giggled, and entranced men left and right, and he looked so impatient with her antics, no one at the Fairchilds' soirée could possibly imagine him infatuated with the girl. It would have been funny to see if it hadn't been so pitiful, and so painful to know the affair that had begun eleven years ago with Miss Higgenbothem had not survived the fortnight of bedded bliss.

A husky contralto voice spoke near Fitz's ear. "Mr. Fitzgerald, what does Ransom think he's *doing*?"

Fitz had thought this woman would never speak to him again. Indeed, she had said she would not, and to his knowledge, she never changed her mind. So he had to carefully contain his spurt of excitement as he answered, "As far as I can tell—and this is a fairly impartial judgment—he's being a fool."

"*I* have come to the same conclusion." Susan,

Lady Goodridge, stood just out of sight behind Fitz's shoulder.

Which might help her avoid his gaze, but wouldn't help her avoid his bitterness. "But being a fool seems to run in the Quincy family."

She didn't reply, but neither did she move away.

"Aren't you going to do something about him?" Fitz asked. "You do like to rush in."

"Where *fools* fear to *tread*. Yes." She took an audible breath. "But I've come to *suspect* you are *right*."

He glanced up at the intricately plastered ceiling. Susan had said he was right—surely this house, and civilization as he knew it, would fall into ruins.

The ceiling looked sturdy, and he didn't speak for fear he would frighten her off—again. Still, she couldn't mean what he thought she meant. Not Susan.

But she said, "I am a *fool*. Or rather—I have been one."

Fitz turned quickly, half afraid it was a chimera that spoke so lucidly, and not his upright, overbearing, arrogant Lady Goodridge. She connected with his gaze for one moment, then looked down, to the side, anywhere but at him. "Do you mean it?" he asked.

A blush crept up from her chest to her forehead, but she sounded remarkably composed as she said, "I would *like* to *reconsider* your *proposal*."

He caught her hand. He moved in close. "I would like that, too, Susan. Won't you look at me?"

He could almost see the effort she put into it: the steadying of her nerves, the gathering of courage.

Then she did look at him, and the calm strength assured him of her resolve.

"Susan." He threaded their fingers together. He smiled with undeniable pleasure. In the low, intimate voice of a lover, he asked, "Why did you change your mind?"

She answered in much the same tone, but with her own special way of articulation. "I *wouldn't* have if I hadn't come back to *London*. But Ransom made me, and I *watched* you *charming* the other ladies and *never* looking at me, and I . . . missed you."

His plan had worked. His plan had worked! He wanted to do a jig on the gambling tables, to laugh in the faces of other fortune hunters. "Did you think about what I said? That a poor half-Irish lover is better than no lover at all?"

"No. That didn't matter. I'd already watched you for *years*, and thought I would *much enjoy* having you in my *bed*."

The shock of that made him sway back.

"But you were my *brother's* friend, and you didn't think of me as anything but an *older* sister . . . until you needed to marry for *your mother's sake*."

That bit of truth had pricked at her, and he said, "I didn't lie to you about that, my dear."

"No, to your *credit*, you didn't. And I am *pleased* to do what I can for the *dear* lady. The air at Goodridge Manor would *improve* her *lungs*, and my cook will fatten her *up*." Susan's mouth got that thin, pinched look he hated. "I confess it was *vanity* which caused me to at first reject your proposal. I didn't like being perceived as *older*, *desperate*, and the *easy mark*.''

She'd surprised him with her acceptance, but now she had astonished him. He stared with what he knew must be goggle eyes. Then, throwing back his head, he burst into laughter.

Mortified, she glanced around at the crowd milling about. ''*What* are you laughing about? *Stop*.''

''Easy?'' he hooted. ''You?''

''*Stop*, I say. People are staring.'' She punched him in the arm, and it was no love pat.

Holding the stitch in his side, he calmed enough to say, ''Better get used to that. They'll always stare at us.'' He couldn't contain his grin. ''My dear Lady Goodridge. My dear Susan—as I've always called you in my mind—you are the epitome of a difficult mark. You are too proper, too rich, too intimidating. That's why no man has swept you up. It takes nerve and skill to approach a woman like you, and the only reason I even dared dream of success was that hint— just a mere hint, mind you—of hunger when you looked at me.'' Throwing propriety to the winds, he slipped his arm around her waist. ''So tell me how long you've lusted after me, and I'll tell you what I plan to do to assuage that lust.''

Her back was so stiff it might crack, and her outrage rolled off her in palpable waves.

What a time they would have, he and Susan! She'd make him rich, and he'd make her happy, and—

''I don't know what you're doing with my sister, Fitz, but I wish you'd stop it for a minute and *pay attention*.''

"The whole damned family can be trusted to have a delicate touch." Fitz swung Susan to face Blackburn. "Do you have to interrupt? We're getting betrothed here."

"I'm pleased you finally convinced her." Blackburn bowed with no ease and much hurry. "But this is a public place and you must have known someone would interrupt sooner or later. I need your help. Someone must watch Adorna for me."

Susan and Fitz exchanged glances.

"*Watch* her?" Susan said delicately.

"She's been passing messages to the French, and I'm afraid someone might try and kill her."

"Ransom, my friend." Fitz placed a hand on Blackburn's arm. "Are you feeling quite healthy?"

"She didn't know she'd been passing messages." Blackburn blew out a sigh. "She still doesn't know, but the spies know and they are ruthless and perhaps vengeful."

Susan and Fitz looked at each other again, Fitz with rising amazement.

"You and that spy rumor. It was really true."

"It really was," Blackburn agreed. "Now, will you watch her? Especially watch out for Athowe. I thought he might be here, but he's not in sight and I'm feeling rather uneasy about Jane."

"Is *she* a spy, too?" Susan asked, too sweetly.

"No, but I thought she was, and she's dreadfully angry about it."

Susan blanched. "You thought she was a *spy*, and you *married* her?"

Fitz experienced a sinking feeling.

"No *wonder* she's angry," Susan said.

"You'll watch Adorna?" Blackburn said with a fair amount of desperation.

"Wait." Fitz glanced from his friend to his betrothed. "How do you know I'm not a spy?"

"Then Mr. Smith will be most pleased we are working together," Blackburn snapped.

"No. I mean"—this wretched honesty was hell—"what if I'm a spy for the French?"

Now Blackburn and Susan stared at each other.

Then, grabbing Fitz's shoulder, Blackburn shoved him into the throng around Adorna. "I don't have time for this. Just watch her and stop trying to cut up."

"I'm serious!"

Susan followed at her own dignified pace. "Fitz, you couldn't even *propose* to me without explaining you were doing it because of my *money*."

Wrestling himself free, Fitz said, "I *am* serious. I talked to de Sainte-Amand about it last night."

"What's your first assignment?" Blackburn asked.

"I didn't get one. He looked ready to flee, so I—"

Blackburn pointed at him. "You're the one that convinced him that they were going to arrest the wrong man, didn't you? You convinced de Sainte-Amand it was safe to stay."

Curiosity prodded Fitz. "Did he stay?"

"He was arrested this morning." Hands on hips, Blackburn looked Fitz over. "You're a lousy traitor, Fitz."

In her usual colorless tone, Susan said, "You trust *Fitz* very easily."

"Of course. He's my friend."

"And *Jane* is your *wife*."

Blackburn stared at her without expression. Then, turning to Fitz, he snapped, "Just protect Adorna and I'll give you my sister's hand in marriage."

As he walked away, Susan breathed, "The man understands at last."

Driven by an ever-increasing sense of unease, Blackburn urged his grays along briskly. What had he been doing, watching over Adorna when any one of a hundred gentlemen would guard her on command? If not a suitor, then the Tarlins, or Fitz and Susan, or even old Viscount Ruskin, who had sat not far away and watched the girl with a bit of a smile playing around his mouth.

Blackburn's place was at home, talking to Jane, making her listen, forcing her to understand what he'd done and why he'd done it. Explaining why he trusted Fitz, that flighty charmer, but not her.

And that would take some explaining, because he didn't quite understand it himself. He suspected it had something to do with his emotions, which he viewed with suspicion, and how they influenced his reason. He had vowed to protect England, but this uncomfortably romantic attachment he'd formed for Jane always seemed to be intruding, distracting him from his duty, modifying his opinions.

He'd heard of men so wild with love they'd betrayed family, home, and country, and a Quincy would not succumb to such an extravagant feeling.

Except he had.

He'd married her thinking her a spy, thinking he had tainted his bloodlines, and thinking none of that mattered as long as he could protect her from the hangman.

Then he had thought she would be impressed by his seeming sacrifice.

Damn. What an ass he'd been.

Pulling up in front of the town house, Blackburn handed the reins to his stableboy and strode into his home. Servants milled about without direction, and they flinched at the sight of him.

His teeth snapped together. *Why* were they cowering?

"Where is my lady?" he demanded of the butler.

Whent's wig was askew on his head, and his hands trembled. "My lord, we don't know."

"What do you mean, you don't know?"

"She was in the library. She had a visitor. And now she's gone out the garden door!"

"A visitor?" This couldn't be happening. "Who?"

"Lord Athowe, my lord." Whent's voice rose in a wail. "My lord, where are you going?"

Running back to the street, Blackburn looked for his little sentinel. She wasn't in her place at the crossing, and her broom lay where it had fallen. "Wiggens!" he shouted. "Where are you?"

In the distance he heard a faint call, and then another, this one a little closer. His bootheels snapped on the cobblestones as he strode to the corner and looked wildly around.

Down the street, her arm clutched to her middle, limped Wiggens.

"Wiggens." Had Athowe hurt her? Blackburn would add that to the score. Hurrying to her, he picked her up. Bones and skin, the child was. "What happened?"

"That toff took Lady Blackburn out the alley, and she a-strugglin' something fierce." The child dragged in each breath, her thin face weary with exhaustion. "I shouted and ran at 'em, but 'e got 'er inside afore I could stop 'im. Then I ran after his carriage until I couldn't run no more. But I lost 'em. I'm sorry, m'lord. I failed ye."

"Nonsense." Blackburn stalked toward his open door and up the stairs. "You couldn't keep up with the horses. But what direction did they go?"

"I couldn't keep up," Wiggens repeated. Tears sparkled on her eyelashes. "But I've got somethin' for ye." Digging in her grubby clothing, she pulled out a sheet of paper and spread it out before Blackburn's eyes. "M'lady dropped it out the window. Does it mean anythin', m'lord?"

Stepping inside, Blackburn handed Wiggens to the hovering butler and took the paper. It was one of Jane's drawings of ships on the open sea. He stared at it and wondered—

"My lord." Whent held Wiggens in his arms, and both of them looked disgusted. "What should I do with the urchin?"

"I ain't no urchin," Wiggens said. "I'm English, same as ye!"

Blackburn drilled Whent with his gaze. "Give her a bath, get her some clean clothing, and feed her as much as she wants."

"A bath!" Wiggens shrieked.

Ignoring the struggle that erupted, Blackburn hastened into the library. There, on the floor by the door, was another loose piece of paper. Perhaps . . . Picking it up, he saw it. Athowe, complete with fangs and hair. Glancing out into the yard, he saw another by the open gate.

Jane had left a trail for him to follow.

Chapter 31

"Jane. May I call you Jane?" Athowe smiled *affably* above the barrel of the small pistol he held trained on her.

"I'd rather you didn't."

"Jane," he said deliberately. "Get out of the carriage now."

His coachman held the door and seemed not to notice anything unusual about the situation. As he probably didn't, if he'd been working for Athowe long.

Slowly Jane stepped onto the step and then down into the muck of the street.

Rank with garbage, the Thames swept by, slapping against the dock that extended into the river. The ship anchored there dipped with the current, and the gangplank rested on the end of the dock, waiting for Jane and Athowe to make their way aboard.

Jane glanced behind her, but she had no chance for escape. Athowe had pulled the pistol in the carriage and taken careful aim at her, and the barrel hadn't wavered since.

She stared ahead at the water that gleamed red in the sunset and wondered if she'd live through a dive. Probably not. If she dove in, and if he shot her, and if she somehow survived the wound, the sewage would probably smother her.

Yet if she didn't dive . . . She swallowed as she considered that gangplank. If she didn't dive, she'd be trapped on a ship with Lord Athowe, a man crazed with greed and—it made her ill to imagine it—with lust for her.

"You only want me because of the guilt, you know," she said in a conversational tone, dropping another drawing and stomping it into the mud. "You're embarrassed that you ran when I needed you."

"That's true." He was quite genial when he was getting his way. "But taking you to Italy is my way of making reparation."

"I don't want to go to Italy," she said for what felt like the hundredth time.

"With me." The gun barrel poked into her back. "I suppose you'd be glad to go with Blackburn."

"He's my husband. It seems more appropriate. Maybe you could get Frederica and we could visit together. Two couples, enjoying the sights." She stepped onto the dock, not knowing what to do, not knowing how to stop this.

"Don't be silly. A Quincy would never visit Italy to see the art. A Quincy would never allow his wife to paint. And that particular Quincy will certainly never allow you to sculpt." The barrel poked a little harder. "Will he, Jane? Will he?"

Ransom wouldn't, of course. She didn't want to go back—indeed, she didn't think she could go back—to a life that stifled her every creative urge. She needed to paint, to sculpt, to draw with all the passion of her heart.

Behind her, Athowe chuckled. "I knew it," he said. "The Marquess of Blackburn doesn't have an unconventional bone in his stodgy body. Now, hurry. We have to catch the tide."

She dropped another drawing and stomped it onto one of the nails that stuck out from the rotting wood.

"What are you doing?" Athowe asked in exasperation, picking up the paper. "Do you really think Blackburn's going to find these?" He crumpled it in his hand. "He's not going to follow you like some bird after a stolen worm. He'll give you up easily enough."

Her future was as murky as the Thames, but she knew the truth of *this* matter. Turning to face Athowe, she said, "I'm afraid you have him confused with yourself."

His pudgy face pinkened. "What do you mean?"

"*You* gave me up easily enough. My *husband* would never surrender his wife."

From the end of the dock came a familiar voice. "How true, Jane."

Jane and Athowe swung about to see Blackburn standing, fists clenched, head down and mouth set. He looked like a man whose most precious possession had been stolen, like a bull about to charge. "Athowe, I'm going to kill you."

His guttural voice projected a menace that made

Athowe flinch, and Athowe made a desperate grab for Jane.

Dodging him she smacked him on the side of the head with the edge of her beloved portfolio. The thump of leather sounded hollow against his skull and sent him stumbling sideways.

Twisting quickly, she rammed him with her shoulder. The gun sailed out of his hand into the river.

Jane had never heard a more satisfying splash.

"Bloody damned woman!" His fist shot out toward her belly.

Blackburn landed on Athowe. The men went tumbling.

Jane went tumbling with them. The thump of fists and the pained grunts were too close. Desperately, she crawled toward the end of the dock. Away from the fighting. Away from Athowe and his madness. Away from Blackburn and his stupid distrust and his unjustified superiority.

Oh, Blackburn was going to win the fight. She knew that. No one knew his strength and muscled form better than she did. Blackburn would to beat the stocky Athowe senseless. Easily. Without a doubt.

So why was she looking back? Athowe landed a blow to Blackburn's eye, and she almost leaped to her feet to help. But then blood flew from the repeated impact of Blackburn's fist to Athowe's nose, and she regained her senses.

Yes, Blackburn would win. Blackburn won every battle he began.

And she really wanted him to win this one. Only . . . she was tired of being his defeated opponent.

Standing, she began collecting her scattered drawings.

Behind her, the steady thump of blows accompanied her search.

Athowe begged for mercy in a choked voice.

Jane tried not to listen.

Finally he quieted, and a large splash reverberated beneath the dock.

When she looked up she wasn't surprised to see Blackburn, fists clenched and bloodied, standing at the edge of the dock and staring into the filthy water.

Just as she knew he would, he had won.

"Ransom." She smoothed the wrinkles out of one of her sketches. "Don't jump in after him. You wouldn't be clean for months."

"Bastard escaped. Jumped." As he stared at her, the fury faded from his gaze, and worry and caution replaced it. "Did he hurt you?"

"No, although he was a little too proficient with that pistol for my tastes."

"Yes." His voice sounded rather odd, choked and rather shaky.

She put it down to pain, and resisted the urge to go to him, bandage his wounds, hug him and give him the comfort a woman should give her warrior.

"Jane?"

She thought he did his best to project appeal. She resisted. "What?"

He sighed. "Oh, Jane."

Walking to the edge of the dock, Blackburn called to his footmen. They came on the run, and he instructed, "When Lord Athowe makes it to shore, pull him out and tie him up. I'll send someone back for him."

The footmen scampered to obey.

Jane ignored them all for the tattered, muddy sketch of the *Virginia Belle*, and mourned its former beauty. She could do it again, of course, but never would she imbue it with the same feeling. Whatever she felt when she worked, it came through her brush and she couldn't hide it. She was an artist. An artist! Nothing could ever change that.

"Jane, I followed your drawings here. I have them in the carriage." Slowly Blackburn moved toward her, behaving as if she might flee his approach.

But why should she run from him? He wasn't that important to her.

Italy was important to her. Italy did beckon, tugging at her like the river's current. If she went to Italy, she could see the great art, touch it, breathe it, and gain inspiration. If she went to Italy, she could grow as an artist, and grow old without the bitterness of wondering what she could have been.

"It was very clever of you to think of dropping them." Blackburn interrupted her dreaming, injecting a note of unwanted reality, compelling her to live in this moment. "Now we'll go home, shall we, before the sun sets completely."

But the dream was there, and it could be real.

And the reality was here. The reality was Blackburn. Lifting her gaze, she scrutinized him openly.

He *was* handsome. Her early infatuation had steered her true. The man moved through life and peeled off layers of elegance, each time revealing a new form, one brighter and more noble. The bruises could not damage the basic structure; they only added character.

She looked at the ship. Its paint was peeling. Its sails drooped. The gangplank sagged. Yet it held the appeal of the unknown, the untried. She could board that ship and leave disillusionment and pain behind.

Blackburn nudged her, trying to catch her attention again. "This is not a safe area after dark."

Turning her face to the breeze, she relished the scent of freedom. So what if freedom smelled of the Thames? At least it didn't reek of frustrated expectations and blighted hopes.

She reached her decision. "I'm here. I'm at the docks. There's a ship. It's going to Europe, and that's where I want to be."

"Jane."

Blackburn was observing her, she knew, trying to decide how to manipulate her into staying. And why? Because he'd be humiliated if his wife left him, of course. Because he had perhaps some small affection for her, and of course because he had a rather pressing lust.

But those were insignificant reasons when weighed against her needs, and he would find another woman soon enough.

When she left, women would be lining up to comfort him.

That thought caused a twinge of something she might have called jealousy . . . if she had cared about him.

So she turned her mind back to herself, to her art, to Italy. Blackburn was the old life; the life she would leave behind, and she didn't care what he thought of her grand plans. "I'm going to live the life I always dreamed of. I'll be gone from England. You ought to be glad of that."

"No."

She ignored him. It was much too late for false expressions of regret. "I'll go to Rome and study art there. I'll paint on the street, and pretend an Italian accent, and sell my paintings to the English tourists."

"Jane, please."

He sounded desperate, but such evidence was not to be trusted, a mere will-o'-the-wisp, a whimsy. "It will be a precarious existence, but no worse than eking out a living as a governess."

"You don't have to be a governess. You're the Marchioness of Blackburn."

She ignored that unwelcome truth. "And a good deal more satisfying, I must say. I can't wait to begin."

"Jane."

Keeping her face resolutely turned away, she concentrated all her attention on the ship. Men scurried up the rigging. The captain shouted out commands. The boards creaked as the ship rose and fell in the current, and beneath Jane's feet that same current nudged the dock.

She was going to do it. She was going to leave England on that ship and never return. For one brief, bright moment, she was eighteen again, when facing the unknown meant adventure and all her life stretched before her.

She lifted her chin, took a breath, and smiled.

And Blackburn said, "Jane, please. Forgive me."

At those totally unexpected words, her head whipped around.

For one second she didn't see him.

Then she did.

He was kneeling. Kneeling in his tailored trousers on the filthy, splintered boards of the dock, his head bent in entreaty. "Please, Jane, listen to me. You didn't deserve my suspicion."

He was kneeling, with every appearance of a supplicant, and that . . . that was more than she ever imagined.

But he still didn't understand. And she shouldn't try to make him. She should just walk away.

Instead, she found herself saying, "It wasn't your suspicion that I hated. It was your condescension."

"Yes, I was wrong."

Somehow his peculiar admission didn't relieve the pressure within her. Rage bubbled in her until she wanted to shriek, to stomp, to pound on him with her fists.

Being Jane, she did none of those things. She'd done it once in her bedchamber, and it had not helped him to understand or her to feel better. She should just board the ship.

Board the ship.

She found her hands bunched into fists, but her voice was steady and, she was proud to note, rather cool. "I'm not noble or rich, but I have more character and more talent in my little finger than you embody in your entire person."

"I know."

"You thought I was a spy." Still Ransom kept his head bent, and Jane imagined it was because he was smirking in that horribly superior way of his. He bent his knee to her, not in supplication, but as the easiest way to avert disgrace. "You dared conjecture I would be grateful that you wed me anyway."

"I was a fool." He looked up at her at last.

And when she gazed into the night sky of his eyes, she realized the foolishness of her every conjecture. Blackburn wasn't kneeling because it was the easiest way to win her back. At any moment he could have swept her off her feet and carried her to his carriage, coercing her rather than pleading with her. He could keep her imprisoned in his home, and because she was his wife, the English law would allow it.

No, he didn't kneel because he had no other recourse. This public display of humbleness was agony for him. He hated it with every fiber of his being. He quivered with the humiliation; he wanted to stand and shout out his antecedents and his pride and his worth.

But for her, he knelt on the dock in front of his footmen, in front of the whores that lolled across the street, in front of the common sailors on the ship.

And he begged. "Jane, please. I don't want you to go. I did marry you thinking you were a spy, but haven't you wondered why? I'd walked away from you before, and I couldn't do it again. You've bound me with your wit and the way you move like a good horse, and when you smile, I realize you don't do it very often and I want to make you . . . find you . . . something to smile about."

A vivid purple bruise swelled on his brow from the

ight, and dirt smudged his chin. His rumpled hair
tuck up in spikes above his forehead, and not even
his valet could rescue this cravat. He looked hot and
disheveled.

He looked beautiful.

"If you want to live in Rome and paint on the
streets, we'll do it together." He shifted as if the
boards were none too comfortable to his knees. "Together, Jane. We could do that. I don't think I can
paint, but perhaps I could sing or—"

"You dance well." *Stupid!* Why had she answered?

"Dance. Yes." His lids dropped to her hands, and
she realized she no longer clenched them in fists.
"Will the tourists drop a penny in my hat, do you
think?"

She was softening, stupid woman that she was. "I
would drop a penny in your hat to see you dance."

"Would you, Jane?"

He looked up at her through those extraordinary
blue eyes and in any other man, she would have said
that expression meant one thing. In any other man, it
would have meant she was his ideal of perfection.

"Or would you stay with me in England, take advantage of my true and sincere remorse—oh, Jane, I
am really so sorry—and let me build you the best
studio any artist ever owned?"

He'd do it, too. One thing she knew, and that was
that a Quincy kept his word.

She must have been quiet too long, for he grasped
her skirt. "Not just one studio. A studio in every
house. You'll have whatever equipment you wish, and

an art teacher. Even a French art teacher.''

Thinking of the glorious, half-finished statue waiting at the Tarlins', she asked, ''Will you pose for me?''

''No other shall.''

Her fingers twitched with that sense of *wanting*. If she could do him in clay just one more time . . .

He must have seen. He must have known victory was within his grasp. Yet he bent his head once more. ''Please, Jane. Forgive me.''

Her hand stretched itself out toward his rumpled crown.

Then she remembered. That first, humiliating rejection. The years of poverty and loneliness. His toplofty behavior when he saw her with Adorna for the first time. His attentions, his seduction, and their marriage. Not because he wanted her, or adored her, as she had mutely hoped, but because he needed to distract the French and all of society from his real objective.

Her hand curved and shook. The tendons grew strained. Her hand clenched.

''Jane,'' he said in a low voice. ''I love you.''

I love you.

I love you?

He'd said *that*?

Oh, but *really*. So what?

She stared at her hand, at the veins and bones covered by fragile skin made white with strain. If she opened it and laid her palm on his head, if she gave her forgiveness for what must be the cruelest betrayal ever dealt to a woman, she would have to be mad.

Or in love herself.

Was she? Was she in love with Blackburn? Not in love like a worshipful child, or in love like a grateful adult, but truly in love?

Slowly, gradually, her fist opened.

Yes. She was in love. In love with a Blackburn who had been stripped of all illusion and still was never less than her ideal.

She placed her hand on him.

He lifted his down-turned head, and her hand slid down over his cheek. He didn't look humble or happy or any of the lesser emotions. Rather, his nostrils flared and his teeth were bared; he was the very epitome of a savage who would reach out and take what he wished.

And he wished for her.

Standing, he wrapped his arms around her waist and brought her close, body to body and soul to soul. His words were a soft growl against her lips. "Woman, you'll pay for making me wait."

He kissed her, a soft, explicit kiss that promised and demanded at the same time, and while she could think, she reflected that his kisses decidedly influenced her in his favor. That, and the sensation of his strong shoulders under her kneading hands, and the way he held her as if she were precious and delicate as fine china when she knew she was strong as an earthenware bowl.

When they separated, she could dimly hear shouting, and when she opened her eyes she realized the ship's crew hung over the railing, yelling crude encouragement to the lovers. "How embarrassing," she said weakly.

"What?" Bending, Blackburn put his shoulder into her stomach and lifted her so she draped him like a scarf.

The shouting intensified as he strode off the dock, and Jane lifted her head and cheerfully waved to the ship.

"I'll let you sculpt our children, too." he said.

"Shall we name the oldest Figgy?"

He didn't pause. "No. But I won't let you sculpt anyone else. Not when you have the distressing tendency to sculpt naked bodies."

Discovering a heretofore unexplored wicked streak, Jane could not resist saying, "You can't stop my imagination."

He halted. "Jane . . ."

He sounded uncertain and not nearly so sure of himself, and she found she didn't like that. In a pleasant tone she said, "But you're the only one I've wanted to sculpt as a nude."

"Really?" He started walking again.

"And if you'll pose for me, I have a statue to finish when we get home."

"I'll pose for you." Setting her on her feet, he grinned at her with the kind of smile she'd dreamed of all her life. "If you'll let me wash the clay off of you afterward."

This marriage, she realized, was going to work very well indeed.